PRAISE |

MW01616922

"Thor, Baldacci, Flynn, Hamburg. Get ready as Banner fits right in!"

AMAZON REVIEW

"Move over Jack Reacher there's a new guy taking over."

AMAZON REVIEW

"Great stuff. Exciting and fast paced. On par with Flynn & Thor."

AMAZON REVIEW

"The writing was superior, the story line was compelling and the action was top-notch. Sorry I could only give this one a five star rating!"

AMAZON REVIEW

BREATH OF HELL

A HARRY BAUER THRILLER

BLAKE BANNER

RIGHTHOUSE

Copyright © 2024 by Right House

All rights reserved.

The characters and events portrayed in this ebook are fictitious. Any similarity to real persons, living or dead, is coincidental and not intended by the author.

No part of this book may be reproduced in any form or by any electronic or mechanical means, including information storage and retrieval systems, without written permission from the author, except for the use of brief quotations in a book review.

ISBN-13: 978-1-63696-318-1

ISBN-10: 1-63696-318-8

Cover design by: Damonza

Printed in the United States of America

www.righthouse.com

www.instagram.com/righthousebooks

www.facebook.com/righthousebooks

twitter.com/righthousebooks

HARRY BAUER THRILLER SERIES

When churchyards yawn and hell itself breathes out
Contagion to this world: now could I drink hot blood,
Hamlet, William Shakespeare

ONE

"Vengeance is mine," he said, and Araminta dropped with a *splosh* into the turquoise cool of the swimming pool. "I will repay, saith the Lord. Romans, chapter twelve, verse nineteen."

I glanced at the brigadier, then returned my gaze to Araminta's liquid form warping like a fish beneath the water in the brigadier's Marbella villa. I spoke absently.

"You're quoting from the Bible?"

"Deuteronomy, the Fifth Book of Moses, originally from the Jewish Torah, but also the Old Testament. Judaism, Christianity, Islam, all branches from the same monotheistic tree. I was brought up an Anglican, obviously. I have since become more of an agnostic." He sighed and gave a slow, reluctant shrug. "There is something of an evidential issue. But, that said, there is much in the Bible that is worthy of thought and reflection."

I watched him while he spoke. Wondering what he was driving at. "Yeah?"

"You may be familiar with the maxim in Budo, 'Look not into your enemy's eye, lest you become your enemy.'"

I nodded. "Sure."

"'Vengeance is mine' runs along similar lines. The idea is that vengeance belongs to God, not to man. Once you seek revenge, you have looked too deeply into your enemy's eye, and you risk becoming the very thing you seek to punish."

Araminta erupted from the water, blowing fine spray from her lips, and pushing her wet hair back from her face. My words were for the brigadier, but I was watching the sun reflecting off her wet skin.

"Where does that leave Cobra?"

"That is precisely the point I am trying to make to you, Harry. We are not about vengeance. We are about cleansing. When you take the rubbish from your kitchen out to the bins in the street, you should not hate the rubbish, or wish to punish it, because you would become emotionally and mentally unstable. It is the same with what we do. In order to decide who is 'good' and who is 'bad,' you need to be a god, an ultimate moral arbiter or judge. Humans are not up to that standard, but we can decide who is a detriment to human society, by a series of objective criteria. Cavendish had to go, not because he was 'bad' and we hated him, but because he had committed acts that meant he was harmful to human society. Harmful, in simplistic terms, means caused more pain than pleasure."

I arched an eyebrow at him. "Seriously?"

"Very seriously. We are mere human beings, Harry. We are the accidental custodians of this planet, and until either a fiery chariot or a flying saucer settles in Parliament Square or on the White House lawn, it's up to us to make the best decisions we can, based on objective criteria. How do we base our decisions on objective criteria?" He raised one hand, palm up, like he was showing me something. "Pain is harm, pleasure is good."

I sighed. "If I had time for philosophy I am sure I could pick holes in that. I might ask you something about how sadists and masochists fit into your argument. But I haven't got time for philosophy, and in any case I have a feeling you are telling me that when I go and bring the colonel back, I should not indulge in wanton revenge against those who took her."

"A suggestion. You may not believe it right now, Harry, but you are extremely vulnerable at the moment, physically and emotionally. As Yoda would have it, you could easily be drawn to the dark side. Your job is not to seek revenge, but to clean out the trash."

I watched Araminta backstroke across the pool with her eyes closed to the sun. I sighed.

"Do you believe that?"

"Just because it is difficult, Harry, doesn't mean it isn't true."

I grunted. "Well, sir, if it's all the same to you, I am going to leave the philosophical, moral high ground to you, and when I get hold of the people who have taken the colonel, I am going to make sure that anyone who hears the story of what happened to them, will think very, very carefully before doing anything similar again."

He arched his eyebrows and nodded. "I should hope so. But that is not revenge, Harry. That is just doing a thorough job. Take out the trash, and make sure the house remains clean. We do not kill to avenge, we kill to clean."

Araminta pulled herself out of the pool and stood glistening and looking desirable in the sunshine, pulling her hair back from her face. Across the lawn, in the shade of the patio, a man in a white jacket with white gloves on stepped out through the sliding glass doors. He approached us and, as the brigadier turned toward him, he said, "Señor, the lonch is ready. Will the *señores* eat out here, or going inside?"

Araminta answered as she wrapped her head in a towel like a turban.

"We'll eat out here, Sanchez. And I'll have a Beefeater and lime first."

He bowed, giving his head a little sideways twist, which made it somehow less servile, and he withdrew back into the shade of the house. Up in one of the palm trees a parakeet laughed at him. It was a harsh, ugly laugh.

After that Sanchez and a couple of cute Spanish girls with

long black hair, big brown eyes and voices about as harsh as the parakeet's went about setting up a table in the sunshine beside the pool, while Araminta sat and browned herself behind large, tortoiseshell sunglasses.

"Who's dead?" she said suddenly, then answered her own question. "Captain Bill Hartmann, your arch enemy in the Ben-Amini affair[1], he's dead. Raymond Hirsch, apparent leader of the 'Find Harry' department of the CIA, he's dead. Captain Seth Campbell, alleged Air Force Intelligence, but according to my research a CIA officer, probably attached to Hirsch's 'Find Harry' team and, indirectly, working for Cavendish—" She paused a moment, having lost herself in her overly long sentence, then shrugged and said, "He's dead too."

I shook my head. "What I don't get is, if Cavendish wanted me alive so he could interrogate me, why'd he send Campbell to kill me?"

She raised a hand to wag a finger at me. "I said *indirectly* working for Cavendish. As I understand it, after Panama[2] Hirsch didn't really care much who you worked for. I think he bought your story that you were independent. One way or the other, he came to the conclusion that your employer was not the problem, you were. Hirsch and certain elements in the CIA collaborated with Cavendish—Cavendish pulled a lot of weight, but ultimately it was a collaboration—and Hirsch wanted you dead. Cavendish wanted to interrogate you but Hirsch was clear, he wanted you dead."

"So Hirsch sent Campbell to kill me in defiance of Cavendish."

"Defiance is probably putting it a bit strong, but yeah, pretty much."

"And Colonel James Armitage?"

---

1. See *The Dead of Night*
2. See *The Silent Blade*

"Nothing to do with Central Intelligence or Cavendish. He is legit 25th Air Force."

"Is he still interested in me?"

She shrugged, with her face still turned to the sun. "Irrelevant. He wants the colonel back, and you are going to bring her back, right?"

"Right."

Sanchez had set the table with a white linen cloth, white linen napkins, silver cutlery and an ice bucket with two bottles of very cold white wine in it. Now he emerged carrying a huge paella pan full of sizzling yellow rice, mussels, prawns, squid and chunks of chicken. The girls followed him in a kind of improvised procession bearing olive oil, vinegar, salt and pepper, and baskets of fresh-baked spongy white bread. The brigadier smiled at me.

"You need building up, old boy."

I smiled, more ruefully than happily, and we moved to the table. As I sat, Sanchez was dishing up the paella for Araminta.

"I'm built up," I said to the brigadier, though it wasn't strictly true. "What I need is to get out and start doing something constructive. I've been locked in here for a week."

Araminta accepted the plate from Sanchez and glanced at me.

"Quit griping, you were a wreck when I brought you here[3]. If you'd gone after the colonel in the state you were in, you'd have been dead inside twenty-four hours."

I leaned sideway to let Sanchez load up my plate.

"You're right," I said, and nodded. "But that was a week ago." One of the cute maids poured wine. When she and Sanchez had left I went on. "I feel OK and we need to start doing something. We can't just sit around..."

I trailed off and shoved a forkful of yellow rice into my mouth. The brigadier wagged his fork at me.

"Just because you are convalescing, it does not mean that we are sitting around scratching our posteriors."

_____

3. See *LA: Wild Justice*

Araminta snorted a short laugh, glanced at me and grinned.

"Posteriors. That's like asses in English. 'Git your posterior over here, boy! Boy, I is gonna whip your posterior!'"

I smiled, but the brigadier ignored her and went on.

"Jane is not as easy to move as you might think. Within the defense and intelligence communities she is relatively high profile, so moving her around requires a high level of control and secrecy, and that itself, ironically, leaves a large footprint. We have been watching the ports, maritime and aerial, the railway stations and roads. There has been no sign of her until now."

Araminta stopped with her fork halfway to her mouth. I said, "Until now?"

"I heard this morning. We are fairly confident the colonel was seen, at about seven AM, boarding a yacht at Puerto Banus."

I scowled. "Why are you telling me now? Why didn't you tell me at the time?"

He raised an eyebrow at me that could have frozen lava. "Because I don't have to, Harry. I am telling you now because it seems to me to be the appropriate time. The agent who saw her knew the colonel well and he reported that he was confident it was her."

"Was she OK?"

He nodded several times as he picked up his fork again. "Oh, yes. She was unaccompanied and boarded the yacht of her own free will."

There was something cold and hard in the way he said it. My scowl deepened. I asked: "What yacht?"

"The *Bucephalus*."

"The who?"

"The *Bucephalus* is a luxury superyacht which belongs to Gabriel Yushbaev, a Russian billionaire with links to both organized crime and, some thirty years ago, the KGB. His worth is estimated by Forbes to be approximately nineteen billion US dollars." He gave a thin smile. "He is one of the few men in Russia to have benefited from the Covid crisis. Some people have benefited, you know?"

"No kidding."

"The *Bucephalus* has not left port yet, though sources tell us it is due to leave very shortly."

I felt a hot jolt of anger in my gut. "Sir, if you had told me this morning…"

Araminta interrupted me, wiping her mouth with her napkin. "What? You could have driven down there, killed everyone, blown up the yacht and dragged the colonel home by her smoking hair?"

The brigadier winced. "Thank you, Araminta." I sighed and started eating again. He went on, "The thing is, Harry, whether I had told you at seven AM or whether I tell you now, it makes little difference, because all we can do at present is watch. Araminta has a point. All we could do right now is storm the boat, and aside from having cutting-edge security and heavily armed guards, it is also under the protection of the Spanish authorities. And we don't really want to get into a conflict with them."

I laid down my fork. "So what do we do? We can't just sit back and watch."

"Clearly." He gestured at me with an open hand. "What do *you* suggest?"

"Do we know where the yacht is headed?"

"Yes, its first port of call is Ano Koufonisi, in the Cyclades islands, about a hundred and thirty miles southeast of Athens. After that it seems they carry on to Istanbul, and after that they may enter the Black Sea, but we don't know for sure."

I frowned. "So not the Middle East. If they are handing off to Al-Qaeda, they're going to do it in Istanbul." They glanced at each other, but remained silent. I said, "What?"

Araminta took a deep breath and sipped her wine.

"The picture has changed, Harry."

I felt hot anger rise up in my belly and fought to control it.

"What do you mean, the picture has changed?"

"Well, for a start the behavior you described."

"What behavior I described? What are you talking about?"

"The way she reacted to you in *Le Jardin d'Eden*,[4] that was abnormal behavior, Harry. And the way she failed to help you, even after you had stabbed Cavendish. She just left you lying there, Harry, and when those men took her away, she didn't put up a fight. But most of all, the way she boarded that yacht this morning, unaccompanied, of her own free will..." She paused, shrugged and drew down the corners of her mouth. "That is not the colonel *I* know. *I* don't recognize that person."

"Are you saying you suspect the colonel of being a double agent?" I looked at the brigadier. "You know her, sir. Are you saying that?"

"No, what I am saying, Harry, is that her behavior is out of character."

"But there has to be an explanation!"

"Of course there has. Clearly, but we don't know what that explanation is, so we can't make any predictions based on it. All we can say is that from what we have observed, the colonel is behaving in an atypical, unpredictable way. We don't know how far that atypical behavior will extend."

I shook my head. "I don't know what you're driving at."

Araminta answered. "What I am driving at, is that we cannot be sure anymore whether the colonel is going to be handed off to jihadists or not." She looked at me with something like pity. "Harry, we don't even know for sure if she is a prisoner anymore. All we know is that they have got her, and we want her back."

I frowned at them like they were crazy. "You want me to *kill* her?"

"No!" It was the brigadier. "Certainly not. I want you to find her, get her and bring her home. That is all."

I ate in silence for a while. I grabbed a piece of bread and tore it in half to mop up the saffron rice.

"Suppose I bring her home and we find she's a double agent?"

---

4. See *LA: Wild Justice*

The brigadier raised a finger. Swallowed and sipped his wine. "In the first place, it is clear from the success rate of our operations that, *if* she is a double agent, she was turned very recently. It stands to reason that if she had been turned earlier, not only would a percentage of our operations have been compromised and failed, but also Cavendish and his associates, not to mention the CIA, would not have been at such pains to find out who you were and who you worked for. They would merely have had to ask her. She didn't inform them and from what we can tell, so far she still hasn't."

I nodded. "That's a good point."

"The second point is that we need to know *why* she has turned—if indeed she has. Is it money? Is it blackmail? We simply don't know, but we need to know."

Araminta had been busy wiping her plate clean with bread. Now she stuffed a piece in her mouth and spoke around it. "But her weird behavior remains unexplained. We need to know what is going on. We can't just ignore it."

I nodded. "OK, point taken."

She shook her head. "No, I don't think you do understand, Harry. This is not about blame. This is about predictability. You were going to die, and she sat there and watched. She did nothing."

"You said that."

"So what I am saying now is, when you try to bring her home, you don't know how she is going to react. She might turn on you. She might alert her...," she hesitated and made inverted comma signs with her fingers, "'captors.' So you need to be ready for that."

"I get it. She is unpredictable right now, and I have to be ready for that."

"So—" The brigadier reached out and helped himself to more rice and prawns. My own plate was still half full. He handed the serving spoon to Araminta with an inquiring lift of his eyebrows and she made an affirmative, "Mm!" and took it from him.

I sighed. "So the question is, how do I get aboard that damned boat?"

TWO

"So what do we know about the yacht?"

Sanchez was clearing away the plates and the girls had brought a big cheese board, a bottle of cognac and a bottle of whisky on a tray, and a pot of coffee. The brigadier cut into the stilton and balanced a piece on a cracker.

"We have photographs, and we are trying to get hold of the plans. It's not easy. It is seventy-five feet long, has three decks and a bridge, two state rooms, four suites and an undefined number of cabins. It has a small cinema, two dining rooms and four lounges. Access is from a rear boarding deck. It has a skipper, a first mate and a crew of six, as well as two barmen, six maids and a butler. Then there are two engineers and Yushbaev's security team who number four. All of whom are drawn from Russian elite special forces. HQ is drawing up a file as we speak."

"As we speak may be too slow."

He shook his head as he poured whisky into my glass and then his. "There is too much at stake to go blundering in all guns blazing, Harry. We need discipline and method."

"Sure." I sipped the whisky and felt it warm me inside. "But discipline and method won't be worth a damn if the colonel disappears into the Russian steppes or the Middle East."

He smiled at me, and after a moment said, "So we need to be disciplined and methodical, quickly." He turned to Araminta. "Would you go to the office, please, and bring the file, such as it is right now, for Harry to peruse it? Call Pleasantville while you're at it. Hurry them up and see if they have anything more."

"Sure." She stood. "Don't eat all the cheese."

I chewed on a dry cracker and a piece of stilton and watched her go inside.

"Could I paraglide in once it's at sea?"

"Drop from a plane?" He made a doubtful face. "It would be hard to do without alerting the crew and the security team."

"Couple of air to surface rockets to the bows of the ship to distract them. I land on the stern and look for the colonel."

"No." He sipped his whisky. "You are thinking like a soldier rather than an assassin. In the Atlantic or the Pacific you might pull it off. In the Med you are never quite far enough either from shipping or somebody's coast guard. Those waters are intensely patrolled, by the British, the Spanish and the Italians. Not least because of the number of people attempting to sail across from Africa. The boat would be swarming with officials before you could get close to her." He shrugged, "And then you've got the other problem."

"Extraction."

"Exactly. How the hell do we get you out of there?"

"OK, drop me with a submersible..."

"Too slow, those superyachts are fast."

Drop me ahead of it. I'll intercept it. I place magnetic mines along the waterline. I pull myself aboard, take the colonel, blow in the side of the yacht, take a lifeboat and get the hell out of there."

"Having damaged the other lifeboats."

"You have someone pick us up in a seaplane."

"Not bad. But very risky, and no plan B. If you miss the intercept, you'll be stranded in the middle of the Mediterranean with egg all over your face."

I stared at the glare of the reflected sun above the turquoise pool. I knew he was right and I knew I had to control my impulse to just do it. Who Dares Wins was our motto, but it belied the meticulous preparation and attention to detail that went before the daring. The wild berserker that lies at the heart of every SAS blade was only allowed to come out when all other avenues were closed. Then, if and when that happened, his opponents had a real problem on their hands. But the time for that had not come yet. I said:

"Then I intercept them at Ano Koufonisi. How do I get there?"

"Fly to Naxos. Hire a yacht there. It is only twenty to twenty-five miles from Naxos to Ano Koufonisi. If you average eight knots you should be there in about three hours or less."

I nodded, then smiled. He had obviously already thought it through and had it prepared. "Can you get a boat at this short notice?"

He returned the smile. "It's already booked, the *Apollonis*, a rather nice fifty-foot Hans 540E. She'll give you eight to ten knots."

"Should be fun. You'll be tracking the *Bucephalus* and you'll let me know where and when she drops anchor."

"Of course. I've booked you in at Charlotte's House, a boutique hotel near the beach at Koufonisia, the capital of the island. It's not much of a capital, a cluster of holiday houses and a couple of restaurants. There is no car-hire there, but I spoke to Charlotte and she said she could arrange a Jeep for you."

We sat in silence for a while eating cheese and sipping whisky. Eventually he said, "What's your plan?"

"Get onboard, kill everybody, sink the yacht, bring the colonel home."

"Good..." He turned as Araminta emerged from the house with a fat file in her hands. As she sat he said, "The island is roughly circular, with Koufonisia located at its southernmost point. Curiously it is not a natural harbor, though a port has been constructed there and is, on the face of it, the most likely place for the *Bucephalus* to drop anchor."

Araminta had been leafing through the file as she spoke and now placed a satellite picture of the island on the table. She pointed at it.

"Here, about a mile and a half from Koufonisia, is Pori Beach, the only natural harbor on the island. It happens to be nice and sandy too, with perfect transparent waters. There is no village, but there is a kind of small tourist resort nearby, Finikias, with a couple of private villas and a hotel on the beach. That's the other place he might drop anchor." She shrugged. "It's more private and secluded, and if he needs anything from town, it's less than five minutes in the launch."

"Pori Beach would make life a lot easier for me."

"For sure, and in the Jeep, if you put your foot down, you could be there in five or ten minutes."

"The million-dollar question now," said the brigadier, "is, how are you going to get onboard?"

I drained my glass and refilled it. "Our starting point is, either they invite me, or I intrude. The chances of their inviting me are remote. So I am not even going to entertain the idea. Which means I have to intrude. I can intrude in one of three ways, secretly, under false pretences, or I can storm the yacht."

Araminta raised an eyebrow at the brigadier. "A one-man storm. If it were anybody else, I'd laugh." She turned to me. "How d'you plan to do that?"

"Swim out at night. Plant magnetic mines forward on the hull. When they detonate, I come aboard aft on the landing platform, move fast to the cabins, kill Yushbaev, find the colonel and leave on the launch. I'd need an assault rifle with a grenade launcher, a P226, a knife..."

"Extraction?"

"I take her to my yacht, then rendezvous with a seaplane. Fly to Rome and pick up an air taxi to New York."

He stuck out his lower lip and raised his eyebrows. He looked at Araminta. "Sounds good to me. Any comments?"

"It's not exactly subtle and surgical. It will attract a lot of attention. The yacht will not sink into the cold, dark depths of the Atlantic. Those are shallow, transparent waters. It will sink eight or ten feet into clear, warm water. When they investigate the frogmen will find not only the pieces of mine on the seabed, they will also find bullet holes and casings, not to mention the bodies of the," she glanced at me, "doubtless *numerous* victims shot to pieces by Captain Devastation here."

I sighed. "Gabriel Yushbaev is known to have connections with the Russian mob. There will be no way to trace whatever they find back to me or Cobra, and it will be assumed that he was attacked by a rival mob. Going in ninja will be much more difficult, require much more preparation and greatly increase the risk element. Not only that, it will put the colonel in greater danger than is necessary. I have to kill everyone on that yacht as quickly and efficiently as possible. That means mines, assault rifle and grenades."

The brigadier nodded. "I agree. Whom do we have in Greece who can provide the hardware?"

Araminta suppressed a sigh. "Nikki Supplies, Athens." She turned to me. "Make a list. You'll need night vision goggles. If you're going all out you might want some C4, ammo..."

"I got it," I interrupted her as I wrote down the things I'd need. "How soon can I be out of here?"

"Tomorrow afternoon. There's just one thing."

"What?"

"Yushbaev has a representative in Marbella who takes care of business for him in Spain. He's not a Russian, he's a Spanish lawyer by the name of Segundo Lopez. You want to find out where Yushbaev is headed after Koufonisi, this guy will know."

"If I ask him, first thing he's going to do is call Yushbaev and tell him I'm after him."

She shrugged and squinted up at the sky, pursing her lips. I looked at the brigadier. He shook his head.

"It's a tricky one, Harry. I can't advise you. We don't condone killing people who are not targets, unless it is in self-defense."

I turned to Araminta. "This guy, Segundo?" She nodded. "Is he just a lawyer on a retainer, or...?"

She was shaking her head before I'd finished. "No, no, no. This guy manages Yushbaev's affairs here. He is not *just* a legal advisor. He is Yushbaev's agent. That means when Yushbaev isn't here, Segundo Lopez *is* Yushbaev."

I turned back to the brigadier. "There is too much at stake to pussyfoot around. I need to talk to this guy and get what information I can out of him." To Araminta I said, "Where can I find him?"

"It's easier if I take you." Then she frowned. "Are you up to this? A week ago we weren't sure you'd make it through the night."

"I'll make it through the night. You can put me in touch with this guy?"

"I know him. I've been observing him for some time on behalf of the Company."

"The CIA are interested in him?"

"Of course, they're interested in Yushbaev, and Yushbaev's point of entry into Europe is Segundo Lopez, via Marbella. So we have met at cocktail parties, events and a few real estate negotiations."

"You have his ear?"

"Up to a point. If I tell him I have a deal for him, he'll be interested enough to meet me."

"OK, tell him it has to be today because I'm going back to the States tonight."

She pulled out her cell and the brigadier stood. "I'll leave you to it." He hesitated. "I don't need to tell you that once you have asked him the question..."

I nodded. "I know. But if I need to choose between this

asshole's life and the colonel's, I don't need to wade through a lot of philosophical angst to reach my conclusion."

"Let me know when you're ready and I'll see you to the plane."

He walked toward the house. He must have been sixty-five if he was a day, but he was tall and strong and moved with the ease of an athlete. At the end of the table Araminta was saying, "Hey, Segundo, my man! How's it hangin'?" She listened a moment and laughed. "Man! That's gotta be painful! Listen, *tío*, I have a good friend here, he's telling me about a sweet deal and right away I thought of you." She listened and laughed. "You bet your sweet ass I'm getting a commission. Do I *look* stupid? But believe me, you are going to like this, and so are your people. You *know* what I am talking about. This is the Persil deal to end all... You don't know what Persil is? Ariel? OK, Ariel. Yeah, yeah, washing powder. So this is the Ariel deal to end all Ariel deals." She looked at me, sighed and rolled her eyes. "It's a detergent, Segundo, a *detergent*. And it *washes whiter*, get it? You do the *laundry* with it...Jesus! Yeah, yeah, you got it. You wash money with it. That's it...good boy."

I laughed quietly and she went on.

"So, listen. Here's the deal. This friend of mine has some land just above Sierra Blanca, roughly where the Quinta Golf Club is...?" She listened for a moment, sighing again. "No, shut up, Segundo. I haven't finished. See, this friend of mine has secured a permit to build a casino on that land. Now, what he wants to do is sell the land to, say, some wealthy Russians, with a caveat in the contract which allows him to reinvest that money into building the casino on that land... Well maybe some other kind of partnership would be of interest to him, but we won't know that unless we talk. But, Segundo? Don't you even dream about cutting me out. I want my commission, *capisci*?"

She winked at me and made like she was listening. Then started shaking her head.

"Nah, that won't do... Because he's flying back to the States this evening... So shoot me! I heard about it this afternoon and the first thing I did was call my good friend Segundo. But hey, if you're too damned busy to spare half an hour to talk, don't sweat it. I'll go and talk to Angeles... Oh," she laughed, "Suddenly you have time, *hijo de puta*? Yeah, yeah. OK, half an hour. No, no, we'll meet at Calle Albinone, at the *Huerta del Fraile*. You know it? Good, be there. Half an hour. And Segundo? This guy has to catch a plane, OK?" She hung up. "Let's go talk to Segundo."

"What is the *Huerta del Fraile*?"

"The Friar's Orchard. It's a big chunk of wasteland on the outskirts of the city. It used to be an orchard, now it's just waiting for the market to pick up so somebody will buy it."

"And that's on Albinone Street?"

"Yup, and on the other side of Albinone Street is a pine forest, about half a mile long and a quarter of a mile across. It's the basically the beginning of the *Sierra Blanca*, the mountains at the back of Marbella." She held my eye a moment. "Don't worry, it's a good place for a quiet chat."

"What about his car?"

"I'll get in his car with him. He'll like that. You follow. When the track starts to get rough, we stop. You have your talk. When you're done we leave him in the car with a used condom and a call girl's number in his wallet. The number will be out of use and untraceable."

"Where do you plan to get a used condom?"

She frowned. "Oh, well, I thought maybe you..." I scowled and she laughed. "It's part of the CIA's basic tool kit. Didn't you know?"

"You done?"

"Don't be silly, stupid, we leave a half-opened condom on the seat beside him. We don't want to go leaving DNA all over the place, do we?"

"You've done this before, I can tell."

She gave a small shrug with a tilt of the head. "Yeah, we tend not to blow things up so much, you know? We're a little more subtle, a suppressor, a knife, bit of misdirection... You know the kind of thing."

"Ninja."

She snapped her fingers and pointed at me. "Ninja."

THREE

THE SUN WAS GROWING HOT AND THERE WAS A BUZZ OF cicadas over the olive groves that Araminta had called the *Huerta del Fraile*. I climbed out of the Cherokee and leaned against the hood, staring down the potholed blacktop, waiting for Segundo Lopez to appear. The passenger door slammed and Araminta appeared walking with her arms crossed and her eyes squinting slightly behind black Wayfarers. I nodded toward the woodland that started immediately at the side of the road on our left.

"Is that it, in there?"

"Yup. A little farther down there's a dirt track that leads in among the trees. About two hundred and fifty yards in there is a small clearing. A car could roll down there and be lost to view, maybe for a few days."

"You got the whole thing figured out already?"

"Yeah, well, while you were sleeping the sleep of the undead, some of us were working."

"So if you had this all figured out already, how come the brigadier didn't mention any of it?"

She looked at me like she wanted to slap me around the back of the head. "You still asleep, Harry? In case you hadn't noticed, Segundo Lopez isn't Lex Luthor. He's a bad man, but he is not guilty of crimes against humanity. So Cobra cannot get its hands dirty with his blood. This is operational, like Bill Hartmann or Hirsch. We do this, not Cobra."

"So you didn't tell the brigadier."

"That's why he got up and left."

I nodded. "OK. Your man is late."

"He's Spanish, the Spanish are always late. Spain will arrive late to Judgment Day. The world will be full of smoldering embers and brimstone, and there will be forty million Spaniards looking around, shrugging and saying, '*Que pasa? Guo'* happening?'"

"You weren't like this in Puerto Rico. You were different."

"That was an act." She grinned. "I did my homework. I knew what you'd like."

The sound of a car made us look down the road. A cream Range Rover approached and stopped a few feet in front of us. The door opened and a short man in a blue suit swung down. He had a yellow bow tie with dark spots on it, and blue-black hair going slightly bald on top, like a monk who'd left his order, and his tonsure was growing back. He strutted toward Araminta with a big grin on his face and his right hand held out.

"Araminta, Araminta! You gonna make me crazy!" He laughed and looked at me. "Always in the last minute! Womens! Womens are always like this! Last minute!" He held out his hand. "Segundo Lopez, at your service."

I took his hand and pumped it enthusiastically. "Good to meet you, Segundo. We have a pretty sweet deal here." I pointed up in the direction of the woods. "Right up there. But I am going to need some help to pull it off. Araminta says you're my man."

He spread his hands wide, hunched his shoulders and grinned. "We gonna talk! Tell me what you want. I tell you if I can do it."

Araminta pushed off the Jeep and slapped Segundo on the shoulder. "You can do it. Let's go have a look. You and me'll go in your Range Rover." She turned to me and winked. "You follow on behind."

Segundo was nodding. "Yeah, OK, OK."

I followed them and after about fifty yards they slowed, pulled off the road and started bumping and rolling up a narrow track among tall pine trees, wild shrubs and ferns. We ground through the dappled shade, lurching over rocks and channels gauged into the dry, red earth by rain and wind, and scorching heat. After four or five minutes the Range Rover slowed and pulled off the track, in among the trees, and stopped. I pulled in behind it, blocking the exit, and swung down from the cab. Segundo was climbing down too, and Araminta was walking around in front of the hood. Segundo had his back to me and was saying, "We cannot do this over a map in a bar?"

Araminta was shaking her head, pointing south, through the trees.

"Are you kidding me? Down there you've got Marbella and Puerto Banus..."

She didn't get any further. I slammed my right fist into his kidneys, took a hold of his collar and kicked his feet from under him. He landed hard on his back and I heard his lungs go into spasm. I pulled my knife from my boot and knelt on his chest. He gripped at my leg, struggling to breath. I showed him the knife.

"Segundo, listen to me. This is really very important for you. Today can end like any other day. Tonight you can have a drink with your friends, have a large whisky and think, 'Man, that was an intense morning. I'm glad it's over.' Or tonight you can be in hospital, on life support, having reconstructive surgery. Or, Segundo, you can be dead in the next minute or two."

He'd been shaking his head since "reconstructive surgery;" now he started saying, "No, no, please, no."

I ignored him. "This is a truly important moment in your life, Segundo. You have many roads ahead of you and you must choose the right one. Do you understand me? Do I have your absolute attention?"

He nodded. "Yes."

"Now, here is what you need to know so you can go home in," I glanced at my watch for effect, "five minutes, if you're smart. Don't lie, don't try to bullshit me, don't try to be clever. OK? That's the don'ts. Now the dos. Do answer every question quickly and precisely. Do tell the truth, the whole truth and nothing but the truth. Do remember that honesty is your path out of this crisis you are in. Understand?"

His breathing had eased. He swallowed. "Yes."

I started with a test question. "Where is Gabriel Yushbaev going in his yacht?"

He swallowed again, hard, and I knew what was coming.

"He is going to a Greek Island, Ano Koufonisi."

I gave him three full seconds because I didn't want to do what I knew I had to do. I glanced at Araminta. She trod on his wrist and I drove the knife through the back of his hand. The scream was the kind of thing that haunts your dreams for the rest of your life. I pulled the handkerchief out of his jacket and stuffed it in his mouth until he'd stopped. Then I pulled the knife out and wrapped the handkerchief around the wound.

"I knew you were going to do that," I said. "I hoped you wouldn't, but I knew you would. I told you, Segundo: the whole truth. But that's only part of the truth, isn't it? I gave you time. I gave you three whole seconds to continue. But you hoped you'd get away with just Ano Koufonisi. Now you don't get to go straight home in five minutes. Now you have to go to hospital instead. And it only gets worse, every time you try to trick me or lie to me, it gets worse. So let's try again, and get it right this time. Where is Gabriel Yushbaev going in his yacht?"

He was breathless, pale and sweating, almost incoherent. "First he is go to Ano Koufonisi. There he is stay a few days. He was not decided, maybe after he is go to Istanbul. He is going to stay in Istanbul a few days. Not decided yet. And then he will go in Black Sea, to Divnomorskoye, on the coast of Russia."

I nodded. "Good, that's good. Now, why? What's he got there?"

Segundo's bottom lip curled in and he began to sob. "I have a lot pain. Please, if I tell you this he will kill."

"I understand your problems, Segundo. It's tough, I know. So answer me and we can get you to a hospital, fast. As to Gabriel killing you, let me assure you he won't, because he will be dead long before he can kill you. My advice? Talk to the *Guardia Civil*, offer to cooperate with them in exchange for protection, because Segundo, your days of helping the Russian Mafia are over. Now, last chance, what has Gabriel Yushbaev got in Divnomorskoye?"

He said simply, "The girls. They bring them from Poland, from Ukraine, other places, Belarus, Turkey. They keep in a big house he have there, in the forest. The girls are stay in luxury, all the time parties and drugs, marijuana, cocaine, heroin. Until the girls is dependent, then he sell them to the clubs."

"Have you been there?"

He nodded. "Yes. Once, when he contract me. He have drugs there, also. He bring from Turkey, from Caucasus, and from his house he distribute. The house is not a house."

I scowled at him. "What are you talking about?"

"Is a palace. It is big, very big, many rooms, three swimming pools, gardens, land, forests..." He trailed off. "Is a palace."

I nodded, glanced at Araminta and sucked my teeth for a few seconds.

"OK, here's the million-dollar question, did Yushbaev talk to you about Colonel Jane Harrison of the United States Air Force?"

He went a sickly pale color. "I really want help you, maybe he use different name. Maybe you tell me what she look like."

"He never mentioned her?"

"I never hear the name."

"A blonde woman, thirties, good-looking. She's been with him these last few days."

"American?"

"Yes."

"Jane?"

"Yeah."

"Yes, she been with him. I don't know she was military. They come to my office couple of times. We go for lunch."

"She had lunch with you and him?"

"Yeah. We have lunch."

I looked up at Araminta and searched her face for something that would tell me I was wrong, that there was some simple explanation. There was nothing there that said that. I looked back at Segundo.

"Was there anything about her, anything that struck you as..." I faltered, not knowing what it was I wanted to ask him. He stared at me, curious even in his terror. After a moment he said, "She not talk much. She was quiet, you know? Serious."

"What was their relationship? Did they give any indication of what their relationship was?"

He looked distressed. "I don't know. I suppose they were lovers. I didn't talk with her. I really need a doctor, mister. I done what you ask."

I could feel Araminta's eyes on me. I stood and said, "Get up."

The report was loud, flat and ugly. His head smacked hard to the side and remained motionless, though his feet and his fingers twitched. There was a neat, scorched hole in his left temple, but lots of blood and gore were oozing out the other side of his head, saturating the dry earth.

I scowled at Araminta. She didn't let me speak.

"Get a grip, Harry. What were you going to do, invite him home for tea?"

"No," I growled, "I was going to take him to his office and collect all his files on Yushbaev. Now you've made that impossible."

She took a step closer. The toe of her boot pressed against Segundo Lopez's shoulder. She poked a long finger into my chest.

"Get this into your head, Harry. You are not the FBI, you are not the CIA. You are not out to investigate or uncover crimes. You have one function and only one. You take out targets."

I curled my lip and snarled, pointing down at the dead meat at her feet.

"Yeah, but he was not a target, remember? And he could have been useful."

"Just stay focused on the job, Harry. Come on, let's get out of here."

I took his cell phone, and we turned the Jeep around and rolled back down the track toward the road. As we lurched back onto the blacktop she said, "I'll go in tonight and get the files. I'll get the CIA's Marbella office to hand them over to the Spanish *Ministerio de Justicia*."

I didn't answer for a while. I knew she was right and I had faltered when I shouldn't have. Segundo Lopez was a son of a bitch who had earned whatever he'd had coming to him. But I had got squeamish and almost endangered the operation. I wasn't about to tell her that, though.

"You know I'm entitled to the spoils of war, right? Now I'll have to take it directly from Yushbaev."

She snorted. "Right, I'm pretty sure you'll manage."

"Yeah, I'll manage."

Back at the villa we found the brigadier in his office. I handed Segundo's cell over to him but before I could tell him what we'd learned, he held up a hand.

"That's fine, Harry. Let me have a chat with Araminta. You'd better pack. I want you in the air before this evening. I'll come up and see you in a moment."

I climbed the stairs feeling unreasonably mad that he wanted to debrief us separately, and packed a couple of cases. By the time I was done he knocked on the door and stepped in.

"We've cleared your gun and your knife, provided they go through in the case. How did it go with the lawyer, Lopez?"

He sat on the bed and I leaned my back against the window frame.

"He's going to Istanbul and then Divnomorskoye, on the Russian coast of the Black Sea. He has some palatial house there where he keeps women he has kidnapped from Turkey, Belarus, the Ukraine, Poland and places along the Caucasus. Lopez had been there. Apparently the girls live in luxury and he gets them hooked on various drugs—coke, marijuana and heroin were mentioned. Once they are totally dependent on him, he sends them out into the world, to the clubs he supplies."

"That is a very expensive way to get prostitutes."

"That's what I thought. It reminds me of the Hashishim. Maybe he's modelling himself on Hassan-I Sabbah, only he's using women instead of male assassins. First he gets their loyalty and obedience, then he uses them."

He made a soft grunt. "A bit farfetched. We'll have to see. Anything else?"

"Yeah, along the same theme, Lopez said Yushbaev went a couple of times to his office accompanied by an attractive American blonde in her thirties who didn't talk much. They also had dinner together and the blonde came along. Her name was Jane."

"That is very worrying. Have they got something over her, or was she, as you suggest, planted in the US Air Force long ago by Yushbaev?"

"It seems unlikely, because we have never been compromised with the Russians or Yushbaev himself..."

"But then we haven't trodden on Russian toes until now. But note how the moment we went after Cavendish, Yushbaev took the Colonel back."

"Did he? Cavendish told me they had been watching her because of her association with me. It looks to me like the Cavendish consortium took her because they wanted to know who I was and who I worked for, and Yushbaev snatched her from the consortium when he realized I was going after her. She was the bait to catch me."

He sighed. "Perhaps. There is no way of knowing for the moment." He paused. "Are you ready?"

"Yeah."

He nodded. "What happened with Lopez? Araminta says you hesitated."

"I didn't hesitate. I was debating whether he would be more useful alive. I thought his files on Gabriel Yushbaev could be useful. I also wanted to screw some money out of him."

"Good." He said it absently, like he was thinking about something else. "Good thinking. Well, it seems the CIA will take the files and hand them over to the Ministry of Justice here in Spain, and perhaps you can screw some booty out of Yushbaev before you eliminate him. Will you deal with him in Greece or follow him through to Russia?"

"As we planned, on the yacht."

"Araminta is worried that you are still convalescing. She's not convinced you're ready."

"That's why there are no women in the Regiment, sir. They worry too much."

He smiled. "Perhaps you're right." He stood. "I'll give you your stuff and last-minute briefing in the car."

"Good." I grabbed my cases. "Let's go."

FOUR

I touched down at Naxos airport at eleven o'clock that night. The place was small and ugly, all whitewash and blue wood, and about as dead as Segundo Lopez the last time I'd seen him. I took a cab to the Iria Beach Art Hotel and slept for eight hours straight. In the morning, after I had showered, shaved and dressed, I took a cab to Naxos City. There isn't a lot to say about Naxos. Narrow streets, some of them cobbled, too many cars and the constant feeling that you're caught in a time-loop and you're seeing the Mediterranean the way it was sixty years ago.

I had the driver drop me at Propopapadaki Street and strolled along the dock to Clive's Mediterranean Cruises. It was set between two restaurants with large terraces where the sea breeze was flapping the tablecloths, and people who were not Greek were beginning to gather to have breakfast.

I stepped through a plate-glass door into a dark blue office with huge pictures of yachts crashing through waves on the walls. A blond, blue-eyed guy reading a magazine behind a desk looked up at me and smiled.

"Do for you?"

He said it in an accent he had cultivated at a private school in the south of England. He smiled and I smiled back.

"You have a yacht reserved for me. The *Apollonis*, a fifty-foot Hans 540E."

"Then you must be..." He waited with raised eyebrows and a smile that I figured came to him easy. I handed him the passport the brigadier had given me the day before on the way to nine airport.

"Bob Foley."

"Super!" He took a look at the passport, compared the likeness and said, "That's you then. Always best to make sure. Your delivery arrived from Nikki Supplies in Athens. Your man said it would. We've stowed it aboard for you. You found us then." This last was said while he rummaged in a drawer. I frowned and he said, "Propopapadaki, not everybody finds it at first."

I laughed. "Yeah, I thought it was a mountain in Mexico, but my cab driver knew better."

"Ha!" he said, "Mountain in Mexico. That's good. Propopapadaki. Pococatapetel. Yeah. Shall we go then?"

I followed him at a quick walk along the dock while he filled me in on how to start the engine, where the insurance papers were and where to find the stores. He also showed me where my delivery had been stashed in one of the cabins, and where the diving gear was. After that he made me sign some papers, wished me luck and told me to give him a call when I wanted to bring her back.

Half an hour later I was pulling out of the harbor, sliding across a flat, creamy ocean, but as I rounded the Stelida headland a rolling swell started, and occasionally she would jump and crash as we split a wave, sending a shower of chill spray high into the air. There are few feelings on Earth as good as standing on a sailing yacht with the sun and the sea breeze in your face and the salt spray spattering your bare skin. It's like flying, only a hundred times better.

Once past Argios Prokopios and Maragakas, the swell increased and the *Apollonis* started to leap and crash, sending explosions of white foam across the bows. I was doing a good nine or ten knots down the west coast, making good time, though I felt in no particular hurry to arrive. *Apollonis* felt like the best company I'd had in a long time, and I would happily have spent the next three or four weeks in solitary island hopping.

But instead of four weeks it was four hours later when I pulled into the small port at Koufonisia, the only town on the island. On the way I had reviewed the kit the brigadier had arranged for me. There seemed to be everything you might need to storm an average-sized fortress. There were the mines I had asked for: each one carried about eleven pounds of explosive and had a total weight of twenty pounds. There were two Heckler and Koch, one with a mounted GLM, a stash of spare magazines, a spare P226, night vision goggles, and four cakes of C4 with corresponding fuses. There was also a waterproof bag for transporting the weapons. It was all in order and nothing seemed to have been left out.

On the way to the airport the brigadier had given me Charlotte's number and I had called her when I was about an hour out of port. She'd said she'd meet me with my Jeep and take me to the hotel.

The port was ugly. It was a bare cement structure reaching out from an arid, featureless stretch of coast. It was not a natural harbor, or even a headland. Its only natural advantage was the relative protection it was afforded by the islands of Kato Koufonisi, about half a mile to the southwest, and Glaronisi, maybe a mile farther to the south.

The port itself was a concrete square with a narrow opening in the southwestern corner, maybe thirty yards across. Beyond the gray cement port there was a broad dirt road that stretched away to the west and to the east, and was lost among scattered pines, gnarled cypress bushes, scorched yellow grass and dry earth. There was a handful of sailing yachts moored at the keys, and a couple of cars parked in the parking lot. One was a dark green Cherokee. By the chunky, square shape I figured it was twenty to thirty years old.

Beyond the beaten earth road there were scattered villas and what might have been hotel complexes. Here and there, there was a glint of turquoise among the whitewashed walls and the parched, russet earth. I could see no houses or buildings older than thirty or forty years.

I lowered the mainsail, then hauled in the spinnaker and entered the harbor using only the engine. As I turned to bring the stern in to the dock I saw a woman climb out of the Jeep and wave. She was blonde and slim, in jeans and a white sweatshirt. She had big, round sunglasses, and a big straw hat on her head. She also seemed to have tied a green chiffon scarf around her hat, maybe it was to keep the flies away. I waved back and she approached the mooring bollard I was aiming for. She had a nice walk, with plenty of hip swing.

I killed the engine, looped the rope around the bollard and stepped ashore.

"Charlotte Fanshaw?"

She held out a slim, pale hand and spoke in what the Brits call cut-glass English. "You must be Robert Foley. How do you do?"

I took her hand and it felt very delicate, so I only squeezed it gently. "I do OK, how do *you* do?"

She smiled with a pretty mouth and I decided she was attractive. "I muddle through. I've brought your Jeep, as requested by your man, but I must warn you, as I told him, there are very few places to drive to on Koufonisi."

"I heard there were a few beaches."

She slid her large glasses down to the tip of her nose and regarded me with very dark blue eyes.

"*A few* might be a bit of an exaggeration. A couple would be more precise. There's this one," she pointed behind her to a small, sandy cove, "and then there's Pori Beach. The rest is all cliffs and rocky shoreline."

"I'll only be here a few days. I guess I'll take a couple of picnics to Pori Beach."

"I guess you will."

"How about places to eat?"

She put her glasses back where I couldn't see her eyes.

"I have the best restaurant on the island. Then there's Mixalios up the road, if you're a carnivore."

"I'm a carnivore. I think it's cruel to eat anything that was not recently gamboling in a field."

"Why am I not astonished?"

"Carrots lead such cruel lives, buried in the soil from birth, and as soon as they break free, they get eaten. It seems inhuman to me."

She suppressed a smile. "Then there's Tis Marias, which is frightfully trad' and friendly, and then there's Guacamole, Burgers and Cocktails, which is exactly as the name suggests. Finally, over on Pori Beach, there is Finikias Hotel which is fun in a rustic sort of way."

I glanced at my watch. It was one forty-five. "So is it too late to have lunch at the best restaurant on the island?"

"Far from it."

She brought the Jeep up to the dock and I loaded my bags in the back. She gave me the keys and we drove to Charlotte's House. The hotel turned out to be no more than four hundred yards away, sitting on the beach she had pointed out to me earlier. It was more like a large, elegant house than a hotel. Five broad steps led up from the sandy beach to an ample terrace where tables and chairs were set out under a creeping Russian vine. Tall, Mediterranean pines flanked the building, sighed in the breeze and scented the air, as well as providing shade.

A couple of large arches gave access to a lobby that was more like a large, elegant drawing room. The reception desk was small, and tucked away on the left. There was a fountain in the center of the floor, and on the right there was a cold fireplace. The furniture was eclectic, an old chesterfield sofa here, an overstuffed calico armchair there, a heavy Moroccan lamp table beside an Emmanuel cane chair, and ferns, lots of ferns in giant terracotta urns. I liked it.

Two more arches at the back gave onto a patio with a pool, and an elegant staircase led to the rooms upstairs.

Charlotte smacked the bell on the desk and while she signed me in to a large red book, a small man of about a hundred and ten took my bags and carried them up the stairs.

"Wifi is a problem," she said, as though I had asked why she used a book instead of a computer. "So is broadband, cable and just about everything else." She raised her eyes and smiled as she slid the book across the counter at me and handed me a pen. "This isn't the virtual world most humans inhabit these days. This is the real one they left behind."

I took the pen and signed. "That's good to hear. I always figured if it was virtual, you were only getting twenty percent of the deal."

"Sight?" I nodded. She said, "So you get cheated out of sound, smell, taste..."

"And touch."

"Kostas has taken your bags to your room. Shall I expect you for a cocktail before lunch in, say, twenty minutes?"

"That sounds about right, Charlotte."

Kostas had put my bags on the big, king-sized bed and thrown open the dark blue French doors onto a small terrace where there was a round table with a couple of chairs. The Mediterranean looked close enough to reach out and touch. A pale haze moved over it in the heavy heat, and mountainous islands, peaks left over from the Flood, rose monolithic out of that mist, like half-forgotten truths about who we were, and where we'd come from.

Kostas pointed at a freestanding wardrobe and a slatted door onto an en suite bathroom, muttered something surly in Greek and left before I could tip him. I had a quick shower, changed my clothes into the kind of cream linen the brigadier would have approved of, and went down for a cocktail and a late lunch.

I found Charlotte in the shade of some palms beside the pool, sitting at a white, wrought-iron table. As I sat, a younger version of Kostas emerged from the shadows in a white jacket, carrying a tray and two menus.

"He knows what I want, what will you have?"

"Will he know how to make a Vesper martini?"

"I shouldn't think so for one minute. Have a dry martini with gin and an olive and be grateful we have gin and martini at all."

"I'm grateful."

She said something to him in Greek and he went away.

She handed me a menu. "I suppose you'll want lamb."

"Coming to Greece and not having lamb is like going to the moon and not having cheese."

She opened her menu and giggled. "That's funny. You'll have lamb chops, we do them extremely well, and we'll share a salad and kalamari to start with. Greek wine is very risky, leave that to me."

I handed her back the menu. "So who do those yachts belong to in the harbor?"

"Oh, regulars who come every summer. This used to be a popular place. June to October it was generally packed, with the harbor absolutely full of boats, and many more anchored at sea or at Pori Beach. Then the crisis struck, credit was cut off left right and center, banks foreclosed on mortgages, cash dried up and the only people who had money in Europe were the Scandinavians and the Brits, and what little they had they spent in Spain. As I am sure you know, Greece practically went bankrupt, and just as we were emerging and tourism was picking up again, bang!"

"Covid nineteen."

"Not back to square one, we'd like to be in spitting distance of square one; no, we've gone back almost to a post-war economy, controlled by Brussels. And things are just getting started. It's going to get a lot worse."

"Yeah? How's that?"

She gave a shrug, like the answer was obvious. "Once the emergency measures stop propping up the European economies, taxes start rising and banks start foreclosing, Europe will implode.

You'll have twenty-seven countries all sucking at the teats of Germany and France, who are in no condition to suckle anybody. This island will shut down. Much of Greece will."

"That's a shame. Will you have to close?"

"Almost certainly, unless I set up some kind of luxury holiday resort for billionaires. The spot's ideal for it, you know."

Kostas Minor reemerged from the building with a tray of bottles and glasses. He served Charlotte with a Beefeater and tonic. Instead of lemon she had two small slices of lime. For me he had a short, fat whisky glass with three big rocks of ice. Over that he poured a generous measure of Beefeater and topped it up with martinis into which he dropped an olive.

Charlotte rattled at him again in Greek and I caught the words, *kalamari, arnaki, katsikisio* and *saláta*. Kostas grunted and ambled away with a face that suggested our lunch somehow proved the basic unfairness of the universe. I raised an eyebrow at her.

"OK, everybody knows what *kalamari* is, *arnaki* is lamb and *saláta* is obviously salad. So what's...," I hesitated, smiling, "catch a kiss-ee-oh?"

"*Katsikisio* is goats cheese, and you know, Robert, it is really quite pointless flirting with me."

Really? Why's that?"

She didn't answer for a while, staring out at the hazy blue horizon. I was about to change the subject when she said, "I'm just not available."

"Oh." I watched her sip her drink, and asked, "Do you get many billionaires here? I guess they pass here on their way to Puerto Banus from Saudi, Israel, Russia..." I paused, then added, "But mainly Russia. I guess Saudi, Egyptian, Jordanian, Israeli, they'd all pass to the south of Crete. You'd have to pull in the Russians first."

"I *was* being flippant."

"Yeah, I know, but it's not such a bad idea. If you have a friendly Russian billionaire you can sell him the idea as a money-laundering scheme. They'd probably finance it themselves. You could have five-star hotels, a casino, everything a Mafioso billionaire needs to blot out the horror of who he is."

She looked at me and laughed. "My dear Robert! What an absolutely horrendous idea. And such bitterness! What has the Russian Mafia ever done to you?"

"Oh, long story and not very entertaining."

She sipped and set down her drink. "As a matter of fact we do have a Russian billionaire who passes this way from time to time in one of those superyachts. He doesn't stop at the port, he usually anchors at Pori Beach. I have no idea if he is a Mafioso, or I suppose in his case it would be a mafioski."

"Does he come ashore and mix?"

"Rarely. Mainly he keeps to himself and stays aboard the yacht."

"He ever come and eat here?"

"Once or twice." She looked at me and raised her sunglasses onto her head. "We are a bit of a nosey parker, aren't we?"

I laughed. "I'm sorry if I am intruding on a sensitive subject."

She didn't answer. After a while Kostas Minor brought out a white linen tablecloth, napkins, heavy cutlery, white wine in a bucket of ice and two plates and glasses. After that he brought a large goat's cheese salad and a dish of *kalamari*.

Charlotte ate the battered rings of squid with her fingers. When she had eaten four or five, and drained her first glass of wine, she said, "I don't normally like Russians. They are far too intense. But Gabriel was somehow different. He broke all the rules, was utterly uncompromising, and once I had been loved by him, nothing else could come close."

FIVE

I SIPPED, WONDERING IF THIS WAS GOING TO complicate my job. "You still see him?"

"Every now and then he drops in if he's passing. But of course I am nowhere near as fascinating for him as he is for me. I run a small hotel on a small, deserted island in a country that is hanging on tooth and nail to the European Union to avoid slipping into the Third World. He is an emperor. He owns palaces, on the land and also on the sea. He owns industries. He has companies preparing to mine on the moon and Mars. My goodness! He owns *people!*"

I arched an eyebrow at her. "He owns *people?*"

"Thousands of employees who work for him, all his devoted followers, he is a visionary. And then there are people like me. He owns me, body and soul."

I chewed on a ring of squid, wondering if she knew what she had said, or if it was just part of her gushing, slightly infantile infatuation.

"You were speaking metaphorically?"

She tried to force a laugh and it came out as a sigh. "Of course."

I shrugged. "There's no 'of course' about it. Slavery is more prevalent now than it has been since the British Parliament passed the Slavery Abolition Act in 1833. Quite a lot of multinationals use slaves in countries where the regimes are willing to turn a blind eye."

Kostas Minor came and took away our plates, then brought a large dish of lamb chops and a stone jug of red wine. He poured me a small amount to try. I was surprised and showed it on my face.

"It's good."

"It's mine. I have a small vineyard on the far side of the island. I age it in oak barrels instead of pine. This one is three years old."

"That's quite an investment for a slow return."

She didn't say anything, and I wondered if I was drinking Gabriel Yushbaev 2018. Two got you twenty I was. I wondered also if she knew he was about to turn up on her island.

"I'd be curious to meet this charismatic guy who makes it pointless to flirt with you."

She laughed. "Well, maybe you'll get the chance if you hang around a few days. He messaged me a couple of days ago to say he'd be passing by on his way to his palace in Russia."

"No kidding? You think he'll descend among the humans for a bite to eat?"

"He might. You never know."

"Tell him you have an American friend who is prepared to invest in a money-laundering scheme for him."

"I think I'll pass on that one. Now, do try the lamb, or Aggy will be very upset."

The lamb was as good as she had promised, and by the time we had finished the platter and the jug of wine, the afternoon was drawing on and the shadows of the palms were lying long across the turquoise pool.

I made my way up to my room, collapsed on the bed with the window open to the dying afternoon, and slipped into a deep, dark sleep. I dreamed, but didn't know I was dreaming. I had that conviction of reality. I was talking to Sheila Newton[1] in the pine forest above Marbella. She looked gray and dead, with dark hollows under her eyes. We were standing over Segundo Lopez's body and she was saying, "If you don't kill one you have to kill the other."

Then I was awake. A full moon was suspended over the ocean outside my window. Its translucent light occupied most of the dark sea, and tinged the deep blue of the sky with green. There was an eerie stillness. I sat up and went to the window. The pines and the palm trees were motionless: tall narrow shadows touched by the moonlight. The only movement now was the winking of the small waves on the shore. The touch of a cool breeze carried the sigh of those waves to me across the sand.

Then there was a light, just a glimmer at first, out beyond the port, but as it inched into view it became clearer, winking in the dark. Then there were two, and three, a ship of some sort. I checked my watch. It was thirteen minutes past five. At first I could not make out the details of the boat, they were obscured by the glimmer of the lights, but as it moved into the moonlight scattered across the ocean its silhouette became visible. It was either a luxury cruise ship, or a superyacht, and there was no doubt in my mind which.

I leaned my elbows on the windowsill and watched it pass slowly west, toward Pori Beach, knowing that Gabriel Yushbaev was onboard, and that Colonel Jane Harris was with him. I wondered if they were sharing the same bed in his stateroom, and I felt the hot coals of anger burn in my belly.

I didn't sleep after that. An hour later I went for a run and worked out on the beach while watching the moon fade into a blue-gray morning sky. I finished up with a swim and strolled back to the hotel at eight o'clock. Charlotte was not there, so I went to my room, showered and changed my clothes, and grabbed

---

1. See *LA: Wild Justice*

the key to the Jeep. I was thinking of breakfast at Finikias Hotel, at Pori Beach.

I timed the drive, taking it easy, and found that at a steady twenty miles an hour, it would take me ten minutes to get from the hotel to the beach. A steady twenty miles per hour was not as simple as it might sound. The road was not asphalt. It was dry, beaten earth eroded by rain, intense heat in the summer and salt winds that blew in off the sea across an almost flat island. There were rocks, potholes, ruts and gauges, not to mention dust, gravel and sand. Twenty miles per hour on that road would be a hurry-up.

The road cut across the eastern half of the island, winding through a russet wasteland of ochre dirt, small gnarled bushes and, here and there, a small pine copse. After about seven minutes I came to what looked like an abandoned, derelict holiday resort made up of ugly concrete boxes piled on top of each other for the factory farming of tourists. Some of the buildings had got as far as being whitewashed, others were in naked, cement gray with gaping wounds where the doors and windows should have been. Rubble, dirty wooden pallets, mounds of sand, all abandoned, starved of the lifeblood of cash, completed the picture of desolation.

Just beyond this apocalyptic holiday resort I came to a small, grassless knoll, topped by another pine copse. Here the road turned sharply to the right and descended a gentle slope to a sandy cove where the water was a cool, lime green and looked good enough to drink. To the left of the track there was another one of those stacks of concrete cubes, but this one had been mellowed with a large veranda onto which had been built a pine structure covered in dry branches to create cool shade. There were red plastic tables and chairs bearing the Coca-Cola logo, a white freezer with a card pinned to the wall above it showing pictures of ice creams, and a bald guy in black pants and a white shirt leaning on the pine balustrade that confined the veranda. He had a red gingham dishcloth in one hand and he was watching me like he wasn't sure whether to be curious or not.

I parked on the sand and climbed the four concrete steps to the veranda. There was a young couple in the far corner. They had a white tablecloth, croissants and coffee, and very orange orange juice. The bald guy smiled at me above his hairy chest.

"*Kaliméra*," he said, like he really wanted me to believe he meant it. "*Kalos ithate!*" He gave a little bow and indicated the red plastic table with both hands. "You sit, sit. What you drink?"

"Coffee, and I'll have some breakfast. Toast?"

"Toast with oil?"

"With butter."

He went inside and I sat, looking out at the small bay. The *Bucephalus* was a little less than five hundred yards out. An easy swim, but the moonlight could be a problem. I'd have to check the time the moon rose and set. The alternative would be to black my face with boot polish, or use air bottles. That was fine as long as nobody spotted the bubbles.

The yacht was big, the size of a small cruise ship. It had three decks and the bridge above the main deck. I figured it was about one hundred and eighty feet long, and electronically it was probably state of the art. Of course, electronics were only ever as good as their power supply, but as long as they had juice, they could be a real problem.

The waiter brought my breakfast and I sat buttering my toast and sipping the strong, black coffee while I watched the yacht. I was thinking it would have been handy to get a look onboard, or at least review the plans of the boat, but the brigadier had not been able to get anything better than a general layout.

I bit into the toast and watched as a dingy was lowered from the stern into the water. A woman and a man climbed aboard and the small boat headed for the shore. The woman was not a blonde, and the way she moved was too affected to be the colonel. As they drew closer I could see she was tall, wore a lime green bikini and had short, dark hair. I wondered if she would die in my attack on the boat.

As they drew up on the shore, the guy jumped out and helped her. She dropped a towel and a bag on the sand. The guy put up a parasol and a folding sunbed. She lay down and he pushed the launch back into the water and returned to the yacht.

As I watched him withdraw across the green water of the cove, I thought that in the absence of a plan of the boat, there was no point in waiting. Further, I had no idea how long they were going to stay. It might be a week, but they might leave tomorrow. I needed to act as soon as it was feasible, and on the face of it, that meant that night.

I finished the toast and stretched out my legs as I put the plan together in my head. After dinner I'd go down and take the *Apollonis* out of the harbor, and sail her round the south coast of the island to Pori Beach. It was about two miles and shouldn't take more than fifteen minutes. I would keep in close to the headland and drop anchor. I figured I could get within two hundred yards. There I'd put on flippers, mask and air bottles, and if I approached from the stern, the chances of the bubbles from the tanks being spotted were remote.

I'd plant the mines on the starboard side, away from the beach toward the prow, one above the waterline, the rest below. Then I would pull myself up on the boarding platform. There I would stow my gear out of sight and prepare my weapons before detonating the mine above the waterline. Once that mine went off it would be a free-for-all. Security and the crew would all charge forward seeking the source of the explosion. Anyone who needed to be protected would be confined to their cabins. They would not be sent to the lifeboats until the nature of the threat had been identified. So, I would head straight for the staterooms, kill any security or crew I encountered, locate the colonel and remove her to a launch, then blow the hull below the waterline.

Simple.

As I was thinking, I had been watching the tall, short-haired woman on the beach. She had got to her feet and crossed the sand to climb the steps onto the terrace. Now she stood talking to the waiter in Greek. He was bowing, goggling at the few bits of her body that were covered, drooling and making the kind of noises you might make after a lobotomy. He seemed to say "Naí," a lot, which sounded like it should mean "No," but probably meant "Yes."

She turned and trotted down the steps again and back across the sand, while the lobotomized letch hurried into the shadows of the restaurant to convey her orders. Shortly afterwards he hurried out again with an ice bucket containing a bottle of champagne. I smiled to myself as I watched him run, stumbling across the beach to place the bucket by her side. He popped the cork, laughed too loud and poured her a glass. Upon which she dismissed him and returned to a book she was reading.

I wondered about going down for a swim and trying to get into conversation, but rejected the idea. I had my plan; anything else now would be a complication. I had another coffee and watched the babe in the green bikini. She didn't do anything more interesting than read and sip her champagne. Nothing much happened on the yacht, either, so I paid for my breakfast and drove back to the hotel.

Charlotte was behind the reception desk sorting through mail when I walked in. She smiled without warmth.

"Have you had a good morning, Robert?"

"Pretty good. I went to have breakfast at Pori Beach. Looks like your friend has arrived."

She looked back at her envelopes. "Really?"

"What was the name of his yacht? This was the *Bucephalus*. A beauty."

She nodded and started slitting open envelopes.

"Yes, I think that was it."

"If he books a table for dinner, I'd love to meet him."

She glanced up with a smile that would have frozen lava. "I'll bear that in mind, Robert. Will you be lunching in the hotel, or will you be taking a picnic? I can get Aggy to put something together for you if you like."

"No, I'll eat in." I glanced at my watch. "I think I have time for a shower. It's hot outside."

She nodded and went back to leafing through her mail. I was clearly not welcome and I wondered what had happened since last night. I climbed the stairs thinking about it. She had said that night that Gabriel Yushbaev owned her, body and soul. He was here, now, and whether he saw her or not, she had to wear her metaphorical chastity belt and give all men the cold shoulder. She was his property, like any of the houses or apartments he owned around the world. He didn't need to occupy them. He just needed to possess them, and keep the door locked; or the belt.

I stopped halfway to the landing and spoke across the empty lobby.

"I was going to ask you if you'd join me for dinner tonight." She looked up at me but didn't say anything. I gave something that might have been a smile. "I guess you'll be on call, huh?"

She still didn't say anything, so I went up to my room.

SIX

I HAD LUNCH AND SPENT THE AFTERNOON ON THE *Apollonis*, checking the engine and the rigging, and going over the hardware to make sure everything was in perfect working order. At five PM I took her for a test run up the southwest coast of the island as far as Pori Beach and had a look at the small coves at the south end of the bay. The cliffs were not huge, but I figured at night they would be enough to hide the *Apollonis* from view. From where I was anchored I could make out a small group of people on the top deck of the *Bucephalus*, lounging and drinking in the sun. The short-haired girl was there, and a tall guy dressed in white, but I could see no sign of the colonel. At six I headed back to Koufonisia, with the small, niggling doubt in my mind as to whether the colonel was on the yacht at all.

When I arrived at the hotel there was a Land Rover Defender 90 V8 sitting at the bottom of the steps. It wasn't the kind of car you'd expect to see on Koufonisi, so I figured Yushbaev had shown up to inspect his property. I wondered briefly if he'd rolled the Land Rover off the boat, but dismissed the idea and figured Charlotte must have been looking after it for him. One piece of property looking after another.

But when I walked into the lobby Yushbaev wasn't there.

Charlotte was standing at the reception desk with a gin and tonic in her hand. She was still and silent, staring at the early evening glow of the doors that stood open onto the terrace and the swimming pool. There was the desultory sound of an occasional splosh laced lazily into the evening song of the birds.

After a moment Charlotte turned to look at me. I said, "Nice car."

"Is it?"

"If you like that kind of thing. I find there is too much that can go wrong with high tech. The more sophisticated it is, the more fallible."

"Are you making some heavy-handed point, Robert?"

"Probably. Something about the shallow allure of apparently impressive things, as compared with deeper, less impressive things that are more reliable and solid."

She surprised me by busting into sudden laughter. She surprised me further because the laughter was not patronizing but genuinely amused.

"Oh, Robert, you know I think I had you all wrong. I think you're actually quite sweet. Are you from Iowa or Wyoming, one of those cowboy states? Are you going to call me ma'am in a moment?"

I smiled and took a step closer to her with my hands in my pockets. "Nope. I'm from New York City, the Bronx, and I might call you many things, most of them pretty flattering, but none of them would be ma'am."

She regarded me with the tail end of a smile on her lips. When she didn't say anything I jutted my jaw at her drink. "You going to offer me one of those?"

"Of course." She rang a small brass bell on her desk. "Martini?"

"Neither shaken nor stirred, just dropped in the glass. You going to introduce me to Yushbaev? Or has the pool been cordoned off?"

A small frown creased her brow. "I don't recall telling you his name was Yushbaev."

"Yeah, well, I'm not just a pretty face. There aren't that many billionaires in this world, and there is only one Russian one called Gabriel."

She sighed and looked back toward the pool. "In any case he's not here yet. His current wonder-fanny is."

It was my turn to laugh. "Wonder-fanny? Short dark hair and all the way up legs?"

"That's the one."

"You think she'd let me engage her in a conversation about Platonic idealism?"

"That's naughty. You don't know, she might be a genius. In any case what she would allow you to do is irrelevant. It's what Gabriel would allow *her* to do that counts."

Kostas Minor came shuffling out and Charlotte gave him his orders. He glanced at me resentfully for no reason I could fathom and shuffled away again.

"He'll take it to you on the terrace. Though I must say I am disappointed."

"Why's that, Charlotte?"

"What happened to your high ideals regarding shallow sophistication and deep, solid reliability?"

"Oh, I am not interested in Wonder-Fanny, Charlotte." She arched an eyebrow at me. She looked nice when she did that. I shook my head. "No, I am interested in the emperor of the universe, master of all things and owner of women, Gabriel Yushbaev."

Her smile dissolved. "I hope you're not going to do anything foolish, Robert. He's..."

She trailed off. I gave a small nod. "I know what he is."

I walked away from her and crossed the broad lounge to step out onto the terrace. The sky was turning dark in the east, but there was still pale blue-white over in the west. One star, Hesperus, hung over the horizon. The moon had not yet risen.

The pool was lapping turquoise in the cooling evening air, and the girl with the short, dark hair was lounging at the edge of it in a wet deck chair. Beside her was a tall drink with a straw. I went and stood eight feet from her head. I looked up at the sky, then down at her tanned body. It was desirable.

"Did I see you at Pori Beach this morning?"

She turned to look up at me. She was not quite expressionless. There was a touch of insolence and a hint of humor.

"Only you can know that. Did you see me?"

The accent was French. "I did."

"Then there you have your answer. You ask your own question and you answer it."

"Is the yacht yours?"

She kept her eyes closed. "The *Bucephalus*?"

"Was there another one there?" Now she turned to look at me. I smiled. "Annoying, isn't it?"

She gave a barely perceptible giggle and closed her eyes again.

"The *Bucephalus* is not mine. It belongs to my friend."

"Lucky friend. Where is he now?"

"He is on the yacht. He will come to this dump soon to have dinner."

I sat myself down, facing her. "I wouldn't call this place a dump. The food is very good."

That got a reaction. Her eyes snapped open and her jaw dropped. "Ha!" she said. "If you had stayed in the hotels I have stayed at in Paris, in Moscow, in Los Angeles…"

"I probably have."

She gave me a patronizing smile that made me want to take her bikini off and tan her fanny.

"I don't think so, Mr…?"

"Call me Robert. You know, expensive and good are not necessarily the same thing."

"Please! I do not need folksy philosophy from your cowboy ranchers."

I wondered briefly if I had acquired a passing resemblance to

Clint Eastwood in the last twelve hours and said, "I am not a cowboy..."

She seemed not to hear me and plowed on, "'Always it begins, my daddy once told me...' and then some nauseating platitude." She gave another giggle. "In France we do not turn to our farmers for wisdom, Robert. We turn to Descartes, Michel de Montaigne, Albert Camus, Jean-Paul Sartre, Simone de Beauvoir, even Voltaire, though he is making us laugh, ha ha ha, he is making us also think. No?"

I couldn't think of anything to say, so I looked at her legs instead. They were still nice legs.

"What we do not do, Mr. American Cowboy, is go to our farmers and ask them, 'Hey, Slim, what did your father tell you about epistemology? Can you tell me? What were your father's thoughts on ontology, while he was digging out the pig shit?'"

"You made your point."

"*Bien.*"

"But I still think you mistake cost for quality. Unless your boyfriend has to spend a lot on it, you don't want it. Am I wrong?"

She muttered something that sounded obscene and closed her eyes again. After a moment she asked, "You are who?"

"Robert."

"Robert who?" She opened her eyes and turned to look at me.

"Robert Foley."

"I have never heard of you. You make money from a ranch or something? *Tu sens la merde de vache!*"

"No, sweetheart, I make money as a highly paid assassin. I get paid to take out pretentious little girls who mistake being rude for being intelligent. If you had half the intelligence and erudition you pretend to have, you'd be capable of having a conversation with a stranger without insulting him every time you open your pretty little mouth. And while we're at it, the only smell of cow shit around here is coming from you." I pointed at her. "Your daddy may have paid for a classical education, kid, but what you know about life could be written on one of your cute buttocks with room to spare for the pictures. Sister, you're as shallow as a puddle of yesterday's piss."

I'd had some opportunistic hope of maybe postponing my attack and trying to get myself invited aboard the *Bucephalus* to do a bit of recon. But I'd given up on that idea almost as soon as I'd started my play. I stood, aiming to go to my room and dress for dinner, but her voice stopped me. It was laced with an interesting blend of curiosity and challenge.

"You think you know a lot about life?"

I took a pull on my drink, savored it and smacked my lips. "No. *You* think you know a lot about life, because you believe you bought that knowledge. I know that what you bought was bullshit. And I know that what little wisdom I have, I have gathered from my own experience. What have you experienced? The fantasy that whatever you want in life you can buy? That's a cheap fantasy. Believe me, if you want expensive, you should try reality. Reality is *really* expensive." I drained my drink, surprised at how mad I'd got, and put my glass down. "Try to enjoy your dinner, even if it's not expensive enough."

I went to walk away. She spoke quickly and suddenly. "My name is Marianne." I stopped and raised an eyebrow at her. "But you can call me Marie."

I didn't answer straight away. "Well, thank you, Marie. You can call me Bob."

"Will you dine here tonight?"

"Yes."

"I will ask Gabriel if you can join us."

"That's nice of you," I smiled, "but what if I have other plans? What if I don't want to?"

Her cheeks colored. "Would you like to join us?"

I made the smile into a friendlier one. "Sure, that would be nice. Thank you."

"I will go and dress now."

She said it like she expected an answer. I didn't have one, so I nodded and went indoors.

Charlotte was standing in the doorway with her back to me. She still had her gin and tonic in her hand. The dark was closing in but the sea was slightly luminous, making her into a shadowy silhouette. She turned as I crossed the lobby.

"Did you get what you wanted?"

"Maybe. It seems your owner is coming to dinner tonight."

She turned away. "Don't be cruel, Robert."

I stepped out beside her and saw that the Land Rover was gone. "Has your man gone to fetch him?"

She nodded. "He bought the Land Rover. It's the least I can do."

"Did he buy the Land Rover, you and the two Kostas as a job lot?" I was surprised at the savagery in my voice. "Does he own the hotel, too?"

"What's it to you?" She looked away at the quickening dark over the sea. "As a matter of fact he does. It's convenient for him, and for me."

There was an empty quality to the silence that followed which told me "convenient" wasn't quite the word. I questioned it.

"Convenient?"

The word hung there between us. She kept her eyes fixed on the ocean. I said: "How the hell did you get into this, Charlotte?"

"Please, Robert, don't patronize me. I don't need a counselor. Life just fucks some people over sometimes. If you happen to be one of the unlucky ones, you take what's coming to you and lump it. That's just the way it is."

"You really believe that?"

She sighed. "Do you believe the sun rises in the morning, Robert? Do you believe you are standing on solid ground? Do you believe we are talking? It's not a question of belief, Robert. It's there. It's real. It's not something you can have an opinion about."

I gave a small shrug. "I always liked the Vikings."

She gave a small snort. "You amaze me."

"They believed that the Nornir..."

"The what?"

"The Nornir, the three Weird sisters, Urd, Skuld and Verdandi, the Fates of Norse mythology. They called them the Nornir."

"Oh." She sipped her drink, frowning at me. "What about them?"

"They were weavers. They wove the destiny of humans and gods alike. But the only points that were fixed in the skein of your destiny..."

She laughed. "*Skein?*"

I fought down a stab of irritation. "It's the thread..."

"I know what it is, Robert, but it's a little archaic, isn't it? *The skein of your destiny* is hardly the sort of thing you expect an American to come out with."

"You asked me not to patronize you. You done patronizing me?"

She looked away again. "Perhaps. What about the skein of a Viking's destiny?"

I felt a sudden rush of bitterness and frustration and was about to tell her to go to hell. Instead I said, "The only fixed point in the skein of your destiny was the time and manner of your death. How you lived and how you died, that was up to you."

She spoke to the darkness, away from me. "You said the manner of your death was predestined."

"Yeah, if you're going to be stabbed through the heart on the ninth of November, 2023, you can take that blade on your knees, begging for mercy, or you can take it standing on your feet, tearing the other guy's throat out with your teeth. That's what I meant by how you die, and how you live."

Far off I saw the glow of headlamps rise and fade. She said, "Mythology, words."

"They're words if you only speak them. But it becomes a way of life if you feel them and act on them."

She turned now and looked up into my face. Then her eyes dropped gradually to my chest and slipped away again, into the dark.

"Perhaps I choose to live and die on my knees, Robert. That may be repugnant to you, but it's a choice I have made. Perhaps I am happier that way."

"Is that why you escaped to a remote island in the Med? Is that why you opened your own hotel? So you could live on your knees?"

Her face whipped around. "You know nothing of me or my life!"

I nodded. "But it's not hard to guess. People who escape are usually escaping from some kind of slavery, Charlotte. And they are usually escaping because they don't like to be slaves. You want to live on your knees, be my guest, but don't kid yourself you like it. My guess is too much self-pity just made you lazy."

"You *bastard!*"

I reached out and cupped the back of her head in my hand, then leaned down and kissed her. She didn't resist, but her left hand rested gently on my shoulder. When I withdrew she spoke in a whisper, "Robert, I can't..."

I kissed her again, softly, then whispered in her ear. "He owns you, Charlotte. He doesn't own me."

SEVEN

The headlamps illuminated the beach, then swung in from the right and the Land Rover pulled up at the foot of the broad steps. Kostas Minor climbed out from behind the wheel and opened the near-side back door. For a moment a pellet of hot coal burned in my gut as I wondered whether the colonel would step down from the back. If she did, I would kill Yushbaev and take her to the *Apollonis* right then. But it was not the colonel. It was a tall, athletic man somewhere in his forties or fifties. He had thick, dark hair swept back from a handsome, mocking face. His eyes were pale blue and insolent, his clothes stank of money, as did he.

While Kostas Minor hurried around to the other side of the car, the man I knew was Gabriel Yushbaev climbed the steps, smiling easily at Charlotte. She gazed at him and held out both her hands. He spoke first.

"Darling, it is wonderful to see you. So nice to return to my little home in the Cyclades."

"Gabriel, it has been far too long. We have missed you."

"I know, I know." I watched him take her in his arms and kiss her, long and deep, while her hands clasped the back of his head.

As he pulled away her hands slid to his shoulders and she whispered, "*I* have missed you."

Below I watched a man who was probably in his late twenties climb the stairs. He was wearing beige chinos and a navy blazer, and also looked expensive, though not as expensive as Yushbaev. Charlotte gestured at me with her hand, still gazing into her owner's face.

"Gabriel, this is Robert Foley, he is a guest at the hotel."

He turned to look at me, like he hadn't noticed me before.

"Robert Foley," he said, as though the name had some meaning for him.

"Gabriel Yushbaev," I replied, in a strange inversion of the usual form. "How do you do?"

"What brings you to Koufonisi, Mr. Foley? Not many people come here these days."

I shrugged. "Just exploring the islands. Looking for adventure."

"And whatever comes your way? An admirable approach to life. Join us for dinner."

I wanted to tell him to shove his dinner where the sun didn't shine. Instead I smiled. "Thank you, that's very gracious of you."

He didn't bother to introduce the guy in the blazer. He walked into the lobby and suddenly, somehow, it was his. It was his lounge, his drawing room, his house and his party, and he was the host. Kostas Minor and two pretty girls appeared with trays of drinks, glasses and a large bucket of ice with two bottles of Krug shoved in it. One of the girls offered me champagne and I told her dry martini. She went away to make it. Yushbaev crossed the room to the French doors that led out to the pool, saying, "I love this place, small, cozy, like home for me."

Charlotte followed a few hesitant steps behind, and the guy in the blazer stepped up to me, holding out his hand.

"Ben Macleod, I'm Gabriel's accounts manager."

We shook. "Bob Foley, I'm a lay-about with too much time on his hands and a taste for easy adventure."

He laughed. "Sounds like fun."

"It is." I jerked my head at Yushbaev. "That's a hell of a big yacht for just the two of you. Don't you get lonely rattling around in there?"

He smiled with limelit pride. "You've seen it? She's a beaut', ain't she? We have a couple other people on board, they're just not here right now. Except..."

He frowned and looked around.

"Marie? She's upstairs getting dressed."

He shook his head and sighed. "Hottest thing on two legs, I tell you. But she is private property."

"Yeah?" I grinned. "Whose?"

"The boss. I'm telling you. I had a secretary, Russian guy, six two, thirty-something, real arrogant bastard. He made a pass at Marie, she told Gabriel and Gabriel beat seven bales of shit out of this guy while Marie watched. He sacked him, had him taken away and I never saw him again."

I could feel the warm burn of excitement in my gut. I gave my head a twitch and smiled. "That's pretty intense. You have to be well connected to get away with that kind of thing."

"Oh." He gave a small laugh. "He is well connected. Take my word for it."

"That doesn't worry you?"

He shook his head. "Nah, the way he's got things sewn up, I figure I have the safest job on the planet."

Her voice came from the stairs, peremptory, sulky, a little demanding.

"Gabbie?"

He'd been talking to Charlotte. Now he turned and looked at the stairs that swept down from the upper floor. She was there, a little over halfway down. I had to admit that she was something to look at. Her short black hair framed a doll-like face, and her tanned skin was set off by long, silver earrings that sparkled with diamonds. A platinum and diamond choker highlighted a neck you just wanted to spend all night gnawing on, and her perfectly proportioned, curvaceous body was being hugged by a simple green silk dress that slid and slipped over her thighs and her bosom when she walked. Whatever your intellect told you about her shortcomings as a human being, your body just didn't give a damn. You wanted her.

Yushbaev crossed the room and received her at the bottom of the stairs. He spoke to her in Russian and she giggled playfully. A Greek maid offered her champagne, which she accepted without acknowledgment, and Yushbaev led her back across the room to where Charlotte was standing, staring at the floor.

I smiled at Ben, who was goggling at Yushbaev with unconcealed awe.

"You have to be some special kind of son of a bitch to enjoy a game like that, huh?"

He added a frown to his goggle and directed it at me. I figured I'd had enough of teenage hero-worship and carried my martini over to the little group. Something in the anxiety on Ben's face told me you weren't supposed to do that unless you were summoned to The Presence by God Himself. I didn't have a damn to give, but if I'd had one, I wouldn't have given it.

"That," I said loudly as I approached them, intruding on their conversation, "is one mother of a beautiful yacht, Gabriel. I have to congratulate you."

He didn't have much choice. He'd already invited me to dine with him and he wanted to play the gracious lordly host, so unless he was going to spoil his own scene, he was going to have to graciously accept my intrusion. That made me smile broadly, while he smiled graciously.

"The *Bucephalus*? It is fun. I enjoy it."

"Fun?" I gave a bark of a laugh and nudged Charlotte with the back of my drink-hand. "It probably cost the annual GDP of a small country!" She winced like I was being vulgar. I knew I was being vulgar, and I was enjoying it like he enjoyed the *Bucephalus*. "How many cabins has it got? I figure two staterooms, right?"

His pale blue eyes said he was about to say something dismissive. So I didn't give him a chance to answer. I turned away from him and started talking to Charlotte, who didn't know whether to look confused or alarmed.

"My brother-in-law down in Texas had one of them superyachts. He's in oil and beef?" I laughed. "He says he can not only give you the steak, he can cook it for you too!" I laughed again. "Whole top deck of his baby was staterooms. Four staterooms with a lounge in the center? And a conch staircase winding down to the deck below. Two hundred feet long, that baby was."

Yushbaev was piqued in spite of himself. He addressed his answer to Marie, who was also staring at me curiously.

"Well, we only have two staterooms, and six cabins on the next deck, but we find it covers our needs."

"Only!" I gave my head a twitch. "You are a master of understatement, sir. What size crew you got? I bet it's about thirty men, isn't it?"

He laughed. "Those, Mr. Foley..."

"Bob, please!"

He winced with distaste. "Those were the older yachts that required a vast crew. But I value my privacy, so my most valued member of my crew is Hal."

"Hal?"

"A small joke. Like the computer in Arthur C. Clarke's *Space Odyssey*. I have a computer onboard, a gift from Bill, which operates just about everything on the yacht. We do still have humans for those little things that require arms and legs, opposable thumbs and independent thought..."

I laughed and interrupted. "But you don't want to encourage too much of that, do you?"

"No, not really. Our crew is just twelve men."

I frowned. "Hal take care of security too? Boat like that is just crying out to be burgled."

"Oh yes, Bob, Hal takes care of security, and the twelve crew are all drawn from elite Russian special forces. Believe me, if you are planning to burgle the *Bucephalus*, you are in for a very nasty surprise."

We all laughed and I raised both hands, crying, "Oh no! Not me!"

While we had been talking, Kostas Minor and the pretty maids had been filing in and out through the doors to the pool. Now he approached us and bowed, and addressed Charlotte in Greek.

"*Servíretai deipno, kyria.*"

She nodded. "Dinner is ready, shall we?"

The question was addressed to Yushbaev. He acknowledged it with a smile as thin as a paper cut and turned to Marie, taking her arm in his, and echoed Charlotte's words. "Shall we...?"

He led the exquisite girl toward the terrace. I raised an eyebrow at Charlotte, though she was looking at Marie, not me, and said, "Looks like you're stuck with me, Charlie, baby."

We followed the divine pair and she glanced at me. "Do you mind telling me what all that pseudo-Texan bullshit was about?"

"Well, ma'am, I don't rightly know what to say. Ever since you told me I was a cowboy, I feel the call of the prairie and the need to yodleee-i-ho."

"You're out of your mind."

"Reckon as how you're right, ma'am."

"Stop it, will you?"

They had set up a long table with six places. Yushbaev had led Marie to the foot of the table and held the chair for her as she sat down, then stepped to the head and indicated to Charlotte that she should sit on his right, effectively making him and Marie the hosts, and Charlotte a guest. He indicated the seat on his left to me and Ben went and sat on Marie's left.

Charlotte sat and the men sat. I glanced at the empty seat on my left. The place had been set with plates, cutlery and glasses. I noticed Marie was still watching me with a lack of expression that managed to convey interest, like a cat watching a mouse. I asked her, "Are we expecting somebody else?"

"The colonel was going to join us, but at the last minute was indisposed."

I smiled blandly. "Maybe he hasn't found his sea legs yet. Have you been long at sea?"

Yushbaev answered. "Just a few days, from Marbella. The colonel, Bob, is a woman. Colonel Jane Harris, of the United States Air Force. Traveling with us to Divnomorskoye, on the Black Sea. Do you know it?"

I shook my head. "I'm afraid not. I imagine you'll pass by Istanbul. That is one town I have never been to, but is definitely on my bucket list."

He settled back in his chair and gave me the kind of smile a mongoose might give a cobra.

"Bucket list?" he said. "Isn't that the list of things you must do before you 'kick the bucket'?"

"That's the one."

"Then you must go as soon as possible, Bob. It is just here, around the corner! Go!"

"You know something I don't, Gabriel?"

He threw back his head and gave a big, Russian, theatrical laugh. "No, my dear Bob, it is simply that we never know what awaits us—not around the bend—but at the next step! Life is a path into the darkness, which we illuminate with every footstep we take. Leave nothing till later. Strike now and make the moment yours! For it is all you will ever have: this moment!"

"Good words. But if it's all the same with you, I'll stick with this moment right now, and do Istanbul next week." I smiled, and gestured at the table with both hands. "Good company, the promise of great food, and a charming, beautiful hostess across from me. This moment suits me just fine!"

Charlotte flushed and looked down at her plate. I felt an icy thunder brewing inside Yushbaev and gave him a big, friendly Texas grin, while carefully ignoring the poisonous babe at the foot of the table.

"Say!" I snapped my fingers just as Kostas Minor and the

maids appeared carrying dishes of seafood and salad. "Speaking of bucket lists and *carpe diem*, you know what I would just love?"

He gave the kind of smile you'd call urbane. "I can guess a few things, but I'd hate to say them out loud in mixed company."

I pointed my finger at him like a gun. "You got me! That's funny! You got me." I dropped the smile. "No, but seriously. And you can just say, 'Bob, no can do, pal,' I will understand. But I would love to have a look on board your rig. I have a passion for boats. Seriously, and I have to say your *Bucephalus* is one of the prettiest boats I have seen in a long time."

He gave a small, indulgent laugh as one of the Greek maids set a plate of fish in front of him and another poured more champagne.

"My goodness, is that all? Come and have lunch with us tomorrow. I'll show you around. I'll introduce you to the colonel. It will be nice for her to meet a compatriot."

"Well that's what I call mighty hospitable of you, Gabbie. I will enjoy that a lot, I am sure."

"It will be our pleasure, won't it, Marianne?" He looked down the table at her. She kept her eyes on me. "Absolutely. I can't wait."

The talk moved on to the latest Broadway shows, and the shows off Broadway too, to Marbella and Puerto Banus's collective status as the two most boring luxury holiday destinations on Earth, but the relative convenience of their proximity to London. From there to the opportunities offered to Russian billionaires by Brexit and the pandemic, plus Yushbaev's theories on the artificial origin of the virus, and its delivery; and from there, finally, to the possibilities of life on Mars and mining there and on the moon. The talk was him talking and everybody else listening and laughing when required. We all played our parts perfectly. I, for my part, had nothing left to say. I had secured what I wanted and I was on fire inside. Tomorrow I was going to see the colonel, face to face.

And tomorrow, if all went well, I was going to kill Gabriel Yushbaev.

EIGHT

It was very tempting to seize on the new conditions, alter the plan and strike right away. It would not be difficult: Come aboard as a guest, and if the colonel came to the table, shoot Yushbaev and his security team, take the colonel and leave. Use the element of surprise to the maximum; and I had slipped the P226 into my waistband, and my knife into my boot, just in case.

But there were problems, too. Russian special forces were not sophisticated, and not all that well trained, but they were as tough as old boot leather, they were ruthless and they were relentless. They would not back off just because their boss was dead. They'd keep on coming until you killed every man Jack of them, and then they'd come back and haunt you as a Russian choir. That meant it was desirable to have a lot of firepower and a powerful distraction —which took me back to my original plan.

So by the time I climbed into the Jeep and headed for Pori Beach for the second time in two days, I had made up my mind to stick to the original plan, unless a perfect, irresistible opportunity presented itself.

When I arrived at Pori Beach at midday, there was a launch waiting for me with a guy who managed to make complete indifference into a special kind of Russian surliness. The truth was, I didn't give much of a damn about his indifference because the only thought I had in my mind, as we skipped across the green water toward the yacht, was whether the colonel was going to be there, and how she would react when she saw me. I had to acknowledge the possibility that she would alert Yushbaev to who I was, and if she did that I would need to act fast and decisively. Yushbaev would have to die immediately, as would his men. The colonel would have to come back with me and be debriefed, and Cobra would have to reinvent itself from scratch.

The brigadier would probably have advised against my visiting the boat. Better to strike by surprise, out of the blue. But the advantages to be gained from a recon were too good to be passed up.

As we moored at the stern, I could see my host in white slacks and a dark blue blazer waiting to receive me. He had a tall drink in his left hand, and Marianne in his right. She was more undressed than dressed, in a mauve bikini that left the essentials to the imagination, but with a lot to go on. Her hair was wet and her skin sparkled with droplets of salty seawater. I climbed aboard and she just watched me while Yushbaev shook my hand.

"Bob, welcome aboard! Let's see if we can satisfy your curiosity today." He gave my shoulder a manly slap. "First, I think, something to refresh you. Then allow me to give you a tour of the boat, and after that, lunch. How say you?"

There was not a trace of the colonel. I did my best to ignore the fact and offered them both a big grin.

"I say that sounds just fine. Do you think your man can make a Vesper martini?"

"Shaken not stirred? Don't tell me you are a fan of James Bond!" He laughed, like it was all he needed to confirm me as an idiot. That suited me down to the ground.

"An arrogant elitist who kills without flinching and is irresistible to women—what's not to like? But if Bond had been based on anyone real, he would have been with the Special Boat Service."

"Perhaps you're right, but fortunately, he is not real."

He led me through plate-glass doors into a large, luxurious lounge with oak-paneled walls, overstuffed cream leather sofas and armchairs and Persian rugs on a parquet floor. At the far end there was a fully stocked bar with a guy in a cream jacket chopping up limes and lemons. Yushbaev addressed him.

"Peter, we want one ounce of vodka, three ounces of Gordons gin, half of one ounce of Lillet Blanc." He turned to me. "The Kina Lillet is no more, as I am sure you know." He turned back to Peter. "Now you will shake this over ice, and serve with a coil of lemon peel. Am I right, Bob?"

"You're not wrong. Do you have an encyclopedia of trivia in your head?"

He chuckled with an ounce of smugness, three ounces of self-satisfaction and half an ounce of ain't-I-just-great. "I am afraid I have an IQ of one hundred and sixty plus an eidetic memory. Tell me something once and I will not only remember it, I will fully understand it and suggest ways to improve it."

He gave one of those big, Russian laughs and we watched the barman, Peter, put together an almost genuine Vesper martini, shaken not stirred. Peter handed it over and Marianne addressed Yushbaev.

"I have already seen this yacht a hundred times, Gabbie. You show Bob. I am going to take the sun."

He shrugged and led the way. Beyond the bar there was a mahogany door with beveled glass panes, and through that an impressive mahogany staircase rose and split into two spirals, one to the right and the other to the left. Before we climbed it he gestured beyond the stairs. "Forward, past the stairs and down the passages, we have the state dining room and the library. We have over five thousand books here. But we will start at the bridge. I think it will be of more interest to you."

I was trying to orient myself and imagine what would be

happening when the mines detonated. I saw a door over to the right of the stairs and pointed.

"I guess that leads to the engine room."

"And storage." He spoke as he climbed, without looking back. "You were curious about the staterooms. We haven't got four like your friend from Texas, only two. But we find them satisfactory."

We'd come to the top of the stairs and here there was another lounge with a bar. This one had a domed glass ceiling and glass walls.

"It's quite fun to have drinks here when there is a full moon or a storm." He pointed toward the prow, where there were sliding glass doors beyond which was an open deck with a swimming pool, and then the large, white structure of the bridge. "Nobody goes up there except me, the captain and his first mate. We have technology up there that is not yet known on the market."

"Yeah? What kind of technology? GPS? Satellite positioning...?"

"No, we have all that, of course, Bob, but this is mainly security: laser technology, electronic surveillance, heat and movement sensors. I would like to show you, Bob, seriously, but it is highly confidential stuff."

I thought I caught something in his tone, but he smiled and turned toward the stern. An archway led through to a lounge area with scattered tables, sofas and armchairs, and just to the left as we went through there was a sliding steel door.

"Through there you have the crew's cabins and recreation area, toilets and so forth, and here is the elevator which takes us up to the staterooms. It is the only form of access, and to activate it, your biometrics must be registered in the central computer."

"So once you're up there nobody can get to you."

He pressed his hand against a plaque in the wall and nodded at me. "Correct."

I laughed. "But if the system fails, you can't get down either."

"The system doesn't fail, Bob." The door slid open and he

gestured me into an elevator car that was eight-foot square of high-polish wood with art deco inlays and hand-carved mirrors. I stepped inside, the doors closed and we began to rise. "But if it ever did, we have lifeboats and an independent power source with which to run radio, radar, GPS..."

The doors slid open and he smiled at me again.

"Our technology really is cutting edge, Bob. More than cutting edge."

We stepped out into what looked like a luxurious hotel lobby from the turn of the last century. It was carpeted in deep burgundy and had a vast chandelier hanging from the ceiling. There were chairs in the same color that looked eighteenth century and probably were. They sat against the walls that were lined with silk. There were gilt mirrors and what looked to my inexpert eye like Old Masters on the walls. A single passageway led from the room. He led me to it.

"Here on the right is my suite, which I call the Emperor's Chambers. I share it with Marianne. I will show it to you in a moment. Here on the left is the Empress's Suite."

Maybe I shouldn't have, but I was getting tired of listening to him. So I smiled and said, "And that's where the colonel sleeps?"

Something happened to his eyes. They were not warm things to begin with, but suddenly they became Antarctic.

"Yes," he said. "She is feeling indisposed today, so she will not be joining us. Come, have a look at the Emperor's Chambers."

The double walnut doors to his Emperor's Suite probably cost as much as my TVR. They were twelve foot tall and the handles and hinges were of solid gold. He pushed them open and we entered what was to all intents and purposes a Rococo drawing room. The only thing missing was a bunch of pampered, lily-white fops in wigs, with painted lips. Maybe that would come after lunch. There was even a marble fireplace with eighteenth-century sofas and chairs positioned about it. One door—a smaller version of the walnut affairs that gave access to the suite—gave onto a bedroom which was more of the same, with a vast, mahogany four-poster with ruby velvet drapes, and another gave access to a large, semicircular terrace where the furniture was more *Star Trek* than Baroque. The same was true of the en suite bathroom in the bedroom, which was all toffee-colored marble and deep blue glass with concealed lighting.

"So, Bob, how does it compare with your friend's superyacht?"

"It's very impressive, Gabriel." I took a little stroll, looking around, peered into the bedroom again, then at the terrace, thinking of the colonel just fifteen or twenty paces away, locked in the Empress's Chambers. I smiled at Yushbaev, thinking I could kill him in a couple of seconds, blow the lock on her door...

"I do not anticipate anybody being stupid enough to attempt to break in and steal from the *Bucephalus*, but if they did," he paused and smiled, like he was trying to convey to me that he knew *I* might try something that stupid, "the problem is not so much getting *in*. After all, you only need to board it and enter, don't you? No," he shook his head, "the problem is *leaving* again once you are onboard. The whole ship locks down into separate compartments, and unless your biometrics are recorded in the central computer, you are a prisoner."

I laughed. "Well I assure you that the only thing I want to take from your yacht is your food and your wine, and some damned fine memories. So I hope you'll let me go home after lunch."

"I would not dream of keeping you a moment longer than you are comfortable. Shall we go and have lunch?"

We retraced our steps, taking a couple of detours to see the other swimming pool, the tennis court, the small cinema and the Star Dome, which was a reinforced glass dome at the very top of the yacht, which was equipped with waterbeds where, according to Yushbaev, you could get stoned, listen to Pink Floyd and lie flying above the stars.

"It is a unique experience. If we had more time I would invite you to try it."

"Yeah, sounds like fun. Do I take it you're leaving soon, then?"

"Tomorrow. Unfortunately I have business to attend to back home."

When we got back to the saloon, the table had been set for lunch. Marianne was still out on a deckchair taking the sun, with huge sunglasses making her look like a particularly attractive ant, and Ben Macleod, in white slacks and a white shirt, was leaning on the doorjamb with a glass in his hand, trying not to look like he was ogling her. He wasn't doing a great job. He glanced at us, said something to her, and came to join us. Through the glass door I saw her sigh and get to her feet to come in.

We didn't talk while we took our places and a couple of his goons in white jackets served us with prawn cocktails and ice-cold Krug in frosted glasses. When they were done and had withdrawn, leaving the ice bucket by his right elbow, he said unexpectedly:

"I don't give a fuck about anybody else's rules."

I picked up my fork. Marianne continued to display a complete lack of expression or interest, but Ben smiled at me, like he was trying to pretend Yushbaev had said something witty. Something told me this was not a new theme of conversation.

I speared a prawn and said, "I'd guess once you have a billion sterling in the bank, you don't need to give a fuck about other people's rules. Or am I missing the point?" Before he could answer I decided to annoy him for a bit by stealing the scene. "Did you know that in Aramaic 'camel' and 'rope' are the same word? '*Gml*' spelt G-M-L. Which casts a whole new light on the whole passing through a needle business, right?" I grinned at him and laughed. "Maybe even you can go to heaven, huh. Gabbie?"

He cleared his throat and stared at me. Marianne paused in her chewing to stare at me too, and Ben frowned a "what the hell are you doing" frown. I ignored them and skewered another prawn.

"I mean, let's face it," I gave a small laugh, "putting a camel through the eye of a needle is something you are never going to do. It just ain't gonna happen, right? But a rope? Now here the metaphor changes completely. Because all you have to do now, is strip away all the excess."

The three of them fell back to eating. After a moment Yushbaev asked, "And who defines what is excess?"

"Well, I guess there are a couple of different ways to answer that. In Texas they'd tell you, 'God decides that, boy.' But I suspect, you being a man of a philosophical turn of mind, might answer, 'I am the god of my own universe, therefore I decide.'"

He paused with a prawn halfway to his mouth and raised his eyes to stare at me. I continued to ignore him.

"And then," I pressed on, "there is the objective view which my Jeet Kune Do teacher keeps repeating to me."

Marianne surprised me by asking, without irony, "And what's that?"

"That heaven is not a place but a state: the state of Nirvana, and the only way to achieve that is by detachment. So every thread of that rope is excess."

Yushbaev managed to express utter loathing with a complete lack of expression for three whole seconds. Then he returned to his prawns and said, "Yes, well, as I said, I don't give a fuck about anybody else's rules. I am rich enough and powerful enough to make my own Nirvana."

NINE

"Listen to me," he said, and raised his index finger. "There is no good or evil, there is no right or wrong. This is not just a controversial opinion. It is a fact. And any man or woman who can face this fact, assimilate it," he paused and stared hard at me, "I mean *really assimilate* it, the way you assimilate the fact of gravity, the need to eat and drink, and shit, any man or woman who can do this—assimilate this reality that there is no right or wrong, has the potential to become a god."

I tried hard not to yawn. He'd brought out his ego to show it off so we could all admire it and say how it was the biggest, shiniest ego we had ever seen. Just like his boat. But I didn't really feel like admiring his ego or his boat, so I stifled the yawn, shrugged and said, "Maybe that is a useful attitude, but I think there is something much more important if a person wants to achieve real power."

He gave an indulgent laugh. "If I were looking for a teacher on how to become truly powerful, I think I might pick the billionaire over the..."

He gestured at me with an open palm, like Hamlet showing Horatio Yorick's skull.

"Incognito," I said, and smiled. "I am an incognito. You actually have no idea how poor or rich I am. You can guess, if you like, but you don't actually know."

He sat back in his chair and arched an eyebrow. "All right, Bob, it is always wise to listen. So tell me, what is this thing that is so important for somebody seeking power?"

I stuck a prawn in my mouth, gave my head a little twitch while I chewed and drained my glass. I handed him my empty glass and sighed.

As he refilled it I said, "I'd go further. I'd say it is the essential, fundamental nature of power. I am not a philosopher like you, Gabriel. But this is something I have observed in the world. True power is the ability to inflict violence. Violence is at the heart of all power. For that reason violence is the most valuable commodity on this planet. He who controls violence, controls everything."

He sat back in his chair again and said simply, "Oh,"

"I would say that is a cardinal truth. So to be really powerful you need three things. You need to be physically able to inflict violence, you need to understand the importance of violence, and you need to be willing to use it."

Marianne had stopped eating and was watching me very closely. Ben was frowning hard at a prawn. Yushbaev picked up his glass and cleared his throat.

"And you say you are not a philosopher. I confess I am surprised, Bob. I did not expect to hear a thing like that from you. It is a deep truth."

I made a circle in the air with my finger, indicating our surroundings.

"You did not achieve all of this, Gabriel, without deploying violence from time to time."

He gave a small shrug. "Sometimes as a threat, sometimes as the real thing. But you are quite right, my power rests on the ability to strike if I have to."

I glanced at Marianne and smiled at her. She still hadn't worked out how to use her face muscles. Ben said, "Sometimes, I guess, violence can take the form of a hostile takeover bid, a repossession, aggressive competition in the marketplace."

Yushbaev nodded. "Of course, but think more deeply, Ben. If you open a supermarket in the same street where mine is, what is to stop me from smashing your windows, burning down your store, even shooting you and your staff?"

"Well, in the civilized world at least, there is the police."

"Bah!" He raised both hands in a gesture of contempt. "So, I shoot the police too. What is to stop me?"

Ben laughed. "Well, you take on the state and I'm afraid you're on a losing ticket, because the government can deploy a hell of a lot more hardware and men than you can."

Yushbaev spread his hands. "So, you see, you have illustrated Bob's point. You can fight through the courts, take out injunctions, compete as aggressively as you like, and yes, they are forms of violence. But the bottom line is, when you use the resources allowed or offered by the law, those resources are backed by the implied threat of violence in the forms of the police and the army. The state *always* reserves to itself the right to use violence. Because, as Bob has explained to us, violence is the source of all true power."

"Which," said Marianne, addressing first me and then shifting to Yushbaev, "makes violence a very profitable business."

I asked, "You trade in weapons, Gabriel?"

"I trade in all sorts of things, Bob, and I certainly don't shy away from weapons. The business is, if you will forgive the pun, a minefield, but if you have the right contacts, it is surprising how easy it can become. The secret is knowing whom you can buy *from*, and whom you can sell *to*." He spread his arms wide in an expansive gesture. "Let's say you want to buy a couple of tanks from me, but treaties and regulations signify that I am not allowed to sell them to you. But I *can* sell them to a company in Marianne's country. Now, these treaties that bind me do not affect Ben's country because he is a nasty, poor Third World dictatorship. So I sell my tanks to the company in Marianne's country, who then sells them to a company you have set up in Ben's country, and that company sells them to you."

"Expensive and roundabout."

Ben nodded. "Yes it is, but the chances are that you and I have either oil, cocaine or some kind of high-value mines, and as well as cash, we can offer concessions and rights that long term are of more value than just money. An expert player who knows how to play these markets can wind up making vast sums."

I made a face that said I found what he was saying interesting, but added, "Dangerous game though. I heard Charles Cavendish was into that kind of business, and rumor has it he was assassinated."[1]

Both Marianne and Ben stared at Yushbaev. He went very still. The goons in the white jackets came and removed the plates and replaced them with four broiled legs of spring lamb in eucalyptus and honey sauce. The wine was a Barón de Chirel Almanzor by *Herederos de Marques de Riscal* 2012, which I knew came in at around eight hundred bucks a bottle. When they were done Yushbaev spoke again.

"Charles was a close friend of mine. He died in a boating accident."

"Really? I heard he'd got in too close with Sinaloa and Al-Qaeda and one of them took him out."

He sliced into the tender meat with a very sharp knife.

"Who told you that, Bob?"

A devil in my head wanted me to tell him I knew because it was me who blew his propane tanks. Instead I said, "Oh, you know, like a lot of Americans I have a weakness for conspiracy theories. Kennedy, the Twin Towers, Roswell..."

"Successful conspiracies, and conspiracies that get blown, like Watergate, get called history. Conspiracies that are only partly successful, or get partly exposed, get called conspiracy theories. It is a very successful second line of defense. Make anyone who

---

1. See *LA: Wild Justice*

espouses the theory look like an idiot. The emperor's new clothes."

"So, are you saying he was assassinated?"

He shook his head. "No, there was a leak in the propane tanks that they used for hot water and cooking. It was an accident."

"Oh," I ate lamb and sipped the superb wine. Then, "So, was it true that he was mixed up with Sinaloa and Al-Qaeda, and involved in all that shady business?"

He chuckled and snorted. "You said yourself, Bob, you don't get that powerful without resorting to violence. He was a master of manipulating the market. He took cocaine, heroin, diamond mining concessions, oil concessions," he made an "on and on" gesture with his hand, "you name it, if he could exploit it, Charles would accept it in payment for weapons. It was an approach that made him fantastically rich, even by my standards. But of course, it was almost impossible to demonstrate a direct connection to him. He was able to maintain this external persona as a great philanthropist, a genuinely good man."

"But he wasn't?"

"As I said to begin with, Bob. When you achieve this kind of power, it is because you have abandoned the idea of good and evil. There is just power and freedom, or weakness and slavery. Up here, we are not in kindergarten."

"Yeah, I get that."

He ate hungrily for a moment, and then regarded me through hooded eyes.

"If he had not had that accident, I might have had him killed myself." I laughed, like he was joking. He didn't, and all three of them observed me very closely. "I am serious," he said. "His death led directly to a huge increase in business for me. People who dealt with him, now deal with me." He returned to his food and asked, "Do you think, Bob, that there are people who undertake that kind of contract for large sums of money?"

I puffed my cheeks and blew, swirling my wine and gazing at the color.

"I don't know what to tell you, Gabriel. On the one hand I'd be real surprised if there weren't assassins of that caliber. On the other hand, it has got to be next to impossible to get at a guy who is that well protected."

Marianne spoke up again. Maybe the alcohol was loosening her tongue.

"I think there is an organization, a secret organization like Murder Inc., which specializes in taking out high-value targets. I should imagine that the operatives, the assassins, work on a free-lance basis for very high fees, and they specialize in either making the kill look like an accident, or shifting the blame for the kill onto other criminal organizations."

I chuckled. "That's a nice idea. Do you have anything to go on, or is it just something you'd like to do?"

She shrugged. "It stands to reason. The United States has Delta Force. They need to get rid of somebody, they send in a team of their special ops men. Or they use the CIA. Other countries have similar setups. But what about organized crime? Organized crime is more powerful and better organized every day. They must have a similar sort of organization."

"Maybe you're right," I said, "it's well above my head. I'm not poor, but I am pretty sure I could not afford to have somebody taken out." I laughed. "How about you, Gabriel, you ever had anybody rubbed out?"

His face was deadpan. "Oh, yes, several times. When I worked for the KGB we used to request terminations quite regularly. When the KGB closed, I remained in contact with several of our operatives, and I used them several times as I was building my empire. Now, I don't really need it so much."

"Wow." I looked at Ben and then at Marianne. Ben was eating, unconcerned, while Marianne was grinning at me, but it was hard to tell what the grin meant. I said, "That's pretty intense. Are you yanking my chain?"

"You were in the army, Bob."

It wasn't a question. It was a statement and it took me by surprise. All I could think of to say was, "I was?"

"It is in your eyes, your look. I have seen this look before. It is in your walk, the way you hold yourself, the way you play your part. Special forces, SEALs, Delta, perhaps Marines but I think not. You have not enough discipline for Marines. What I am wondering is, why are you hiding it?"

"I'm impressed."

"Yes, so why do you hide it?"

I shrugged and spread my hands. "Force of habit, Gabriel. There are a lot of memories, a lot of things you did, that you don't especially like to think about or talk about. And people think of special ops guys as a kind of superheroes who can do all kinds of crazy things, but we're not. We're just regular guys who are well trained to perform certain tasks."

I paused. He was watching, waiting, unsatisfied with the answer. I flopped back in my chair and sighed.

"You go to a social gathering and from the guys you get one of two reactions. Either they hero-worship you and ask you a lot of dumb questions like, 'Did you ever kill a guy?' or 'What was the most dangerous spot you were in?' or they want to pick a fight with you. And the women either find you disgusting, or want to screw you because they think you must be so fit you can keep going all night."

He threw back his head and laughed out loud. Marianne was giving me a look that said she was in the second category. She said:

"So who were you with, the SEALs? Delta?"

I was about to say Delta. I knew a lot of guys from Delta, and the Regiment had a pretty close relationship with them. But I remembered the brigadier, and my instructors telling us over and over, "Keep your lies to the minimum. Nothing is more believable than the truth. Lie only about what is essential." So I took a calculated risk.

"Neither. I was with the British SAS."

Yushbaev's reaction was nothing more than a fraction of a second. It was a minute freeze, and then a smile.

"You hide it well. Whom do you work for now?"

"I don't work. I just bum around, taking it easy, making up for lost time."

He chortled. "I think we both know that's a lie. But you are entitled to your secrets, Bob. I have no wish to pry. But if you ever feel like undertaking some gainful employment, keep me in mind."

I made like I found the proposal interesting. "You serious?"

"Very. I have a great deal of respect for the SAS. We have been on the receiving end of their skills a few times."

I nodded a few times, aware that Marianne was not taking her eyes off me. "Well, that could be interesting. How can I contact you?"

"Ben will give you a number before you leave. Perhaps I'll drop in on you tomorrow, after you've had a chance to think it over."

"Yeah, that would be good. Terms would be crucial."

"I can be generous, Bob, when I think it is worth it."

"I believe you."

We had coffee, cheese and dates helped along by some very fine Macallan. We talked about this and that, current affairs, nothing of importance, but I tried to act like I was out to impress him, motivated by his idea of employing me.

A little later I said farewell and he had one his surly identity-goons take me ashore. I jumped down onto the sand and the goon pushed the boat back out into the water. Beyond him I watched Marianne walk out onto the deck in the late, russet light of the afternoon. She stood watching me watching her for a moment. Then gave a small wave. I returned it and walked away, pushing through the sand toward my Jeep.

TEN

I SAT DRUMMING MY FINGERS ON THE STEERING WHEEL, looking through the dusty windshield at the figure of Charlotte sitting on the sand by the shore. I swung down from the cab and slammed the door. She must have heard it—aside from the sigh and lap of the waves, the late afternoon was silent. I approached across the sand. She had a white, semi-transparent blouse on that was tinged with gold from the declining sun. It flapped listlessly in the salty breeze. Her feet were bare, and surprisingly white, digging into the gray, damp sand.

I stood next to her, but she didn't look up.

"How was lunch?"

"Interesting."

"Did you satisfy your curiosity?"

"Partly."

"What were you today?"

I frowned at her. "What?"

Now she looked up at me. "Californian beach boy? A cowboy from South Dakota? Tough guy from the Bronx? Or were you sticking with the Texan friend to oil billionaires?"

I smiled. It must have looked like an unhappy smile, because she turned back to the sand, picked up a stick and started drawing geometrical shapes, then rubbing them out.

"You're a bit harsh, aren't you?" I sat cross-legged, casting a long shadow across her feet. "I was curious about him. You painted a pretty crazy picture for me. You said he owned you, body and soul." I shrugged. "So I played a stupid game."

She didn't answer right away. Eventually she gave a small shrug. "It's none of my business, really. I own a hotel. You're a customer. He's a man I once had an affair with. Now we just have a business relationship. It's just shitty, cruel life, rolling along."

"I'm sorry you feel that way."

She looked at me, like she was vaguely surprised. "Are you?"

"Yeah. I like you. You're a pain in the ass and you complain too much, but I still like you."

She laughed, not a lot, but enough. "I'm sorry. It's a bad habit. You don't complain much, do you?"

"It was beaten out of me in the Regiment. If things go badly you haven't got time to complain. You have to fix them, usually pretty fast. When I left it was a choice: take up residence at Grand Central, or get busy doing what I did best."

"What was that?"

I looked out at the sea, and the horizon beyond it. The blue was turning to violet. I shrugged. "Special operations."

"Oh."

"I made a lot of money working in private security. Enough to retire. But before that happened the going got pretty tough. When the going gets tough, you have to think about the solution, not the problem."

"Good grief, Bob, that sounds like something out of one of those dreadful self-help books."

"No." I shook my head. "First time I heard that was from a Kiwi sergeant. I can't tell you where I was because I wasn't supposed to be there." I smiled. "Your government sent me there illegally, to do something even more illegal. We did it—"

"This illegal thing?"

"Yes, but on the way to the extraction point we were spotted and attacked, and had to escape into the wilderness. I was very young and had very little experience. The sarge saw I was becoming a danger to myself and to the other guys, so he grabbed me by the scruff of the neck, shoved his big, bearded face into mine and snarled at me," I did my best New Zealand accent, "'Listen to me, you sniveling little shit! Do *not* think about the fuckin' problem! Focus on the fuckin' solution!' I will never forget it. I am probably alive today because of those words."

She smiled, then gave a small laugh. "I suppose that does rather put it into a different context."

"He's not a good man, Charlotte."

"Who, your sergeant? He sounds excellent to me."

"Gabriel." She drew a few more geometric shapes. I went on. "He is not a good man, and he is not good for you."

"Don't." She became serious and scrubbed out a pentagram. The sun slipped behind the headland to the west and she shuddered. I saw the goose bumps on her arms. "The last thing I need is another man to become dependent on."

"I agree. But another thing I learned from my Kiwi sergeant was that one thing is depending on a friend, and another is becoming dependent. I could use a coffee. You want to join me?"

"Oh Lord, why do you Americans have to be so nice? Can't you be bitter and cynical sometimes?"

I stood and she gave me her hand to pull her up. We turned toward the hotel and she slipped her arm through mine. I gave a listless shrug.

"Oh, sure, cynical, like *that* would make any difference."

She laughed and briefly leaned her head on my shoulder as we walked. And that was nice.

After coffee I walked down to the port to give my preparations one last review. I checked the mines, checked my weapons and went over the layout of the boat a hundred times, rehearsing what I would have to do at every stage. I had finished putting the assault rifles and ammo in the waterproof bag with a few other bits and pieces when I heard feet up on deck. I stepped out of the cabin and locked the door as a familiar female, French voice called down.

"Bob? Are you there?"

"Yeah."

Dusk had fallen and there was a translucent evening sky making her into a dark silhouette as she came down the steps. She paused on the last one, with one knee bent. Even in that half-light she looked exquisite.

"You don't look so pleased to see me, Bob."

"Am I obliged to, Marianne?"

She shrugged. "If you want I'll leave."

I approached to within six feet of her and half sat on the table. She was in a low-cut white dress that hugged her skin and told you she had nothing on underneath.

"Did you come to see me, or did you come for me to see you?"

"Why do you have to be so mean?"

"I don't know. You seem to bring it out in me. What do you want, Marianne?"

"I am bored, I want you to take me to dinner."

I thought about it for a second. It wasn't such a bad development. Whether it was rational or not, the Regiment had always been pretty clear that we did not wage war on women or children. If I could take Marianne out of the equation early on, that would make things easier. I smiled.

"OK, but I have two conditions."

She arched an eyebrow. "*Conditions?* You don't put conditions..." For a moment she was lost for words. "*I* should put conditions on *you!*"

"Yeah, maybe that's the way it works in France, but I am not French. First, we don't eat at the hotel. I want you to show me somewhere more interesting."

"Fuh!"

"And second. I have had about as much as I can take of people —including Gabriel Yushbaev—telling me how goddamn amazing Gabriel Yushbaev is. We talk about anything you like, but not Gabriel Yushbaev or how amazing he is."

She smiled and it was almost a grin.

"You and me both, Bob. I thought I was a total narcissist, but *mon dieu! C'est impossible!* This man is totally in love with himself! Totally!"

"Deal? Because right now you are talking about how amazing Gabriel Yushbaev is."

She laughed. "OK, deal." She stepped down the last rung and came up close to me. "So what shall we talk about, how amazing you are?"

"Nah, we can talk about how amazing you are. I'm comfortable with that."

She poked me in the chest. "You try to come across as a stupid, foolish man who knows nothing. Naïve, innocent. But it is a lie. I was watching you, listening to you. You are an actor, a bastard. I don't know what is your game, but I can tell you are a big bastard."

I took her small, silky chin in my hand and kissed her. Then I whispered in her ear, "You have no idea."

She shuddered and giggled.

AN HOUR later we emerged from the *Apollonis* and climbed into the Jeep. The moon had not risen yet, but there was a glow of starlight off the sea. The air was balmy, with an occasional waft of cool air off the ocean that made your skin shudder agreeably. She'd brought Yushbaev's Land Rover, but I refused to use it and insisted we go in the Jeep. She pretended to be annoyed, but gave in easy enough.

We went to the To Steki Tis Marias. It was on the beach on the far side of the port, a half mile drive across the scattered buildings and dirt tracks that tried and somehow failed to be a town. We could have walked it, but I wanted to have the car handy as soon as I needed it. I was improvising and I still didn't know how it was going to play out.

Tis Marias was a nice place. It was a traditional, blue and white Greek building on two floors, with at least two big terraces and large, chunky wooden tables with gingham tablecloths. We sat at a table on the top terrace and a waiter in jeans came and greeted Marianne with a small bow and stood jerking his knees, waiting for us to order. She ordered a dry martini and a gin and tonic in Greek and he went away.

"How many languages do you speak?"

"Six, and I am studying Chinese."

"How does Yushbaev feel about you having dinner with me?"

"You said we were not going to talk about him."

"Yeah." I nodded. "But I don't get this. He's supposed to be this anarchic, possessive, territorial guy who is so dangerous to cross. But here you are."

"Who said he was territorial and possessive?"

"Charlotte." She made a dismissive noise. I went on, "And Ben, he said he beat seven bales of shit out of some tough guy who made a pass at you. And everyone keeps talking about how he owns people. Are you on loan for the evening or what?"

She made a face that was oddly ugly, with the corners of her mouth drawn down, and shrugged. "He beat Igor because he was disrespectful, not because he was jealous. Gabriel does not own me. I am along for the ride. This is a unique experience. I live in supreme luxury, in exchange I have sex with him sometimes. It is not a problem for me. I enjoy sex. He is good-looking. He is an OK lover. But I will get bored and I will move on."

"And he's OK with that?"

"Sure, why not?"

"Because ownership is a big deal with him. I don't know if you've noticed, but he likes to own things. People included." She shrugged and looked away at the sea. I insisted. "Have you had a good look at Charlotte?"

"Charlotte! Charlotte! You are so obsessed with Charlotte, why don't you dine with her instead of me?"

"Don't be childish. I'm trying to show you what happens to women he is through with."

"OK, so you showed me. Now, no more Gabriel and no more Charlotte."

She had neatly avoided my question. I had little doubt he had sent her, but I was going to have to wait and see what for. Her next question told me I wasn't going to have to wait very long. The waiter delivered our drinks, she ordered kalamari and roast lamb without consulting me, picked up her gin and tonic and sipped it, eyeing me over the rim of her glass.

"So what are you really doing here, Bob?"

I sighed. "You know what? It is not so strange for a guy like me, who has spent eight years almost nonstop in combat zones, behind enemy lines, when he leaves the army to look for a way of life that has a bit of an edge to it: a bit of adventure, exploration in remote places. It is not so strange. He sent you to pump me, didn't he?"

She pointed her finger at me like a gun. "Mention him again and I will get up and leave. He does not own me, Bobby. To tell you the truth, I am getting a bit bored with him. I am curious about you. I want to know for me, for myself."

It was almost convincing. I sipped my drink and sat back in my chair. "OK, I apologize. The real reason I am here is to escape; to escape from the city, to escape from my past, to escape from the kind of people who live in the hive." I paused, watching her eyes to see what they said. They said she was curious, so I went on. "I am trying to escape from face masks, smoking bans, people who believe they have the right to make rules for other people's lives, political agendas and people who try to define their identity by using ever longer acronyms."

"Wow, you are definitely not woke."

"I am definitely not asleep, either."

"You don't think your sexual identity defines you?"

"No. I haven't got a sexual identity. What the hell is a sexual identity, anyhow? I am me. I like sex. I like women. How complicated can that be?"

She laughed. "You are a little primal, Bob. Current thinking..."

"Screw current thinking. How many identities do I need? Do I need a food identity, a drink identity, a clothing identity? How about a breathing identity?"

"OK, OK...you made your point. So you came here to escape from a crazy world that has lost touch with reality. It was pure coincidence you arrived here the day before we did."

I threw my head back and laughed out loud. Several people glanced over. "Boy, that really is narcissism taken to a whole new level. You believe I flew New York, London, Athens, Naxos and then hired a yacht and sailed to Koufonisi, all in a desperate attempt to be in The Divine Presence for just a few hours? Come on, Marianne, get real. Where do you people get off? He has a lot of money. That is about as interesting as Gabriel Yushbaev gets. There is exactly nobody I would fly halfway around the globe to pretend to bump into. But if I did, it would be somebody a damned sight more interesting than your ego-freak boyfriend."

"Wow." She gave a small, humorless laugh and I saw that her cheeks had colored. "You are some kind of a son of a bitch. Do you have to be so intense? 'Don't be silly' would have been enough."

"Sorry."

"He is not so bad. He is an interesting man."

"Well, he sure thinks so. Shall I tell you why I came here, Marianne? I came here not for Gabriel Yushbaev Almighty, not for you, not for anybody else. I came here for me. Because I was tired and burned out, and I wanted a rest on a remote Mediterranean island. So now you know I wasn't spying on Mr. Fascinating, have you lost interest in dining with me? Do you want me to drive you back?"

She sighed. "No. I am sorry. Perhaps I have been living with him too long and I am infected with his idea that the universe revolves around him. We shall start again. When you are not oblivious and ignoring billionaires in the Mediterranean, what are you doing? What fascinates you? What makes you happy?"

ELEVEN

WE MANAGED TO GET THROUGH THE NEXT COUPLE OF hours in comparative peace, and even laugh a bit. We avoided the subject of Yushbaev, but talked about pretty much everything else. I had decided she had been sent to find out if I was any kind of threat, and she had come to the conclusion I wasn't. So all I had to do now was put her to bed in the hotel, go and terminate Yushbaev and collect the colonel.

We'd moved on from roast lamb to cheese, dates, black coffee, cognac and whisky and Marianne had just drained her glass. She was about to signal the waiter when I said, "You fancy a nightcap at the hotel?"

She pouted with half a smile. "You want to get rid of me already?"

"No, I was hoping you'd stay."

"Don't you think Charlotte will mind?"

"You'd have to ask somebody who gave a damn."

She giggled. "OK, that sounds nice. But will you allow me one *envie*?"

I managed to frown and arch an eyebrow at the same time. "I might if I knew what an 'on-vee' was."

"A caprice?"

"Sure, what do you want?"

"There is, just here, two hundred meters, no more, a bar on the corner. It is a small bar, with only tables outside. From there we can see the moon rise over the sea and have our first nightcap. Then we can have another in your room. OK?"

The damned moon. It would be halfway to its zenith by the time I reached Pori Beach. It was not fatal to my plan, but it sure as hell would not help. I smiled.

"That sounds like a beautiful idea."

I signaled the waiter, paid the check and we strolled back to the Jeep. We climbed in and slammed the doors, and I fired up the engine. The headlamps laid amber funnels on the dusty road and the world around us slipped into deeper darkness. I lowered the windows and we rolled down the path at a steady twenty miles per hour. Marianne was silent, looking out at the stillness through the open window. We covered the two hundred yards and the road turned left, following the coastline. I slowed. To the right there was a small harbor with a handful of fishing boats pulled up on the sand among low, rocky outcrops. Opposite, in the crook of the bend, there was a small, whitewashed building, a kiosk, not quite a house but bigger than a shack, with a small veranda out front. It was dark and closed up. I said:

"Looks like your bar is closed," and it sounded unnaturally loud in the darkness.

She said, "Stop the car."

I slowed to a crawl, looking at her face. "Why?"

She smiled. "We could go down to the fishing boats and watch the moon rise from there. We could swim naked..."

She trailed off. I returned the smile. "OK, Marianne, I'll give you your *petit envie*."

I killed the engine and we climbed down from the truck. She took my hand and led me to a narrow flight of uneven steps that had been hewn from the rock and wound their way down some six feet to the sandy cove. The air was cooler down there, and the only sound was the quiet ripple and sigh of the tiny, transparent waves as they lapped the shore. She took both my hands in hers and kissed me softly.

"Look," she whispered, "the moon is just rising from the horizon. It is like lava, boiling up from the center of the Earth. It is like your feeling for me, and my feeling for you."

I turned to look. The cool breeze touched my face and I saw the fat, warping ark of orange light swell above the horizon.

"I am sorry," she said. I frowned down at her, but she was looking past me, up at the road. There was no expression on her face and I went suddenly cold inside. I turned to face the road and saw the fan of light from some approaching headlamps. There followed the hum of an engine as it slowed and stopped. I gripped her arm and scowled. "Why?"

"Come on, Harry. You didn't really think we bought all that Bob Foley bullshit, did you? He's been waiting for you to show up since you killed Cavendish. When you showed so much interest in the yacht we were both alerted, and when you started talking about the rumors concerning Cavendish's death, that was the clincher. That and the fact that Bob Foley and Harry Bauer have lived exactly the same lives."

Four doors slammed like gunshots above us. Four guys with that unmistakable look of Russian special ops thugs appeared at the top of the steps. Two dropped to the sand and the others skipped down the steps.

I would not have used her as a hostage, but she didn't know that. She yanked her arm free from my grip and ran toward her boys. One of them grabbed her and pushed her toward the stone steps. She didn't climb them. She sat and smiled at me.

"Time to die, Harry."

It is not advisable to engage in wisecracks when people are trying to kill you. Instead I slipped my right foot forward with my left hand open, up by my chin and my right fist aimed toward my target. I am not left-handed, but I'm a southpaw. I like to have my heavy artillery up front to get the job done as fast and as decisively as possible.

I scanned my opponents. There were four of them, in their late twenties, tall and powerfully built. The guy on my far right had a shaved head and was hunched forward with a big bowie knife in his hand. By the way he moved I figured he liked to wrestle. He'd try to take me to the sand and gut me.

On my far left was a guy I'd seen on the yacht. He had short black hair and a goatee. He was lean and athletic, and he also had a bowie knife. There was no mistaking the intention to put an end to Harry Bauer that night.

In the middle was a muscular blond who was gym-fit and eager to show what he thought he could do. Him and the goatee would be throwing kicks and punches. They were probably from Tae Kwon Do. To his right was the boss of this rag-tag band. He was older than the other three, maybe in his early thirties. He was more muscular, more sure in his movements. His strength and his skill didn't come from the gym anymore. He'd learned what he knew by killing people.

These two also produced knives and came at me.

The slow burn in my gut told me I might die that night, right there on the beach. The immediate presence of your own death is a powerful motivator. I shuffled back to where the sand was damp and it was easier to move.

As a general rule of thumb, if you have your right side forward, any movement you make to your left will tend to open your guard. So it's best to move to the right, back foot first. The guy I wanted was the boss, the big guy in the middle. So I moved fast, like I was going for him, then crossed my left leg behind me and charged into a low side kick and smashed my heel into the bald guy's right knee. I felt it crunch and before my foot hit the ground I had smashed my right fist into his jaw. His fight was over.

Mine wasn't, but I had at least flanked them and now had all three of them in a line, scrambling in the sand, the goatee and the blond harmless behind the boss. He charged me, the knife held low in his right hand. I sprang back in a long step, then took a short step and lunged forward and to his left, away from his knife. I smashed my rear, left heel into his right knee and as my foot hit the sand I flicked my hip and drove a right hook right through his jaw.

That left two of them. They both looked worried. I didn't stop to pick up a knife. The blond started for me. I pushed my right foot forward like I was lunging in a fencing match, then drew my rear foot in, put all my weight on it and smashed my right instep into his balls. He went down on his knees, wheezing. I put my hand in his face and pushed him aside.

The goatee knew that if he went back without my head, he was dead meat. He rushed me, thrusting the knife fast and hard at my body. I don't like knife disarming techniques. The risk is too high and the benefits are dubious. A knife is only marginally more dangerous than a well-used fist, unless you try to grab it. Then it becomes a real danger.

So I leaned back, like he'd thrown a cross, and trapped his forearm against his body with my left hand. Then, fast as a viper, I stabbed my fingers deep into his eyes. He dropped the knife he had intended to kill me with and groped at the ugly mess that was his face. He was making ugly noises, high-pitched and pitiful.

I bent down, picked up his blade and thumped it hard into his back, deep into his heart. Being blind wasn't a problem anymore. He fell face down, jerked a couple of times and rattled his goodbye into the cool sand.

I bent and wiped my prints from the handle. Behind me I heard the roar of a powerful engine. I ignored it. I knew it was Marianne, running. I went to the big boss guy. His leg was broken and he was semi-conscious, groaning softly. I drove his knife through his neck and death came quickly for him. I killed the other two in the same way, wiped my prints off the weapons and made my way back to the Jeep.

I drove to the hotel and sat a moment drumming my fingers on the wheel. Marianne would be back at Pori Beach by now. She would have called Yushbaev and warned him what had happened.

There was no way I could get to them and plant the mines before they took off. I had to reformulate my plan. I had to think it through and intercept them either in Istanbul, or follow them all the way to Divnomorskoye.

I swung down from the Jeep and walked into the hotel. The lounge-cum-lobby was empty, but for Charlotte sitting in an Emmanuelle-style wicker chair by the door to the pool. She had a tall gin and tonic in her hand and looked like she might be slightly drunk.

"Hello," she said. "Did you enjoy your evening? Was Marianne entertaining for you?"

I ignored her, picked up the brass bell on the desk, and rang it hard. Kostas Minor shambled out of what I figured was the kitchen and jerked his chin at me.

"Whisky, bring the whole bottle." He stared at me and I turned to Charlotte. "Tell him to bring me a whole bottle of the best damned whisky you have. And a glass."

She said something in cool, languid Greek and Kostas Minor shambled away, back into the bowels of the kitchen.

"You look upset, Bob. Bad date?"

I went and stood by the open doors, looking out at the pool. The dark sky above was paling in the light of the rising moon. A moon that would no longer be a problem. She watched me a moment.

"Are you going to talk to me, or shall I just talk to myself while you stand there and look moody?"

"I don't know."

"Well that's something."

"What do you do for cops on this island?"

Her eyebrows shot up. "Cops? Nothing. There's no crime here. If we need the police, which we never do, they come over from Naxos." She hooted a little laughter. "Don't tell me that little bitch has stolen your credit card!" She trailed off and a look of horror, tinged with delight, came over her face. "Don't tell me you... You haven't *raped* her, have you?"

Kostas Minor shuffled in with a tray bearing a bottle of the Macallan and a large tumbler. I took the bottle and the glass and addressed Charlotte without looking at her.

"Tell him to go away."

She said, "*Fyge!*"

I poured myself a generous measure and pulled off half of it. As the warmth of the spirit spread through my belly I realized I needed her help.

"No, I didn't rape her. But there are four men lying dead on the beach to the right of the port." I turned to face her. She was staring at me, expressionless. "They are four of Yushbaev's security goons. He sent them to kill me. I had to kill them. It was self-defense."

She sat forward, blinking. "You killed four men? And now they are lying there, on the beach, dead?"

I drained the other half of my drink.

"Yeah."

"Yeah? That's it? *Yeah?* What the hell are you going to do about it? What *on Earth* did Gabriel want to kill you for?"

I sighed. "It's a long story."

"But, I mean..." She looked at me helplessly. "I'll have to phone the police in Naxos! I'll have to phone *him!* He owns this place! He'll have to come –"

I cut across her. "Get a grip, Charlotte! Stop babbling. Yushbaev will already be pulling out of the island on his way to Istanbul. He and Marianne will have cast-iron alibis long before the cops get here, and you can be damn sure he will not be investigated."

She was quiet for a long moment. It was dawning on her what I wanted. She said, quietly, "Why did he want to kill you?"

I poured another drink and sat.

"He'll sell this place. He'll want to disassociate himself from it in every way. I can guarantee it will be on the market by tomorrow morning."

"Bob, why did he try to have you killed?"

"Listen to me! I can have this place bought for you, in your name, and the deeds sent to you within a week. I just ask one thing in return." She didn't say anything. She just stared at me. I said, "If anybody ever asks, I took my yacht and left this island earlier today at midday."

"You're after Gabriel, aren't you? You want to kill him."

I shook my head. "No, he has a friend of mine on his yacht. He knew I was here to recover her. So he used Marianne to lure me to the beach, and then his four goons showed up."

"Who is your friend?"

I knew I shouldn't tell her, but who would believe her anyway? I smiled. "A United States Air Force colonel."

"You must be CIA or something."

"Something. Are you going to help me?"

She stood and walked to the sliding doors and stood framed in the waxing light of the moon. "In exchange you will buy this hotel for me, and it will be mine?"

"Yes."

She shook her head and turned to face me. "No," she said, and there was cold rage in her eyes. "I want something more."

TWELVE

I WAS STANDING BY THE POOL. THE MOON APPEARED TO be under the turquoise water, looking up at me from a luminous, liquid sky framed by warping palms. On the other side of the pool, beyond the lawn and the patio, the sliding doors stood open onto an empty lounge, where Charlotte sat in a wicker chair, staring at her third gin and tonic. I dialed the brigadier's number. When he answered he had a frown in his voice. He knew the timing was wrong.

"Harry?"

I sighed, and for a second wallowed in self-pity. "I blew it."

"Explain."

"They were expecting me." I told him how Marianne had come to the *Apollonis*, how we'd hit the sack and then gone out to dinner. "I was overconfident, sir. I bought her act as an arrogant, naïve narcissist. She was convincing. They both were."

"Learn from it and move on. So what happened?"

"We had dinner and she said she wanted to go to a small bar on the beach before bed. My plan was to take her to my room, put her lights out and go and get the colonel."

"Good."

"But she and Yushbaev were several steps ahead. She took me

down to a cove and four of Yushbaev's boys joined us with knives."

"Are you hurt?"

"No. I killed them. But she told me they had never believed the Bob Foley story. Yushbaev had been waiting for me ever since I killed Cavendish. When I asked to be shown the yacht it alerted them Bob Foley was probably Harry Bauer." I sighed. He didn't say anything. I went on. "I was uncomfortable boarding that yacht without some kind of recon. I thought I could fool them. I was wrong. They were smart."

"If it's any consolation, I would probably have done the same. It's in our training, Harry. Prepare, prepare and then prepare some more. After that..."

"Prepare again."

"Precisely. What you probably didn't need to do was respond to Yushbaev's arrogant provocations. Am I right? Did you show off?"

"Maybe a bit, yeah."

"Didn't we teach you to be meek, and whimper and simper when necessary? It's an essential part of counterinterrogation."

"Yeah, my mother sent a note that day."

He grunted. "What you see as a strength, Harry, is a weakness. It may have cost the colonel her life. Make it right. If you haven't already run out of time. It may be too late."

"I know."

"Now, what about Charlotte?"

"Yushbaev owns her hotel, or at least one of his companies does. I am pretty sure he is going to want to sell it now, to distance himself from the shit storm that's about to hit the fan. He will instruct his people to sell it tomorrow. I told Charlotte we'd buy it in her name if she'd alibi me."

"What did she say?"

"She said it wasn't enough. She wanted me to kill him too."

For a moment he sounded alarmed. "Did you tell her about Cobra?"

"No. She assumes I am CIA."

"All right. I'll get the finance department onto it now. Tell her to expect somebody in the next forty-eight hours. But, Harry? You pay for the hotel. We'll handle it, and we'll explain the terms and consequences of any breach of the agreement. But this is on you. You pay, and you had better make damned sure the colonel has not been hurt as a consequence of this."

A wave of hot shame washed over me. The brigadier was about the only person on the planet who could do that. I said, "I understand."

"I know you do. Now, go to Naxos. There will be a plane waiting for you. Go to Istanbul. Make this right, and no more showing off."

I hung up and went inside. Charlotte raised her face and watched me with big, wet eyes.

"It's a deal. I'm going to leave now. The hotel will be bought and put in your name sometime this morning. Somebody will come and see you in the next forty-eight hours. They will bring the deeds and explain the terms of this agreement."

"You mean they'll threaten to kill me too if I don't comply."

"No." She gave a dry laugh but I ignored her. "They might ridicule you, attack your credibility, maybe even sue you for libel or slander. But all we want is for you to forget that this ever happened. We had a party, we all drank too much. I left early in my yacht. You slept the night through. What you assume is that four of Yushbaev's boys left the boat, got into a fight, either with each other, or with some local guys. Nobody will ever know for sure." She nodded and I drove it home. "Try and implicate me and we'll prove you're lying. They'll make you look like a crazy, alcoholic conspiracy nut."

"I don't want to implicate you. I like you. Just find him and kill him."

I nodded, turned and left the hotel with a dull ache in the back of my head and a sick feeling in my belly.

I TOUCHED down at Istanbul International Airport at noon the following day, feeling pretty ragged. Cobra had booked me a room at the 10 Karakoy, a luxurious brown and beige marble boutique hotel a stone's throw from the Golden Horn, where it meets the Bosphorus and the Sea of Marmara. It was, however, a good half hour's drive from the airport—in spite of the driver's attempts to reach warp speed ten—some fifteen or twenty miles to the north and west of Istanbul.

The million-dollar question, once I had got to Naxos, was what to do with the hardware I had stashed onboard. I had assumed the brigadier would have his man come from the mainland and collect it. But he had said no. He'd have someone collect it and take it to Kabardinka, a holiday resort on the Black Sea, just twenty miles from Yushbaev's palace. It seemed crazy to me, but I figured he knew what he was doing. He usually did.

I checked in, had the bellhop take my bags up to my room, gave him fifty bucks and told him not to let anybody disturb me for the next four hours. That was how long I allowed myself to sleep the sleep of the dead.

I awoke at five in the afternoon, had a long shower alternating between scalding hot and cold, and emerged feeling almost human, but in bad need of food.

Down in the lobby, I was planning to go and get a drink and some food at the Atakoy Marina. Some rough mental arithmetic had told me the *Bucephalus* would be doing anything up to forty knots to put nautical miles between herself and Koufonisi. That would give her an average speed of forty-five miles per hour over a distance of about three hundred and ninety miles. That meant that the *Bucephalus* would have been arriving in Istanbul about eight and a half hours after she left the island—about four hours before I had.

A call to the brigadier from my taxi had confirmed that they had satellite images of the *Bucephalus* docking at the Atakoy

Marina, about six or seven miles from the mouth of the Bosphorus. After I had slept, I figured it would be a good idea to take a stroll down there and have a look. But like Joseph Heller said, nothing ever works as planned. Which means that the only point in making a plan, is so you can adapt it to all the things that go wrong with it from the moment you start to execute it.

What went wrong as I crossed the lobby was that the concierge hailed me and said, "Oh, Mr. Bauer, you have somebody here to see you."

I approached the desk. "Somebody to see me? Who and where?"

"Mr. Armitage, sir. He is in the bar. You told us not to disturb, so I advised him he might have to wait a while."

I nodded. "Good, thanks."

Armitage. It took me a few seconds while I moved toward the bar. Then it came to me. Colonel James Armitage of the United States Air Force. He'd shown up at my apartment in Los Angeles just after the colonel had disappeared, asking about my relationship with her.[1]

The bar had wooden walls, subdued lighting and potted palms. I found Colonel James Armitage sitting at a table with what looked like a large Scotch in front of him. He had an attaché case beside his feet and he was reading a file. He was not in uniform. He looked up and removed a pair of reading glasses from his nose when I leaned on the back of the chair across from him.

"Mr. Bauer, good of you to see me." He laid the file on the table in front of him. "Would you like a drink?"

"I haven't much time, Colonel. What's this about?"

"May I give you some advice, Mr. Bauer?"

"I guess that depends on the advice."

"Make time."

He held my eye and I knew I had no choice. I had to find out what he was doing there, and why he wanted to see me. I signaled

---

1. See *LA: Wild Justice*

the barman. "Macallan, double, no ice." I pulled out the chair and sat. "Are you following me?"

He gave a small laugh that was not entirely humorless.

"You say that as though it were an easy thing to do. We have been trying to follow you. Have you heard of the Five Eyes?"

I had heard of the Five Eyes. It referred to an intelligence alliance between the United Kingdom, the United States, Canada, Australia and New Zealand, founded on a treaty for joint cooperation and signals intelligence. Departments within those five governments had also come together to form Cobra, the very special kind of NGO I worked for. Its brief: identify the trash, and take it out.

I knew what the Five Eyes was, but I said, "No, what is that, Lobsang Rampa with glasses on?"

If he got my allusion to the author of *The Third Eye,* he didn't show it. Or he didn't think it was funny.

"We share intelligence and cooperate with Britain, Canada, Australia and New Zealand. It means if I want to watch the airports in those countries, there are protocols we follow and if you enter or leave any of those countries by train, plane, ship or automobile, I get to hear about it, very quickly. I also have access to CCTV footage, and all other forms of intelligence."

"You have my number, you could have just called."

"Are you a funny man, Mr. Bauer? I haven't got a great sense of humor. Especially at the moment. Jane was a friend of mine, and I am still not one hundred percent convinced that you didn't kill her."

The waiter brought my drink and set it in front of me. I looked at it a moment and sighed. "So you tracked me across two continents—"

"No, you dropped off the radar in California and nobody saw or heard anything of you until MI6 spotted you in Greece, and then again in Turkey. I have no idea where you have been in the meantime."

"MI6, huh? All right, so you found me. What do you want?"

"I want to know why you are here, in Istanbul, and, above all, I want to know where Jane is."

"Why I am in Istanbul is none of your damn business, or the United States Air Force's for that matter. And I have no idea…"

He raised a hand. "Stop right there, Harry." The gesture, and the use of my first name, pulled me up short. "Let's cut the bull-shit. We both know that you left Los Angeles to look for Jane. You can take it as read that the Air Force has me investigating her disappearance because I am not stupid. So I would take it as a kindness if you would show me the minimal courtesy of not treating me as though I am an idiot."

He paused and took a breath, looking down at his drink. He picked it up, thought about taking a sip and put it down again.

"When we spoke in Los Angeles you told me you were talking to the Cavendish Foundation about providing Third World children with clean water, or some similar project." He paused and held my eye. "A couple of days later Charles Cavendish was killed aboard his yacht fifty miles off Arroyo Grande."

I was shaking my head and frowning. "Wait a minute. What are you talking about? He wasn't killed aboard his yacht. His yacht exploded because of a faulty gas fitment. The propane tanks exploded."

He shrugged in a way that was overtly dismissive. "If you like. The point is, I do not know how those two facts are connected, but I am damned sure they are. There is also the fact that his personal assistant was gunned down in your apartment, and you disappeared at exactly the same time that Cavendish was killed, a couple of days later."

"That he died."

"Two days after his assistant was murdered in your apartment."

"None of which means that I know where the colonel is, and none of which means I had anything to do with her disap-pearance."

He gave his head a brief shake. "No, in fact I don't think you had anything to do with her disappearance. We checked the CCTV footage from the hotel. What you said was true. She climbed out of your TVR and entered the hotel. But the cameras inside the hotel lobby did not capture her coming through. It was as you said in Los Angeles. Whatever happened to her, happened between those two sets of doors. But none of that takes away from the fact that you are in some way involved. It's just too many coincidences."

I was quiet for a moment. "She doesn't enter the lobby."

He shook his head. "No."

"But somebody leaves."

His eyebrows twitched and knit momentarily. "Yes, somebody leaves. Two people."

"And one of them was carrying a long coat, a gabardine perhaps?"

Now his frown deepened. "How could you know that?"

"Because it would be the only way to conceal the very striking dress she was wearing. They must have put the coat on her and hustled her out to a waiting van or car." I hesitated a moment, then, "So if you don't think I had anything to do with her disappearance..." I spread my hands.

"People have a habit of either dying or disappearing around you." He pointed at me. "I believe you were there for Cavendish, and I believe you are here looking for Jane. And before you try to deny it, let me tell you that would be pointless."

"Colonel." I picked up my glass and swirled the contents around for a second. "Assuming for a moment that you were right —and I am not admitting anything—assuming you were right, why *would* I admit it to you?"

"The way I see it, Harry," he paused, "do you mind if I call you Harry?" I gave my head a small shake. "The way I see it, Harry, is that you have information about where Jane is that I need. And I have resources that are second to none in the world. We might be able to help each other."

I nodded. "That would be great if I was looking for her, but I am not, and I have no information as to her whereabouts." I made to rise but stopped. "Have you spoken to the local CIA representative?"

He gave me a very steady look. "No, they don't know I'm here and I would like to keep it that way." He reached in his pocket and pulled out a brown leather wallet. From it he removed an embossed card and handed it to me. "I have a feeling you are going to change your mind. If you do, this is my private cell number. Call me. I am not here in an official capacity, and this mission is not sanctioned, so I would be grateful if you called me Jim."

"Thanks for the drink, Jim."

I drained my glass but before I could stand he said, "I know about your background, Harry. I know about Captain Hartmann and Ben-Amini. I have friends in the SAS. I did a couple of training exercises with them when I was younger. I know what happened and I know what kind of man you are."

"What's that supposed to mean?"

"That the chances of your letting Jane's abduction go unanswered are somewhat less than one in a million. If you are in Istanbul, it's because you think she is." He stood and drained his glass. "I'll be waiting for your call."

THIRTEEN

THE AFTERNOON WAS ON THE BRINK OF EVENING. THE sun was just a few inches above the horizon, its light had acquired a coppery hue and it was making long shadows across the parking lot of the Ataköy Marina. Some of those shadows were the warped shapes of the few cars that were parked there. Others, more abundant, were from the trees that fringed the lot, providing me with cover but allowing me to keep an eye on the *Bucephalus,* moored just fifty paces away from where I was sitting in the Corolla I had rented from the hotel. It was a car without virtues, except that it was anonymous. And right then that was the best virtue it could have had.

I had positioned myself at the northeastern end of the lot so that I had the dying sun reflecting off my windshield and driver-side windows, effectively hiding me from view; assuming anyone aboard the *Bucephalus* could see my car beyond the wall of trees.

I waited an hour. During that time I saw activity aboard, but I didn't see anybody I recognized, just crew members and staff. Then, just as the western horizon was turning flame red, I saw Yushbaev emerge onto the rear boarding deck. He was talking over his shoulder. Immediately behind him came Marianne. She stopped and turned back and that was when I saw the colonel emerge. She was in jeans, with a white blouse, a brown leather jacket and a leather bag hanging from one shoulder. She stopped to talk to Marianne and Yushbaev. There was no particular feeling to the way they were talking. They might have been discussing arrangements for dinner, or a shopping list. After a moment she put her hand on Yushbaev's shoulder and kissed him on the cheek, then she walked down the gangway onto the quay.

I was aware the rate of my breathing had increased, and I had hot coals in my belly. I watched her enter the parking lot and I saw the lights on an F-Type Jaguar flash. The colonel approached it and climbed in behind the wheel. The engine roared, I let her cross the lot and then followed her out onto Kennedy Avenue, headed east. I held back and allowed her to pull ahead. At the Ayetkin Kotil Park she took the exit onto the overpass and I followed her to the Ekrem Kurt Boulevard interchange. The streets were busy, anyone who has driven in Turkey knows that Turkish drivers believe traffic accidents are an American myth devised by Hollywood to undermine the Turkish economy, and that anyone inside a car is in fact invulnerable to death or mutilation. And that's how they drive.

The roads in that part of the city were broad and attractive, and there was an abundance of trees and green spaces, and lights which were widely and cheerfully ignored. I followed her around the circus and into Aksu Osmaniye Yolu Street, where things became more narrow and crowded and I had to fall right back to avoid her noticing me. We moved, stopping and starting, along a two-way street that was wide enough for one car. At Adelet Street she took a left and I followed her past two and three-storey apartment blocks with balconies and bright awnings. There the ground floors were all occupied by hardware stores, butchers, grocery stores, cheap clothes stores and cell phone shops, where the merchandise spilled from the shop out onto the sidewalks and groups of women gathered in clusters to view them and argue about the prices. And in every doorway that was not a store, there seemed to be an old woman sitting on a chair on the sidewalk, chewing on her gums and watching her neighborhood roll by.

We picked our way, stopping and starting, past the Osmaniye coffee shop, the Eczane drugstore and the Süleymanoğlu Inşaat just-about-everything-and-anything-you-can-imagine-shop, which had just that in the window, and a little more out on the sidewalk: from old TVs and bicycles to tubs of paint, sheets of Styrofoam and plastic tubes for plumbing. There was even a guy leaning on the doorjamb wearing a djellaba, and a hongma on his head, smoking a cigarette.

She turned right then up another narrow street that was bustling with women buying fresh produce from grocery stores where the fruits and vegetables were stacked high in crates out on the street. Interspersed with the stores there were terraced cafés where all the customers were men. I wondered briefly if it had dawned on them that they had taken half the fun out of going to bars if you were only ever going to meet other guys there. Then I remembered you could only buy booze after ten PM, and you were limited to three pints per person. So there went the other half.

We turned into a narrow, cobbled street and she followed it to the end, where it met a broader avenue. A red sign on the wall opposite the intersection said it was Cöreki Street. There she turned in and parked. I kept going, past a shop selling cheap, plastic toys for kids, and found a place to park in the shade of some large trees.

In my mirror I saw the colonel climb out of the Jaguar and enter a two-storey building with a large patio covered by an awning. At first I thought it was some kind of a restaurant, but I turned the car around so I could park facing the building she'd entered, and noticed the minaret at the back, and it slowly dawned on me that she had gone into a mosque.

I felt my skin go cold and clammy. My stomach burned, not just with anger, but with a nauseating fear; a fear of something that made no sense, and which I could not understand. I took several photographs with my phone.

I waited ten minutes and saw the colonel emerge again, accompanied by a guy in a djellaba and a hongma, and another guy in jeans and a black leather jacket. The guy in the djellaba had a big beard and was probably somewhere between forty and sixty, it was hard to tell. The guy in the leather was probably in his mid-twenties. They stood at the gate talking for another five minutes, I took a few more shots, then the colonel and the younger guy got in the Jag and pulled away.

I followed.

I let them get well ahead of me and followed them east, past the hippodrome along Fikret Yüzatli and then down 56th Street, dodging the crazy traffic, the kids on bikes and the people who spilled from the sidewalks apparently unaware that there was traffic on the roads, unaware, in fact, that there was any distinction between the sidewalks and the blacktop which at times were paved the same.

At 58th Boulevard she turned right and headed south. Here at least the road was asphalt and the sidewalks were paved, but the people were as abundant as ever, and as reckless about traffic. We snaked along, among buildings that all looked like they'd been thrown up in the '70s, plastered with advertisements, miniature billboards and signs stuck in windows. I had no idea what they were offering, but I figured it was everything and anything from dental services to legal, employment agencies and private investigators.

Pretty soon the road forked. The left branch made a right angle and the boulevard continued, semi-pedestrianized, with restaurants and pavement cafés lining the sides. Here the Jaguar came to a stop and I saw the colonel and the guy in the leather jacket climb out and cross the sidewalk toward a restaurant with a red sign that read, Ekin Simit Evi. I pulled in to a side street on the right, parked the car and made my way back to where I was within sight of where they sat. I saw they had taken a table on the terrace and the colonel had her back to me.

I glanced around. I had two options. There was a café across the road that also had a terrace. Getting there and sitting outside both risked being seen. The other option was the Simit Sarayl, which was right next door. The front was open and I could sit just inside, in the shadows, keep an eye on them and avoid being seen myself. I stepped inside and ordered a coffee and a kebab.

I waited a while, but they just seemed to be talking, so I took out my cell and called the brigadier.

"Harry, any news?"

I smiled to myself. "Hi, honey, yeah, I'm finally here. I am currently sitting on a terrace having a coffee and a kebab on 58th Boulevard. You wouldn't believe how busy it is at this time of the evening. Not cold at all."

"I gather you can't talk freely."

"Well, to be perfectly honest, darling, I am not sure, but personally I would rather not."

"All right, have you any news?"

"Oh, absolutely. The weather has been gorgeous and the sun has been blazing. And you should have seen the sunset. I couldn't take my eyes off it."

His voice became tense. "You've seen Jane?"

"Technicolor."

"Have you still got eyes on her?"

"Oh certainly, sweetheart, ever since sundown. Where have we been? Well let me see, I think the best thing is if I send you some photos. The mosque was of particular interest. It really is quite spectacular. Hang on a sec', sweetheart..."

I sent him the photographs I had taken, then put the phone back to my ear. He was very quiet.

"I have to tell you, honey, I have no idea what is going on."

He was silent a little longer, then, "Have you been able to hear anything?"

"No, not yet, but I'm hoping to do a bit of swimming soon."

"This is very unsettling. Is she speaking Turkish or Arabic to this man?"

"I was wondering the same thing. Did she ever tell you she could do that?"

"No, and it's not on her CV—résumé—which you would rather expect it to be, all things considered."

I laughed, like he'd said something funny. "No argument there. I mean, it makes you wonder, sweetheart, doesn't it? Do we ever really know *anyone?*"

"I need to think about this. I am not sure how objective I can be at the moment. Is she there now?"

"About thirty or forty feet. But you know she's not alone in that, darling."

"She's still with the young man in the leather jacket?"

"Oh, I couldn't agree more."

"Stay with them. See where they go, if anyone joins them... You know the drill." I heard him sigh heavily. "I am going to have to leave this up to your discretion for now, Harry. I am afraid I have been rather wrong-footed and I can't trust my own judgment. Keep me posted."

I sighed back. "I know how you feel, kid. I feel the same way."

"Should I relieve you? Send somebody else?"

"Nah, I won't be here long enough. And besides, if that job has to be done, then I don't want anybody else to do it."

"No, no, I suppose not."

"We'll talk soon, sweetheart."

"Yes, talk very soon."

I hung up and sat staring from the shadows at the blonde head just fifteen or twenty feet away. After a moment I saw her lean forward and something changed hands, after which she placed something in the pocket of her jacket. The guy in the black leather stood and I watched him cross the sidewalk. When he got to the road he hailed a cab and drove away.

I called the waiter and paid, and carried my kebab back toward the Corolla. I could see the colonel speaking on the phone to somebody. I sat on the hood of my car eating, waiting for her to do something. I had assumed that when the guy in the leather jacket left she would follow. But she didn't. What did happen was that five minutes later, as I was stuffing the last of the kebab in my mouth, a Q7 pulled up, two of Yushbaev's special forces goons jumped out of the back and went to where the colonel was sitting. The Q7 took off again. The goons spoke to the colonel for a moment, she got up and they followed her to the Jag.

I tailed them south down to the Kennedy Highway which ran along the coast. I settled in about ten cars behind them and followed through the dense, evening traffic, among the flow of headlamps, as far as the port at Türkmenistan Park, and there they turned north up Namik Kemal, under the railway bridge and into the kind of neighborhood where even hope can't give you a solid reason to keep trying. Squalid and run-down was what you got after giving this place a face-lift.

The Jag turned the wrong way into Küçük Langa and pulled up outside a grotesque gray, three-storey building with dead, gray-green glass panels all over the second and third floors, and dirty gray granite all over the first floor. The entrance was on one side: a cavernous gaping maw of an arch with encrusted dirt on the floor, possibly last year's vomit, among crates of empty bottles and various other kinds of filth that was hard to identify.

I crawled past as the three of them climbed out and went inside. I watched double doors swing open onto a dimly lit room that, at a glance, looked like a nightclub which had not opened to the public yet. Then I was past and couldn't see anymore.

I found a space a hundred yards down the road, parked my car and sat wondering. Was she delivering whatever the guy in the black jacket had given her, to some contact in the club? Were they separate errands? And why the hell was she doing errands for Yushbaev anyway? More to the point, and more worrying, was this new? Was this the first time she had run errands for him on her own? If not, maybe the two goons who were with her now were not watching her, but guarding her. They were her bodyguards.

My mind struggled to make sense of it. She was one of the founders of Cobra, the brigadier had known her and trusted her for years. And he was not some simple, naïve teenager. He was a longstanding senior officer in the SAS who had seen it all and done it all. How could she have pulled the wool over his eyes so completely?

And yet, there she was, in the club, holding whatever it was the guy in the black leather jacket had given her. And the image came back to my mind of the colonel on the yacht, just before she'd left, her hand on Yushbaev's shoulder as she kissed his cheek. It had come so naturally to her. All of her behavior, since she had been spotted in Puerto Banus, in Marbella, and while I had been following her here in Istanbul, all of it had been so relaxed and natural. It spoke to one thing, one thing I could not accept—did not want to accept—that she had been a double agent for years. She was intimate with Yushbaev, she was one of his operatives and had been planted not only in the Air Force, but with Cobra.

I felt sick to my stomach with a sense of rage and betrayal. But forcing myself to look beyond that, if I was right, if it was true, the consequences for Cobra, for all its operatives and for the brigadier and myself would be catastrophic. Unless...

I looked down the street at the entrance to the club. A sign in neon lighting flickered and came on above the door. It said *Rio de Janeiro Copa Cabana Club*. A hot slow burn started in my belly and I spoke the words aloud to myself.

"Unless I kill Yushbaev and her."

FOURTEEN

I GOT OUT OF THE CAR, SLAMMED THE DOOR AND shouldered my way through the crowd. I moved into the entrance arch and found a set of large, double doors. I pushed through them into a foyer that was carpeted in stained, dirty red. Over on the right there was a cloak room with a black wooden counter. On my left there was an empty ticket booth and to the right of that there was a stretch-belt barrier. I ignored it, entered the foyer and looked around.

Behind the ticket booth there was a red-carpeted staircase that rose to the upper floors. Over on my right, across the foyer, were the johns, and straight ahead of me was another set of double doors which I guessed led to the bar and dance floor. I crossed and pushed the doors open. The place was big, dark and even uglier than the exterior.

The bar itself was a large square in the middle of the floor. At the far end there was a dance floor flanked by two large cages where I figured naked women would probably dance. The rest of the place had dark purple wall-to-wall carpet, a plethora of low tables and chairs, and walls painted black. The ceiling was peppered with what looked like lenses, which I imagined projected colored lights and lasers. There was nobody there so I let the doors swing closed and made my way up the stairs.

Up on the second floor there was a small landing that led immediately to a broad lounge with a bar. Like the rest of the place, it was empty. The windows, a dirty gray, overlooked the street below. There were low tables and chairs scattered here and there, and either side of the bar there were large double doors. I pushed one open. It gave onto a broad, semicircular balcony that overlooked the bar and dance floor below.

I went back to the empty lounge and made my way to the far end. There I saw the johns, and to the left of them a short flight of five steps up to a heavy, wooden door with a brass plaque on it that read, *Özel*. I thought about it a moment and decided that *özel* meant private in Turkish.

I climbed the steps, and with a hot burn in my belly I knocked. The door opened and one of Yushbaev's boys stood looking down at me. He produced a frown of confusion that turned into a cumulonimbus scowl before he growled, "*Tchyo za ga'lima?*"

I smiled and nodded. "Hi, I'm looking for Jane. Is she here?"

He spat elaborately at my feet, "*Otva'li, piz'dad err'mo!*"

I didn't need to speak Russian to knew that he wasn't saying he liked what I'd done with my hair. His expression suggested it was more about my sanitary condition and the gender of my face. Perhaps, if I had been serious about achieving some credibility as a woke, twenty-first-century guy who was in touch with his feminine side, I might have invited him to have a full, frank and searching dialogue. But in my view, woke men are second only to vegans in nutritional value, and I have no feminine side, so I flexed my knees slightly and drove my fist into his balls in a very savage uppercut. As he bent forward, with his jaw hanging open in painful astonishment, I smashed a right hook that traveled all the way from my feet, through my hips and my waist right into his dangling chin and shattered his jawbone.

I stepped over him, where he lay whimpering on the steps and said, absently, "See? That's what you get for calling a guy an *Otva'li, piz'dad err'mo.*"

I was in a small lobby with a desk and a couple of chairs. To the left of the desk was a door. I took hold of the handle, turned and pushed. It was an office, and not a particularly large one. There were a couple of grimy open windows that looked out over a filthy back alley. In front of the window was a desk and behind the desk was a man in a shiny, gray, double-breasted suit. He had curly black hair that was so thick with grease he probably didn't need to wear a hat in the rain. He had insolent black eyes with long black eyelashes, that were staring at me and wondering about ways to cause me pain. He was not alone in the room.

Leaning against the window frame was a man who was not yet fat, but he was working on it and had mastered flabby with an "A" grade. He was wearing jeans and sneakers and a dirty gray T-shirt that hung over his belly like a tent. He'd lost the hair on the top of his head, but the ring he had around the back, from ear to ear, was thick, greasy and curly, like his friend's.

Leaning against the wall, just seven or eight feet to my left, regarding the world with an air of easy superiority, was the other one of the two Russian boys. This one must have been descended from the Rus, because he was easily six four, had platinum hair and very pale blue eyes. He gave me the kind of astonished frown his friend had tried on me and muttered something that sounded very like, "*Ty che, blyad?*"

The fourth person at the meeting was Colonel Jane Harris of the United States Air Force. She sat in a burgundy vinyl armchair, staring up at me not so much in astonishment as in fear. I smiled down at her.

"Hello, Jane."

She didn't say anything, but the big blond snarled, "*Idi syuda!*" Which must have meant something like "Come here," because he came at me, reaching for my collar with both hands. Then he growled, "*Po ebalu poluchish, suka, blyad!*" Which I figured meant he wanted to dismember me and eat my heart.

I let his fingers grip my lapels before I stepped back. Fights need to be short. They need to end quickly and decisively. So as I stepped back I brought both forearms down hard on the crook of his elbows and hugged them in toward my chest. His forward motion helped, and before he knew what had happened I had driven my right fist into his oncoming chin.

A decent blow to the chin, however big or tough a man is, will put out his lights, and it did that for Ivan the Rus. I gave him a gentle shove and let him drop in front of the door, effectively locking the colonel in the room.

The whole thing had taken no more than two seconds. Now I smiled at the guy behind the desk and stamped hard on the back of the Rus's neck. His legs jerked and kicked for a couple of seconds, then he lay still.

The guy by the window was still gawping. I had taken two strides before he started fumbling behind his back with his right hand. I took a handful of his collar with my left hand and a handful of his crotch with my right and pivoted him out of the open window. He only had time for a high-pitched squeak before he hit the alley with a sickening thud. The colonel was hunkered down now, grabbing at the Rus's cream linen jacket and trying to pull two hundred and fifty pounds of dead weight away from the door.

The guy with greasy hair had lost the insolent look in his eyes. He was getting to his feet with both palms held out and pushing at me as he yammered something inarticulate. I raised my right knee and drew the fighting knife from my boot.

"Do you," I said loudly and deliberately, "speak English?"

He shook his head rapidly. "No English, no English."

"Wrong answer."

I took a long step forward and drove the blade deep into his heart. He gasped and fell back into his chair. I wiped the blade on his shiny jacket and walked back to the door, where the colonel stopped dragging at the Russian's jacket and stared up at me.

"I think you have some explaining to do, Jane."

She shook her head. I nodded.

"I'm going to tell you what we are going to do. I am going to take your arm and shove a Sig Sauer P226 in your side, and we are going to walk quickly, without causing a fuss, to my car. There, you are going to get behind the wheel and drive us to my hotel. We will go up to my room and there, while we wait to be collected and taken home, you will tell me in minute detail what the *fuck* is going on."

Her eyes were wild. Her breathing was ragged. She swallowed three times before she spoke.

"You have to get out of here. Go back to New York. You have to let me go. Open the door. Let me go."

I wasn't amused, but I laughed.

"Yeah, sure. But that's in another universe, Jane, where the bunnies teach physics, the trees dance jigs and the camels all smoke pipes and ride bicycles. In this universe you and me are going to go and talk, and you had better make a lot more damned sense than you are making right now. Come on, get up!" I reached down and dragged her to her feet. Then I held her real close, gripping her shoulders. "I don't know what the hell is going on, and I am still just about prepared to give you the benefit of the doubt, though Christ knows, after what I've seen in the last few days, you do not deserve it. But push me, just push me an inch, Colonel, and I will shoot you stone dead, right here where you stand." I pointed out toward the street. "Or out there in front of a hundred witnesses. So just do as I say and don't try to run, because I will kill you." I reached out my hand. "Give me your purse."

She handed it to me and I tipped the contents on the oak desk. There was no weapon and nothing of any interest. I frisked her from head to toe and found nothing. So I grabbed the Russian's shoulders and heaved the body away from the door far enough for a person to fit through. I grabbed the colonel's wrist and squeezed through, dragging her behind me across the lounge toward the stairs.

Halfway across the bar she suddenly stopped dead and tried to yank her hand free. She seemed to be on the verge of tears.

"For God's sake! You *have* to let me go! Please just *leave!* Go away! Go back to New York! *For God's sake, just go away and leave me alone!*"

I turned on her and yanked her savagely to me. "You think after what you've done I'm going to go away? Are you out of your mind? You'd better get real, Colonel. You had better start thinking about best-case scenarios, and the best-case scenario for you right now is where you spend the rest of your life in jail. You need to identify your friends, and start cooperating with them. Because as of this moment there are a *lot* of people who think you should be dead. And that number is going to be growing. So wise up!"

"You can't do this to me."

"Wrong." I growled, "Move!"

I pulled the Sig from my waistband and shoved my arm around her waist under her jacket, then walked her toward the stairs.

"Let's be clear. Try to run, scream, call for help, I will shoot you and throw you in the back of the car. Make it hard for me and I will shoot you stone dead on the sidewalk. Do you understand?"

"Yes."

We moved down the stairs to the main lobby, pushed out through the swing doors and into the bustling street. I pulled her close and spoke into her ear. "Lean in to me and make like we are having an intimate conversation. Walk quickly."

We moved back up the road, pushing through the crowds. I had the Sig pressed hard against her side and her left arm gripped in my left hand. When we got to the car I opened the driver's door and shoved her in. Then I climbed in the back, behind her and slammed the door.

"Drive."

"Where?"

"I don't know yet. Head down to the coast. Follow the

Kennedy Highway around the horn and take the Galata Bridge. You know the 10 Karakoy Hotel?"

"Of course."

"That's where we're going. But take it slow and easy. I'll blow your spine through your belly if you do anything stupid."

She pulled out and cruised slowly down the road toward the intersection, among the interminable people spilling from the sidewalk and milling among the cars. She turned right and started moving south down Namik Kemal. I was suddenly overcome with a sense of the situation being surreal. I had taken this woman out to dinner in New York less than a week before, she had been about to come back to my house for a nightcap, possibly more, and now I was holding a gun to her back, threatening to kill her. On a sudden impulse I said, "You haven't addressed me by name since I walked in on your meeting."

Her eyes flicked at me in the mirror, but she didn't answer. I felt a cold prickling in my scalp. But I didn't ask what I wanted to ask. Instead I said, "What was your meeting about?"

"Heroin. And guns."

"You buying or supplying?"

"Gabriel has a poppy plantation about fifteen miles northeast of Divnomorskoye, in the foothills of the Caucasus. He also has a lab there for producing heroin, and other variants..."

"Gabriel?" She glanced at me again, and again didn't say anything. I couldn't keep the bitterness from my voice. "What is he, your lover?"

"No."

"Just your employer, huh?" I paused, looking at her reflection. "Any reason I should believe you?"

"No."

We moved on, weaving slowly through the traffic, past the seedy shops and the dirty roller blinds. We passed under a concrete railway bridge and her face fell into darkness. We emerged and passed a used car lot, a gas station on the right, and dull light washed over her face again. I noticed she was staring at my reflection and felt a sick hollow in my gut, and cold fear crawled through my scalp.

"Do you even know who I am?" She shifted her eyes back to the road. I said, "So Yushbaev supplies heroin to Turkey?"

"The Mexican cartels are finding it increasingly hard to reach the East. With his connections..." She hesitated. "Yushbaev can farm very large areas of remote Russia and produce very large quantities of opium, and process it too. Aslan, the man you killed—"

"Which one?"

"The one you stabbed because he didn't speak English. He was proposing a distribution network that would run from Poland all the way to the Pacific. Yushbaev had clients who needed weapons for a jihadists group. He was trying to put together a drugs for guns deal."

"That two-bit punk was going to run a distribution network?"

"He wasn't going to run the network, he said he had contacts who would be willing to cooperate."

"So what was your role in this drugs for guns deal?"

"To hear Aslan's proposal and take it back to..."

I interrupted her and loaded the name with bitterness. "To *Gabriel?*"

"Yes."

"When does he expect you back?"

She took a ragged breath. "Some time tonight." She looked at me in the mirror and her eyes flooded with tears. "You have to let me go."

"Why?"

She didn't answer and we wound on through the night, with darkness and feeble streetlight touching her face by turns.

FIFTEEN

I CLIMBED OUT OF THE CAR FIRST, KEEPING MY WEAPON concealed in my jacket as I opened the door for her. I could see her eyes searching wildly as she climbed out. She was searching for a way to escape, and that drove home for me the painful fact that this was no misunderstanding, no double bluff or clever rouse. She, like Charlotte and Marianne, belonged to Gabriel Yushbaev.

We pushed through the doors into the lobby and crossed to the elevators. I kept a tight grip on her and let her feel the cannon of the P226 in her side. I smiled down at her and whispered in her ear: "You know me well enough to know that I will do it, Colonel. There is a better way out. Don't make a mistake."

She pressed the elevator button and searched my face with her eyes.

"Is there?"

"Being cryptic and feeling sorry for yourself will not help you. We are going to talk now, and you are going to tell me everything."

I was aware as I said it that all feeling had drained from my eyes. It was a lack of feeling I recognized. When you are behind enemy lines, when you are in the immediate presence of death, sometimes you have to do things that require you to lose your humanity, if only for a while. When that happens to a person you can see it in their eyes. They shut down their empathy and their compassion and they look at you differently. She saw that in my gaze and she recognized it. I saw her go pale and pasty. The elevator doors slid open and we stepped inside.

"Are you going to kill me?"

"That depends on you."

"Are you going to torture me?"

I felt myself falter inside. "I have never tortured a woman or a child."

I let the ambiguity stand and we stared at each other until the elevator came to a halt. We stepped out and I led her to my door. I slipped in the card, the light turned green and I shoved her inside. As I closed the door behind me I said, "You have a choice, strip naked or I take your clothes off. One way or the other you take off your clothes."

"What are you going to do?"

"Take them off now."

She stripped, I took her clothes and threw them in the bathtub, with both faucets open full. If there was any kind of bug or listening device in there, now it was dead. Then I called reception.

"Mr. Bauer, what can I do for you?"

"My wife has joined me unexpectedly and I need a transfer to a suite. I need it to be immediate and I need it to be completely confidential. I don't care how much it costs, I do need it to be in the next five minutes."

He said, "Oh," a few times, then gabbled, "The, the, the Terrace Suite is available, Mr. Bauer. It is...um..."

"I don't care how much more it is. Reserve it for me now for a week. Send me a bellhop with the key in the next five minutes and I will demonstrate my gratitude in a way you'll remember."

I hung up while he was still telling me he would do that. The colonel had wrapped herself in a toweling dressing gown and was sitting on the bed with a cushion in her lap. "How do you expect me to make it to the suite dressed like this?"

"We'll manage."

I dumped my stuff in my bags and five minutes later there was a tap at the door. I opened it and a young woman in her early thirties, dressed in a pale blue suit with a white blouse, smiled at me.

"I am Miss Demir, assistant manager of the hotel, I have your key, Mr. Bauer. I can show you to the Terrace Suite now…" Her eyes traveled to the colonel. "If you are ready."

"Yeah, can you step inside for a moment?" I closed the door behind her and gestured toward the colonel sitting on the bed. "My wife has just had a very distressing experience. She was robbed at knifepoint, her purse and all her baggage were taken, and there was an attempted rape…"

Miss Demir looked alarmed. "In the hotel?"

"No, out on the street. It *has* been reported and the police *are* dealing with it. You don't need to concern yourself with that." She gave a small involuntary sigh and a smile. "But as I am sure you can understand, the experience was very traumatic. So here is what we need from the hotel. The clothes that are in the bath are all that she has left, but she can't bring herself to wear them. Please, dispose of them, incinerate them, whatever. We will dine in the suite tonight and my wife will not be going out for the next couple of days while she recovers."

"Of course, I understand—"

"And, please, if anybody comes asking for us, we checked out and left the country tonight. The hotel has no idea where we are. I am prepared to pay extra for the incognito if that is necessary. I just want her to feel safe and protected."

"Of course, I understand perfectly, Mr. Bauer, that is no problem."

"Now, can we get to the suite discretely, without drawing attention…?" I gestured at the colonel in her bathrobe.

"Not a problem. The elevator is right here and goes directly to the suite."

The transfer from the bedroom to the suite took no more than ten minutes, and while we were in the process the cleaners were summoned to collect and dispose of the colonel's clothes. If they were bugged, and I was pretty sure they were, we would soon be off the radar, at least for a while.

When Miss Demir had gone I called room service and ordered a couple of steaks and a bottle of wine. The colonel dropped onto the sofa and I poured her a glass of cognac and a glass of whisky for myself. I handed it to her, but stayed standing. She cupped it in both hands, with her elbows on her knees, and stared at the carpet while she bit her lip.

I gave her a moment, but she didn't say anything so I spoke instead.

"I'm going to call the office in a moment. When I do that they'll send somebody to get you. You'll spend the next few months being debriefed. What happens after that is anybody's guess." I waited a moment. Only her eyes moved. They flitted over my face, like it might tell her something more than my words. "You need to get to grips with something, Colonel. It's over. You can never go back. You can never go back to how it was, and you can never go back to Yushbaev."

She took a deep breath and sighed. "You..." She bit off the words, then snapped, "You don't understand!"

"So make me understand! Believe me, Colonel, from where I am standing there is no great mystery, except how the hell you managed to be so convincing. How you pulled it off is the only damned mystery in this for me. The rest of it is real clear. You are a traitor. You were planted in the US Air Force and worked your way..."

"No!" Her eyes blazed, but then she closed them and bit hard down on her teeth.

"No?" I waited. She sighed again. "Listen to me. You are a highly intelligent woman, but right now your behavior is nothing short of rank stupidity." Again the blaze in her eyes, but this time she held my gaze. "There is only one path for you." I held up one finger. "One path! You start cooperating with me right now. You tell me *everything*. And maybe there will be leniency for you. Be obstructive and refuse to cooperate, and you are looking at a charge of treason and spending the rest of your life in jail, if the Company don't take care of you first."

She looked away. "I can't."

There had been a creeping doubt in my mind, and now I gave it voice for the first time.

"Do you know who I am? Do you know me?"

She didn't answer straight away, but finally she said, "Of course I do."

"Who am I? name me!"

"Harry..." She moved her glass around a bit, then took a swig. She swallowed and said, "What, you think I'm a double?"

"What's the name of our organization? Who runs the show? What was my last job?"

"This is ridiculous. You're Harry Bauer, Alex—the brigadier to you—runs the show, though he has superiors you don't know about. We work for Cobra, I am a cofounder and I briefed you on your last job just before... You were briefed to eliminate Charles Cavendish."

"Just before what?"

"You won't believe me, but just before they took me."

"Who took you?"

"Sinaloa, but they were working for Gabriel Yushbaev."

"You knew him from before." It wasn't a question, but she shook her head. "No."

"You called him Gabriel. The first time you mentioned him you called him Gabriel."

"He plays mind games. He indoctrinates people."

"Did he seduce you?"

"No."

"Are you in love with him?"

She scowled at me. "No!"

"Does he own you?"

She scowled harder and drew breath to answer, then stopped,

closed her eyes and sagged. "I don't know. Perhaps. I don't know."

"What is this bullshit?"

I pulled my cell from my back pocket and video-called the brigadier on the secure line. His face appeared on the screen.

"Harry."

I switched the camera so he could see her. The colonel looked away. I snapped, "Look at the camera!"

She turned toward me, stared at the phone for a moment, then looked away again. I said, "I followed her from the yacht, like I told you, after the mosque she went to a nightclub, the *Rio de Janeiro Copa Cabana Club* on Küçük Langa to negotiate a distribution deal for the opium and heroin Yushbaev is producing in the foothills of the Caucasus, about fifteen miles northeast of Divnomorskoye, and also to try and work a drugs for guns deal for a bunch of jihadists in the Middle East."

His voice was dry. "She was negotiating the deal?"

"Yes, representing Yushbaev. I entered the club. It was not open yet and there was nobody there except for the colonel's two Russian bodyguards, Aslan, the Turk they were negotiating with, and his muscle. I killed them and took the colonel. She is not cooperating much, and I need you to send somebody for her soon. You need to take her home and debrief her."

"Have you asked her what she was doing at the mosque?"

"Not yet."

"All right. Do what you can. I'll have a team there in about an hour. Where are you?"

"10 Karakoy." I explained the arrangement I had made, then told him, "I'll inform the front desk that my cousin is coming with some friends, and to let them up. So have your man tell them he's my cousin."

"All right."

"You take the colonel home. I am going to fly to Divnomorskoye."

"No, they are bound to be looking out for you there. Fly to

Anapa International Airport. It's about fifty miles as the crow flies from Divnomorskoye. I'll have the team bring you some documents when they collect the colonel, rent a car at Anapa. Meanwhile we'll see if we can get the colonel to cooperate and keep you posted on anything we learn."

I nodded. "OK."

I hung up and she spoke with her eyes closed. "You have to stop this."

I raised an eyebrow at her. "What makes you say so?"

She took a deep breath, still with her eyes closed. "You just *have* to let me go and stop this!"

"Do you realize how stupid that sounds? Do you seriously think, after what you have done..."

She turned on me, eyes blazing. "Stop saying that! What? What have I done, Harry? I got abducted! Aside from that, *what have I done?* Have I compromised Cobra? Have I compromised you? Have I *ever* compromised you or Cobra?"

"Have you compromised me? Are you serious? On Koufonisi Marianne almost had me gutted by four of your lover boy's goons!"

"Marianne, not me!"

"On your information!"

She stood, her face flushed, stabbing her finger at me in the air. "No! On the bloody noise you make every time you make a hit! Yushbaev, who is not stupid by a very long shot, knew that you were coming after him and probably me! He used me as bait so that you would follow! You blundered right into his trap and started spouting about the Cavendish kill and how you suspected it was murder. They laughed at you, Harry! They laughed at the way you were chronically incapable of not boasting!"

"Boy, you really admire this guy."

"I do *not* admire him and he is not my *lover boy!* Why can't you get over your *gigantic* ego for two minutes and *listen* to me? He used me as bait! Can't you see that? Even today he was using me as bait!"

"So talk! This guy is so damned brilliant and he was one step ahead of me all the way, using you as bait! How could he not be with you in his pocket drooling at his feet and telling him everything he needed to know?"

"Oh, God *damn* you, Harry! You are so *obstinate!* How many men did they send?" Before I could answer she held up her right hand with her thumb concealed. "Four! They sent four men! Seriously, knowing you the way I do, *how many goddamned men do you think I would have sent if I wanted you dead? You asshole!*"

She made a gesture like she was going to hurl her glass at me, but drained it instead and sat back down on the sofa. Then she waved her finger at me.

"No! Not six, not eight! Because you are such a damned savage you'd find a way to blind and maim them all and you would come out of it, covered head to foot in blood and gore, none of it yours! No, if I had wanted you killed I would have had Marianne kill you. Or I would have had them bring you to me on the yacht, fed you a goddamn sob story, and I would have poisoned you. But I didn't, and as far as I am aware, in all the time Gabriel Yushbaev has had me in his power, Cobra has *not* been compromised, neither have you and neither has the brigadier."

My head was reeling. It wasn't just that what she was saying made sense; I knew, just from looking at her face, that she was telling the truth. I exploded, "Then what the hell are you doing, Jane? What the hell are you playing at?" She just shook her head. I pointed savagely toward the docks. "I *saw* you at the mosque talking to that guy in the leather jacket. I *saw* him give you something!"

"A shopping list of weapons."

"I *saw* you negotiating with those guys at the club, you have admitted that's what you were doing, and I *saw you, goddamn it, kissing that bastard on the cheek!*"

She nodded. "Yes, Harry, you saw all of that."

"Explain it, Jane! Tell me what the hell you are doing!"

"Please, Harry. It would take too long, and you probably

wouldn't believe me anyway. You have to let me go. Just *trust* me, Harry!"

I shook my head, feeling a hot knot in my belly that told me I was making a mistake. "I can't. How can I?"

"All right, we'll do this the slow way, then. I will tell you every-thing that happened from the moment you dropped me at the hotel. And then you have to help me, Harry. You have no idea what is at stake, and there is no time to do things by the book."

"OK, so tell me."

I was about to sit opposite her when there was a rap at the door. I called, "Who is it?"

"Your meal, sir."

And I went to open the door.

SIXTEEN

THE KID SET THE TABLE, OPENED THE WINE, POURED IT and left, ten bucks richer. The colonel rose from the sofa and carried her cognac glass to the table, where she sat. I sat opposite her. She sagged back in her chair.

"What I am about to tell you will finish me forever. Left to my own devices with Yushbaev, I could have redeemed myself and proven my loyalty to Cobra, but what you are forcing me to do will rob me of that chance."

"I'm sorry, this is the only way."

"Yushbaev is blackmailing me."

"Blackmailing you how? What the hell could he have over you?"

"You don't know everything about my student years, do you?"

"No, I know practically nothing about you or your student years."

She picked up her knife and fork and paused a moment before cutting into the steak.

"I was not always such a prudent, well-behaved girl."

I had to fight to repress the smile. "Really?"

"Really. I dropped out of college for a couple of years, hooked up with a Hell's Angel in California and rode with the gang for almost two years."

I was frowning hard, trying to see it. It wasn't as hard as I might have expected. "You're serious?"

"Yes, for two years I was a one hundred percent biker bitch. I wasn't just his old lady, I did the whole thing. We grew marijuana in the basement of his house, sold coke..." She shook her head. "You name it, I did it. I had a crazy two years. My parents had no idea where I was or what had become of me. They must have gone through hell."

"So you smoked some dope and snorted some coke..." I shook my head in disbelief. "It's a shame, but in our culture these days a lot..."

I stopped because she was shaking her head. "No, Harry, I did not smoke some dope and snort some coke. I crawled out of bed every morning at eleven or twelve and rolled two joints, one for me and one for Bull, and probably smoked a dozen more before I crawled into bed at four the next morning. I was permanently drunk on beer, whiskey and vodka, and for every ounce of coke I snorted, we sold a K to some pusher. We used to drive down to Arizona to collect the stuff, then take it back to California and sell it."

"What happened?"

She shrugged and made her first cut into her steak. "I woke up one morning with one suicidal hangover too many. Bull was sleeping like the dead, I rode my bike to the bus station, called the cops and told them where Bull's stash was in the house, and went back home. I made up a story for Mom and Dad about where I had been. It was pretty much the truth, but I left out the drugs, and I made out like Bull had forbidden me to contact my family. They bought it, because it was the best possible version of the truth." She gave another, smaller shrug. "I cleaned myself up, went back to college, and joined the United States Air Force."

"So how did Yushbaev come by this information?"

"I don't know exactly, but he and Cavendish, among others,

were watching you, and they noticed that you occasionally had dinner with me. So they decided to investigate my background and they found that there were two years missing from my otherwise well-ordered life. They started digging and they found Bull."

I chewed on a hunk of steak, then drained my glass of wine. As I refilled it I asked her, "Why didn't you tell the brigadier?"

"Why would I? I had all but forgotten about it. But as I walked through the doors into the hotel, two men closed in on me. One placed a dark coat around my shoulders and the other showed me a photograph of me on the back of Bull's bike. It was a photograph he had taken, which I would give a lot to destroy. I was in such a state of shock I didn't know what to do. As they led me out I was praying you would still be there and do something, but you had already gone. They took me to a van, saying there was somebody who wanted to have a brief chat with me. The rest is history."

"Wait a minute." I shook my finger at her. "That only goes so far. It does *not* explain how you have come this far without compromising the brigadier, me or Cobra,"

"That's bullshit and you know it, Harry. I just did exactly what you did in Panama. I told them I worked for the CIA's Special Activities Center. They didn't believe me—not entirely—but Yushbaev said it didn't matter. If he gave me a loose enough lead, you would eventually come sniffing after me."

"So why did he run in Koufonissi instead of taking me out?"

"Because he had just lost four men and realized he had underestimated you. He decided to draw you to his home base. Again he underestimated you. Please don't look smug. He thought you would try and come aboard and take me from the yacht."

I was skeptical, but the question I really wanted to know was more important. "OK, supposing I buy all that. There is one thing that just doesn't make sense. Why are you so desperate to get away? Why are you compounding this by acting like you're part of his gang? Like you have some loyalty to him?"

She put both hands to her forehead like it hurt from battering it against my stupidity.

"Because, Harry, you may have taken me, but he is still alive and his organization is in full working order. You haven't rescued me, Harry you have captured me in very damning circumstances. And to compound that, he will now publish the information he has on me and send it to my commanding officers in the Air Force and, to put the cherry on the damned cake, the Air Force will now investigate me and could find my ties to Cobra."

I sat staring at her, thinking for a long while. Finally I said, "Yeah, a Colonel James Armitage has been chasing me chasing you."

"He is very good. Don't underestimate him."

"Can you prove any of this?"

"Of course, but I don't need to. The FBI and, or, Air Force Intelligence will prove it for me, and they will then prosecute me to the full, punitive extent of the law, and the very best I can hope for is that I will be disgraced and lose my career. The worst can happen is that I will go to prison for the rest of my life. In either case, Yushbaev's organization will come after me and kill me." She heaved a heavy sigh and shook her head. "If you had just let me do things my way, I would have sorted this. You of all people should understand that."

"I should understand that? Perhaps. What I don't understand is the kiss, living on his yacht like one of the gang..."

"No? You don't understand that? Well cast your mind back to one May Ling, or how about Rachida, AKA Mary Jones?[1] Or Diana AKA Helen[2]? Should I continue? If you had been spotted in your more intimate moments with those ladies, how do you think that would have looked, Harry?"

"It was essential to the operation..." I trailed off because it sounded lame even to me.

---

1. See *Dying Breath*
2. See *Quantum Kill*

"The difference being that you were sent on a job, whereas I was abducted?"

"If you had gone to the brigadier, or me…"

"*After* I was abducted?"

I sighed, feeling helpless. "If what you're saying is true, we can work something out."

"No." She shook her head. "All we can do now is wait for the storm, and when it breaks I will be disgraced, I will go to prison and I will then probably be murdered."

"That's not going to happen."

"Your trust in the system is touching. Excuse me."

She stood and made her way past me toward the bathroom.

Someone once told me, trust no one absolutely. It's not fair on them. Nobody is that good that they can be trusted no matter what. But I guess trust is a hard thing to overcome. We all want to believe that particular person will be there for us, come what may. We all want to believe that *that* particular person will stand by us unconditionally, regardless of what life throws at them. We all need to believe that *that* particular person will not betray us, even when they already have. But the man was right. It is not fair to expect from somebody else a standard of honor and integrity no human can achieve.

The pain—the physical pain in my head—lasted only a fraction of a second. My skull split open, there was a violent flash of white light and then blackness and stillness, and oblivion.

Pain only exists in three dimensions, and as I returned from that shapeless, timeless place in my mind, so the pain returned. It came first to my head, sharp as shards of glass, it pierced my skull, and then settled to throbbing down through my neck and set about getting itself generalized into my whole body.

The next thing I was aware of was the cold, wet discomfort of water spilling from my face down onto my collar. I moved my face and wiped it with my sleeve, sending a few more shards of glass through my skull.

I opened my eyes and looked up from the floor at the ceiling.

There was a blurry face in the way, frowning at me, like it disapproved of my position, splayed on the floor. I agreed and tried to sit up. It was a bad idea, with painful consequences. I saw it through anyway and sat, groaning, and scowling at Colonel James Armitage of the United States Air Force.

I managed to say, "What the hell are you doing here?" before I got to my feet, staggered to the bathroom and threw up.

I rinsed my mouth and stuck my head under the cold shower for fifteen seconds, then went back to the suite, drying my hair with a towel. Armitage was sitting at the table with a glass of whisky in front of him, watching me. He managed a smile that actually contained some humor.

"In answer to your question, Harry, I am not as stupid as you look right now."

"Thanks. Care to enlarge?"

"I've been tailing you, as I have no doubt you know. After you got back to your hotel, I asked for you at reception. They told me you and your wife had checked out already and left the country. I knew that wasn't true because I hadn't seen you leave. Obviously you had paid to change your room and for the discretion of the hotel." He shrugged. "It's what I would have done."

I sat and reached for my glass. "That easy, huh?"

He shrugged. "It was a good plan. It would have worked if I hadn't been stuck to your tail."

I tried to think through the pain. "Colonel Harris, where is she?"

"She's gone."

"Gone where?"

"I don't know. Presumably back to the *Bucephalus*."

I stared at him a moment. "How the hell did you know what suite I was in?"

He gave a modest smile. "Combination of luck and deduction, Harry. I figured if you were looking for anonymity you'd have to pay more, not less. More meant a suite. This is a boutique hotel, there are only three suites. This was the second one I tried, the door was open, you were on the floor."

I tried to frame a question that made sense, but the pain in my head kept breaking it up. In the end I said, "Jane..."

He handed me two pills. "I found these in the bathroom cabinet. It's Panadol, they call it Paracetamol here." I washed them down with the whisky while he kept talking. "She left the hotel while I was talking to the front desk. I didn't recognize her to begin with. She was dressed in pants and a shirt that were much too big for her, and she had big black sunglasses on. She wasn't so much trying not to be noticed, as not to be recognized. The penny dropped as she went out through the door. I went after her, but she was climbing into a cab, and by the time I reached my car she was gone. I assume she went back to the yacht, and the yacht will make off tonight. My hunch is they'll leave somebody behind to deal with you. Probably tonight."

"How do you know about the *Bucephalus*?"

"I told you, I've been tailing you."

"I didn't notice you."

He smiled. "Yeah, well, the CIA isn't the only organization that trains its operatives well. The Air Force does a pretty good job too."

I grunted. I was mad at myself. I had screwed up on Koufonisi and I hadn't stopped screwing up since. This case was about as hard to understand as female logic expressed in Chinese algebra.

I rubbed my eyes and took another pull on the whisky. The pain in my head and neck began to ease. "There are too many departments involved in this case, all pulling in different directions, and nobody has all the facts."

"I agree. I hope you'll cooperate with us now."

I ignored his comment like I hadn't heard it. "Nobody but Colonel Jane Harris."

"You think she has all the facts?"

"I know it."

"She told you something?"

"Yeah, some. How long have you known her?"

"A few years."

"You ever had any reason to be suspicious of her?"

"Never. This whole thing has come out of left field."

"Let me ask you something, since she disappeared—I know it is not long—but since that happened, have you had any sign that 25th Air Force or any of its operations have been compromised?" He hesitated, looked away at the black glass in the window. I pressed him. "You want us to cooperate, but you want me to do all the cooperating. Is that the way it is?"

He sighed. "No, but as you say, it is early days."

"Maybe, but I know Jane pretty well, and I don't believe she's working for Yushbaev or the Russian Mafia. She's been with you a long time, and I am pretty sure, however hard you look, you will not find anything to suggest she was giving information to anybody, or sabotaging operations."

"Then what the hell is she doing with this guy? He's letting her go around on her own, she's kissing the guy on the cheek..." He shrugged and spread his hands. "What are we supposed to think?"

I pointed at him. "You said it right. What are we *supposed* to think. We're supposed to think the same thing he does. That she's either gone over to him, or that she's been working for them all along. But the question I am asking is, where's the damage? Where is the damage she's done us? Where is the payoff for Yushbaev and his gang?"

He grunted. "So if she's on our side, why did she crack you on the head with a vase and run?"

"Because our intelligence community is so obsessed with compartmentalized security that no department knows what the other departments are up to. So when we went after her, to rescue her, we actually jeopardized her mission. Hell! I was going to arrest her. I imagine you were too."

"That's insane."

"It also happens to be the explanation she gave me, and the only one that makes any sense."

He looked into his whisky and pulled down the corners of his mouth, like he was skeptical it was really whisky. "So who, exactly, is she working for?"

"Us, but she refused to be more precise than that."

"Did she tell you what her mission was?"

"Yeah," I lied, "to get close to Yushbaev and kill him."

SEVENTEEN

He took a pack of Camels from his jacket pocket and showed it to me.

"Do you mind if I smoke?"

"You can burst into flames as far as I'm concerned."

He smiled and nodded as he pulled a silver Zippo from the other pocket and flipped it open. "The old ones are always the best."

He lit up and inhaled deeply. As he blew the smoke at the ceiling he pulled a Glock 19 from his jacket and laid it on the table.

"Harry, I am going to need to know who you are."

I looked at the weapon a moment, and then at Colonel James Armitage.

"That may be so, Colonel, but I don't need to tell you. I thought we were pals now and we were going to cooperate."

"That's precisely why I need to know who you are. There are too many unanswered questions about you. I'm assuming you're from the Company, but the CIA deny your existence and you have not confirmed you're with them. You simply haven't denied it. So before we go any further, I want to know who you are. I have a team five minutes away who will happily take you to the

Incirlik airbase where we will waterboard you until either you talk, the CIA claim you as their own, or you vomit up your lungs, which is probably the most likely outcome of the exercise."

"Or I could break your damned neck and throw you off the terrace."

"You could certainly try, but the condition you're in, and the shape I'm in, I wouldn't recommend it. Also," he looked thoughtful, "something tells me you're not a guy who'd find it easy to kill an American officer who was simply doing his job."

I sighed. "You have a better opinion of the CIA than most Americans have, Colonel."

I pulled my cell from my pocket and dialed the brigadier.

"Harry, the team is on its way."

"Yeah, there's been a development. The colonel has left."

"What?"

"And Colonel James Armitage is here with me. He found me on the floor with the remains of a broken vase around my head."

"She attacked you?"

"From behind. But here's the thing. Colonel Armitage believes we should collaborate. As an alternative, and if I can't prove to him that I am with the Company, he proposes to take me to the Incirlik airbase and waterboard me until either you claim me, I start talking or I vomit up my lungs."

"I am inclined to let him do that. How the hell could you let her get away?"

"She was wearing a towel…"

"You *slept* with her?"

"No, sir! Look, can we discuss this later? The colonel is getting away, we are wasting time and I don't want to throw Colonel Armitage off the terrace."

"No, you have made quite enough blunders for one day, Harry. Don't compound it by killing a US Air Force colonel. All right. I'll see what I can do, but getting legitimate CIA papers at this short notice… Tell him to stand by. Where did she go?"

"Colonel Armitage believes she went back to the yacht. He has people watching it to see if she turns up."

"You don't agree, do you?"

"You might well think that, sir, but time is of the essence."

"All right."

He hung up and I looked at Armitage. "He said to stand by."

"Who is he?"

I shook my head. "Uh-uh, not even your boss would let you know that. You find out who I am, and then you forget."

"Suits me."

It was a long, tedious half hour, after which there was a knock at the door and I went to open it. I wasn't all that surprised to see Araminta there with an attaché case.

"Good evening, Harry. Can I come in?"

I stood back and gestured to the dining table. Armitage stood. I said, "Colonel James Armitage, US Air Force, this is Jane Doe. Jane Doe, meet Colonel James Armitage." To her I said, "Can I offer you a drink?"

"Sure, bourbon, two rocks." She laid the case on the table and sat.

"OK, Colonel, I have a number of documents here, one of which will satisfy your curiosity, if you get to see it." She reached inside her dark blue jacket and pulled out a leather case, which she handed to Armitage. "I am a CIA officer, Araminta White, and I am authorized by the Central Intelligence Agency to provide you with information regarding this man's operation, in so far as it affects the Air Force's attempts to recover Colonel Jane Harris. However, there is a condition."

"There always is with you people."

"You must accept, in writing, that you are aware, and it has been made clear to you, that the information I am about to give you is subject to Title Eighteen of the United States Code, Crimes and Criminal Procedure, Chapter Thirty-Seven, Section Seven Ninety-Eight, Disclosure of Classified Information. Do you understand that, and are you willing to sign said document?"

He handed back her badge. "Yes, I understand, and I am willing to sign your document."

She opened her case and slid a piece of paper across the table to him. He glanced over it and signed it, then handed it back.

"This is Ronald Eastman, he is an officer with the Central Intelligence Agency investigating the disappearance and subsequent reappearance of Colonel Jane Harris of the United States Air Force. He is not, I repeat not, authorized to collaborate or cooperate with any other government agency or department in this investigation. In fact, if we could, Colonel Armitage, we would request that the Air Force suspend its investigation until we are done. But we can't. Is there anything else I can help you with, Colonel?"

He had been staring at me throughout. Now he shook his head. "Eastman, huh?" He sighed. "No, there is nothing you can help me with. But you can be damned sure we will not suspend our investigation, and we will be watching you, Mr. *Eastman*, like hawks."

He stood and made his way to the door. There he stopped and looked back, smiling. "That'll be one for the club, huh, Harry? SAS man turned CIA officer rendered unconscious by a female US Air Force colonel."

He closed his eyes to laugh more thoroughly, then opened the door and left. Araminta turned to look at me and burst out laughing too.

"That's funny, real funny. Even I can see the humor in that." I picked up my glass. "Oh, wait, I was wrong. No, I can't."

"The great and fearsome destructive force that is Harry Bauer..." She hooted. "Mr. Primal, Macho Man himself!" She hooted some more.

"Are you done? Your hooting is hurting my head."

She toned it down to a chuckle. Then said, "The brigadier is not happy."

"He can join the club. I am the president."

"How'd it happen?"

"Why should I tell you?"

"Because he told me to tell you to tell me so I could tell him."

I narrowed my eyes at her. "Have you been practicing that on the way here?"

"No, I'm a double Gemini, we find that kind of thing easy. Now what happened?"

I went through it in detail, then told her, "Once we got back here she said she had been blackmailed by Yushbaev."

She looked skeptical. "Jane, blackmailed? How?"

"That's what I asked her. Apparently there were a couple of years when she dropped out of college. She was a bad girl back then and hooked up with a Hell's Angel by the name of Bull. That was in California. She rode with the gang for almost two years."

"Jane?"

"I know. It's hard to imagine. I'm just telling you what she told me. She described herself as a one hundred percent biker bitch. They grew marijuana in the basement, sold coke, did all the stuff crazy bikers do. Her parents had no idea what had happened to her. We should check if there was a missing persons report filed by them at that time."

Araminta shrugged. "So she smoked some dope and snorted some coke. I did a lot worse than that, I told my superiors, assured them I had left all that behind and that was the end of it. Hell, if we sacked everyone in the intelligence community who has smoked dope and snorted coke, we'd have to close down national security!"

"Yeah, I know. I'm not sure I share your bleak view, and besides, the Air Force is not the CIA. But she did a lot more than smoke cannabis and snort coke. According to her she smoked maybe a dozen joints a day before, as she put it, crawling into bed at four in the morning. She was permanently stoned and drunk, but the worst part is that she trafficked the stuff."

"Colonel Jane Harris trafficked marijuana? I can't believe that!"

"And coke. Apparently they used to drive down to Arizona, collect it from the Mexican border, then take it back and sell it."

"So why did she stop? How did she miraculously transform into Miss Driven Probity?"

"OK, tone it down, Araminta. I'm just telling you what she said. And try to remember she's a friend of mine and I care about her."

Her eyes narrowed to slits. "Did you let her go?"

"Will you just shut up and listen?"

"Fine, shoot."

"According to her, she woke up one morning with, in her words, one suicidal hangover too many. She took her bike, rode it to the bus station, called the cops and told them where her boyfriend's stash was, and went back home to her parents. She cleaned herself up, went back to college, and joined the Air Force."

"Her boyfriend was called Bull? That's what that story is, a load of bull. Jane is not a bad girl. She is Miss Driven Probity and has been since she was born. I'm sorry if you don't like me talking about her like that, Harry. I do happen to like her, but there is no way she was driving around on Harleys when she was eighteen, smoking dope and snorting coke. I don't buy it."

"Have you read her file?"

"No."

"Then shut up."

"So how did Yushbaev get this information to blackmail her?"

"We know Cavendish and his Sinaloa pals were watching me and sharing information. Apparently Yushbaev was in on that too. Cavendish told me on his yacht that they had noticed I had a relationship with the colonel. So Yushbaev investigated her background and found there were two years missing. They dug a little deeper and found Bull."

"Well if Yushbaev found Bull, so can we, and check if he was prosecuted back when Jane was eighteen or nineteen."

I nodded. "We need to do that, and we need to sanitize her."

"Sanitize her? After what she's done? Are you out of your mind?"

"What has she done, Araminta?" I found myself echoing the colonel's own words. "She just did exactly what I did in Panama, with you in fact[1]. She told them she worked for the CIA's Special Activities Center. She did not compromise us."

"If all of this is true, Harry, and you seem to be willing to buy it, why is she so desperate to get away? Why did she crack you over the head with a vase and run? And if Colonel Armitage is right, she went running right back to Gabriel."

"Because Yushbaev has information, and photographs which, if she does not go back to him, he will send to the Air Force brass. She could face prison time, she could be found guilty of spying for the Russian Mafia, and if the Air Force digs deep enough they could find her ties to Cobra. In her words, the best she could hope for was that she would be disgraced and lose her career. The worst would be to go to prison for the rest of her life. In either case, Yushbaev's organization would come after her and kill her. What she wanted was for us to let her deal with it her way. I got the idea her intention was to kill Yushbaev. She said I of all people should have understood that, and she's right."

"Then she cracked you on the head, stole some of your clothes and escaped."

I nodded. "She did what I would have done. And that's interesting."

"Interesting. Yes, I guess you could say it was interesting."

I pointed at her. "She behaved like a badass biker bitch."

Her eyebrows shot up. "Huh..." She made a face, sipped her drink and smacked her lips. "So, what now?"

"Her cracking me on the head notwithstanding, she is not me, and if she tries to kill Yushbaev the consequences will be unthinkable."

"Yeah, well, your ill-concealed feelings for the colonel

---

1. See *Silent Blade*

notwithstanding, there is also the fact that her innocence is far from proven with that crock of shit she sold you. And even if it is true, there is the fact that if Yushbaev gets tired of playing her as a bait to try and catch you, he might just start cutting bits off her until she breaks and tells him everything he wants to know."

"That is another way of looking at it. Either way, I have to go and kill Yushbaev before she tries to."

She opened her case and withdrew a familiar manila envelope which she dropped on the table in front of me.

"Anthony Sams, if anybody asks, you play the stock market, you're an entrepreneur based in San Francisco. You're in Russia on holiday but scouting for investment opportunities. But ideally, don't talk to anybody. Just find him and kill him. By the way, the *Apollonis* is moored at Kabardinka, only now it's called the *Lady Jane*."

"How appropriate."

"I told him it was a bad idea, but he insisted. The brigadier has his moments of whimsy. It's got the same cargo it had in Koufonisi, only there is some additional stuff. I have rented you a Range Rover which you can pick up at the airport. You're booked in at the Primorskiy, Ulitsa Mira Five, in Kabardinka, where the yacht is moored. And Harry?"

"What?"

"Get it right this time."

"Count on it. Do we have any intel on the house, the grounds...anything?"

She shook her head. "Zero, nada, zilch, squat. Well," she danced her head from side to side, "I'm exaggerating. We have a few fuzzy satellite photographs."

"Good, good, that's great."

"And there is something else."

"What?"

She looked at her watch. "It's two AM, and you fly at ten tomorrow morning. It's an air taxi, you're really pushing up your expense account on this job, pal. Flight time is about an hour, so you'll get there at eleven. Collect your baggage and your car, you should be at the hotel in time for lunch. Orders from the brigadier: Take the afternoon to formulate a plan. Execute it that night or the next day at the latest. He told me to tell you, there is no time."

I nodded. "I am aware. The plan is, break into the palace, kill everybody and bring the colonel home."

"Seems to cover it."

I sighed and drained my glass. "I'd better get some sleep."

She nodded but didn't move. I frowned at her. She sucked her teeth and looked at the wall for a moment.

"Harry?"

"What?"

"You might not come back."

"Thanks. I know that."

"I like you. I'd kind of miss you."

I scowled for a moment, then said, "Thanks."

"Do you think you might need some help getting to sleep?"

I was about to tell her to go to hell, but then wondered why I would do that. So instead I said, "Yeah, maybe. And you can drive me to the airport in the morning."

EIGHTEEN

Anapa International Airport was not what I had expected. I had expected a grim relic from the Soviet era, but it was big, bright and modern, and milling with people in Bermuda shorts and open shirts. I collected my Range Rover from the rental parking lot and, at just after eleven thirty, I pulled out of the airport complex and onto the M25, headed south and east toward Kabardinka and my yacht, the *Apollonis*; now renamed the *Lady Jane*.

I mused, as I cruised through the dry, yellow fields with scattered copses of trees I did not recognize, that the brigadier should have known that it was considered bad luck to rename boats. I doubted he'd bothered with the whole renaming ceremony, but who knew? The Brits were by and large crazy, and Brits like the brigadier were crazier than most.

As I came in sight of the sea I intoned, "Oh mighty ruler of the seas and oceans, to whom all ships, and those who venture upon your vast domain, are required to pay homage, I implore you in your graciousness to expunge for all time the name *Apollonis*, which has ceased to be an entity in your kingdom. As proof thereof, I submit this ingot bearing her name, to be corrupted through your powers, and forever be purged from the sea."

I smiled. I couldn't remember it exactly, but it was something like that. I would have to cast a bottle of wine and a silver dollar into the sea to appease Poseidon when I climbed onboard. I am not superstitious, but it pays to be careful.

After half an hour I arrived at Novorossiyskaya Bay. It was about nine or ten miles across, shallow, with the Novorossiysk port at the western end, and the small holiday resort of Kabardinka at the eastern end. There was no word for what I saw of Novorossiysk other than just plain ugly. The best you could say for it was that it had a lot of trees. But you couldn't help feeling that was purely accidental in a town that had worked so hard to eradicate all human warmth from its architecture, design and city planning. It was an industrial port that had humans in it because they were needed to make the port work.

Kabardinka was different. It was almost pretty. As I entered the town I had the sudden feeling of having slipped through a warp in space-time and wound up in rural northern California. It was leafy and green, laid-back, with curious, eclectic architecture and roads that rambled through suburban woodlands just because it was nice to do so, not because they had to get anywhere.

At the market on *Ulitsa Revolyutsionnaya* I turned right into *Ulitsa Mira* which led among abundant trees, roadside cafés, restaurants and gift shops, to the beach and eventually my hotel, the Primorskiy.

It was a small, cozy guest house on the outskirts of the town, overlooking the southeastern end of the bay. It had a small parking lot at the back of the building, where I left the Range Rover, and a flight of seven broad steps rising to an entrance porch with shiny brass handles on shiny, plate-glass doors.

Inside, the foyer was functional in beige, but clean and comfortable. There was a small lounge with a TV through an arch on the left, and a melamine reception desk on the right with a woman behind it whose forehead sagged under the weight of her single eyebrow.

I handed her my passport. "Anthony Sams,"

She consulted a computer screen, pushed over a document for me to sign and handed me an old-fashioned key with a wooden tag with the number five on it beside a big letter "B," 5B. Then she pointed up the stairs.

She said, "*Tvoya komnata, naverkhu! Naverkhu!*" and jabbed her finger up the stairs. "*Naverkhu!*" Then she opened her palm to display five fingers. "*Pyat! Pyat!*"

I figured my room was upstairs and it was number five. I pointed at the numeral on the tag and said, "*Pyat.*" Then I pointed up the stairs. "*Naverkhu.*"

She nodded, I smiled and she stared at me to see what I would do next. I climbed the stairs. She called after me something that sounded like, "*Vasha lodka!*" I waved in a way that said that was nice, and went to find room 5B.

It was unremarkable. It had an en suite bathroom immediately on the right as you came in. Then there was a spacious room with an ample bed, a desk, a TV and a big window with good views of a pretty town on a pretty bay.

Araminta had explained to me on the way to the airport that the *Lady Jane* had been moored at the Primorskiy's own jetty, down on the beach. By presenting my passport at reception and asking for it, they would give me the key and the papers. Maybe that was what "*Vasha lodka*" meant, "What about your damned boat?"

I unpacked, hung up my stuff, showered and changed my clothes, grabbed the satellite photos of Yushbaev's palace, and went down to find out. The primal being was still at the desk. I smiled at her and said, "My boat?" I made motions with my hands like a boat going over waves. She stared at me. I grinned and made the outline of a yacht, made the sound of waves with my mouth and finally took out a pen and drew a boat. She said, "*Vasha lodka.*"

I nodded, still grinning. "*Vasha lodka.*"

She shook her head. "*Net.*"

"*Net?*"

I stared helplessly at her, shrugged and shook my head. She threw her head back and laughed louder than anybody I had ever heard laugh, and pounded the desk with a huge, powerful hand. She turned and reached in a pigeonhole, still shaking her head and laughing, and brought out a manila envelope and a couple of keys on a piece of string. She placed them in front of me repeating, "*Ya govoryu, 'Vasha lodka,' ti govorish, 'moya lodka'!*"

Something told me it was all about my boat your boat. Family life at Mrs. Primal's place must have been a barrel of laughs. I said, "*Spasibo*," a few times to show I was grateful, and took the keys and the papers out into the midday sun with me.

Across the road there was a gate in a white wooden fence. I went through it and followed a sandy path down to the beach. There were several jetties reaching out into transparent green water. Some had small sailing yachts and rowing boats attached. The farthest on my right had the *Apollonis* moored at the end, with *The Lady Jane* stenciled in gold letters either side of her prow.

I climbed on board and went below. The hardware was in the cabin where I had left it. The brigadier's addition had been a Maxim 9 internally suppressed semiautomatic, a takedown bow with a dozen carbon fiber hunting arrows, and a dart rifle with a couple of boxes of tranquilizer darts. He didn't like people killing dogs.

There was also an extra ten pounds of C4 which I was happy to see, and he had thoughtfully added a dozen polythene bags of ball bearings. He didn't like killing dogs, but he had no problem with people. I had absolutely no idea how I was going to get into Yushbaev's compound, let alone his palace, but it is a sound rule of thumb which the brigadier understood well, when you don't know what you're going to do, take a bow and a lot of explosives. With the one you can take out the guards silently, and if all goes wrong you can blow everything up and get the hell out of there.

That is not Regiment policy, it is just my basic approach, and the brigadier shared it.

I went to the galley, made some coffee and spread the photographs on the table. The house was set within a rectangular compound in the middle of a deep forest about three and a half miles by mountain road to the east of Divnomorskoye. The compound was about one hundred yards across and maybe fifty or sixty deep. It was fringed by trees, but most of the compound was lawn, offering great visibility from the house.

The house was, from what I could make out, on three levels, with a gabled roof at the top, a large, south-facing terrace on the second floor, and a sprawling first floor. Gardens at the back didn't seem to offer much in the way of cover, and at the front of the house there was what looked like a gravel drive that led to a gate and then wound through the forest to the road.

Dots on the terrace and on the lawns suggested people. At least four of them were dressed in dark clothes and seemed to be carrying assault rifles. I was pretty sure there would be more than four of them, but how many more was anybody's guess.

I rubbed my chin. It would have to be a booby-trapped distraction near the southeast corner of the wall, followed by a second booby-trapped distraction at the southwest corner, while I breached the compound from behind, in the north, and entered the rear of the house using the gardens for what cover they could provide.

I rose and fetched myself a glass of scotch from the galley, then stood looking down at the images. But before the first booby-trapped distraction, I would have to take out the power lines and leave the house without electricity, and disable the electronic security system. I had noticed since I had landed that most of the power cables here were still overhead, not buried. That was a good thing. If I could find the nearest pylons to the house and blow them, I could deprive the compound and the security system of its main power source.

However, they were sure to have a backup system. So while they were responding to the second booby-trapped distraction, I would have to strike at the emergency generator, before entering the house. I scanned the photographs, trying to figure out where the emergency generator was most likely to be. I decided it had to be either a large shed at the back of the house, which seemed too big to be just a tool shed, or in the basement of the house, in which case there would have to be some kind of ventilation system. But the satellite images were neither clear enough nor close enough to give that much detail.

I made my way back to the hotel, climbed back in the Land Rover and cruised my way gently back up *Ulitsa Mira,* past all the gift shops selling inflatable rings, flippers and airbeds, past all the cool terraced restaurants and cafés, set in the cool shade of the ubiquitous trees, until I came again to the *Revolyutsionnaya Ulitsa*. There I turned right and followed it out of town, past a suburban district of cute villas on the left and rolling woodland on the right.

There the *Revolyutsionnaya Ulitsa* connected with the M4 and I hit the gas, climbing steadily into the forested foothills of the Caucasus Mountains. After four miles I passed the coastal town of Gelendzhik, perched on the shore around the natural harbor of Gelendzhik Bay. I kept going and after another four miles, just before the small village of Svetlyy, I turned right onto a road that was as hard to pronounce as it was to read, but I knew it would lead me to Divnomorskoye, the town above which Yushbaev had his so-called palace.

After another three miles of winding, tree-lined road I broke out into a spectacular, sunlit view of the small seaside town, with small clouds riding in a perfect blue sky above the expanse of the Black Sea beyond. Past the town I began to climb again and the view of the sea was hidden by dense forest that spread out all around me, obscuring every bend in the road so that I had to drop down to no more than forty miles an hour.

I wound through the woods for about three and a half miles, then slowed right down, scanning the far side of the road for a track through the woods that would lead to Yushbaev's place, his palace, his center of operations.

It wasn't hard to spot and for a moment I was tempted to cut across the road and follow the track to the gates of his compound. But I figured there was not much point, and the risk of alerting them to my presence was too great. Instead I kept on driving and three hundred yards down the road I came to an intersection which I had seen in the satellite pictures.

Straight ahead the road wound on into the forest. To left and right it was more of a broad track of beaten earth. I turned left and followed it in among the tall trees. Another four hundred yards brought me to a spot where the road widened and formed a clearing. There I pulled into the left and found a spot where I could leave the car and it would be invisible from the road. I killed the engine and swung down from the cab, mentally checked the photographs and began to push through the thick undergrowth of bushes and tall ferns that grew among tall pines and wild oaks. It was very quiet in the deep green shade.

After a quarter of a mile, and about fifteen minutes of moving with great care not to leave tracks, I came to a tall, redbrick wall, ten or twelve feet high. It looked surreal in that setting, in that vaulted, green silence. The pines were tall enough and close enough, if you could climb them, to get you onto the wall, except that the top of the wall was covered in razor wire, which, by the way it was hooked up, was also electrified. And every fifty feet or so there was a camera looking along the wall. That was the first line of defense. Breaching the wall was the first problem.

Once over, as Yushbaev had said about his yacht, that would be when the real trouble began. If I knew anything about Yushbaev, that wall was not to keep people out so much as it was to keep people in. So he could deal with them without the interference of the cops.

I pulled back a bit into the cover of the trees and found a suitable pine tree to climb. I hauled myself up and scrambled and heaved my way along until the tree started to bend and creak. Then I lay on my belly on a branch that looked like it would hold my weight, pulled the binoculars from my pocket and started to inch my way forward.

I saw what I had expected to see from the photographs, only a little more of it. On the other side of the wall there was a lot of well-tended lawn stretching for a long way. There was virtually no cover and there were men, I could see two of them, in black uniforms patrolling with assault rifles and Rottweilers.

About two hundred feet away I could see the side of the house. It was hard to make out any detail except that there was an ample, balustraded terrace on the second floor, which I had seen from the photographs, and a garden at the back which was extensive and pretty elaborate, and did seem to offer more cover than I had expected. That surprised me.

I smiled and began to snake my way down the tree again. A plan was forming in my mind that might just work. I needed to get another couple of angles on the house, and then I would go back, get a few hours' sleep, and return with the hardware. Tonight Yushbaev would die, and tonight I would take the colonel back to New York.

That, at least, was the plan; and you know what Joseph Heller said about plans.

NINETEEN

I HAD SLEPT THROUGH THE AFTERNOON AND AS THE sun was setting over the Black Sea, and the sunburned holiday makers were starting to spill into the evening streets, I had taken the Range Rover down to the jetty. There I had packed the water-proof bag with all the kit the brigadier had provided, and slung the bag in the rear of the truck. After that, at a leisurely pace, I had retraced my steps and driven back up *Ulitsa Mira*, along the Revolutionary Way and out into the darkness of the forests toward Gelendzhik, Divnomorskoye, and Yushbaev's palace in the woods.

The roads were deserted, and if anybody bothered to notice me leave Kabardinka, they didn't bother to follow me.

I found the track that led through the woods to Yushbaev's place, and then the intersection, where I turned left as I had that afternoon. I turned in, killed the lights and followed the track to the clearing. There I pulled into the gap behind the trees and the ferns, where I had hidden the Range Rover earlier that day.

I climbed out of the truck. There was no moon yet and what little light there was from the stars was filtered out by the trees, infusing the forest with an impenetrable darkness. I slipped on the night-vision goggles, slung the bag over my shoulder and started to pick my way through the woods, now a deep green and black, using always an irregular, broken rhythm, and pausing often to listen.

After fifteen minutes I came to the eerie, monolithic wall that towered among the trees, hunkered down behind the ferns and spent ten minutes watching and listening. Beneath the mantle of quiet the woods were alive with small rustles and scuttles, the small sounds of nature's predators, where killing and devouring another life is no big deal.

I identified the cameras up among the barbed wire, satisfied myself that I was not in their scope and crouch-ran up to the wall. Then I inched my way along to the corner. There I packed two one-pound blocks of C4 against the wall beside one of the mines I had originally intended for the *Bucephalus,* taking care to focus the center of each blast some distance from the corner of the wall itself, where the explosion would not be absorbed by the perpendicular wall. I set the detonators to the number nine on my cell, then took another pound of explosive, packed another detonator and couple of bags of ball bearings into it and buried it in a shallow grave eight feet from the wall. I set that detonator to eight on my phone.

A five-minute loop through the forest took me to the far end of the wall, about a hundred yards away. There I placed another two packs of C4 on the wall with another mine. I set those detonators to the number seven.

This time I placed the booby-trap concealed against the trunk of a large pine tree about fifteen feet from the wall. This one contained three bags of ball bearings. The resistance of the tree would direct the blast, and the three hundred scalding steel balls, in an infernal funnel of death upon anyone standing within twenty or thirty feet of the damaged wall. That detonator I set to the number six.

I had no idea how many men Yushbaev had at the palace, but by the time they had investigated these blasts, he'd have a good few less. That was a cert.

The next part of the operation was more difficult and took longer. I made my way to the rear of the compound. There I moved along the length of the wall, staring up at the eerie, black and green trees, identifying the ones that either overhung, or came close to the top of the wall. None of them was perfect, but there were a couple near the center of the wall that might do the job. I picked one, scrambled up to about twelve or fifteen feet, where the thick, lower branches sprawled up and out, and snaked my way along one of the thicker ones until I was suspended some three or four feet over the razor wire which topped the wall. Fifty paces across a floodlit lawn I could see the elaborate gardens that were at the rear of the house, and the tiered structure of the palatial building, with its ample terraces and glowing amber windows.

There, with great care I reached down and dropped four burgers of C4, each with a detonator set, like the first charge on the front wall, to the number nine on my cell. They would go off at precisely the same time as the first explosion, remove the razor wire and, with a little luck, they would go unnoticed.

I had just one thing left to do. I left the bag in the tree and scrambled down with four magnetic mines stuffed into a canvas bag.

The power lines entered from the intersection where I had turned onto the dirt track, on wooden pylons, and from there fed a handful of villas to the east of the track. At roughly the point where I had hidden the Range Rover, the cables were taken up by taller, steel pylons that stood at about twenty-five feet and carried the wires above the treetops and over the redbrick wall, into the grounds of the house.

I had counted a total of three pylons: one where I had left the car, one a little less than halfway and the third about fifteen or twenty paces from the wall, on the east side where I had first arrived. This was my first target.

I scrambled up the steel tower until I was about a foot from where the power cables connected to the pylon. There I placed two of the magnetic mines. I scrambled back down to the base and there I placed another two against two of the uprights, with the detonators set to one on my cell.

Finally I returned to my tree, scaled it again and slung the two Heckler and Koch rifles over my shoulder, one with its grenade launcher attached. I hooked some spare magazines to my belt and slipped a belt of grenades around my shoulder. The Maxim was under my right arm and my Sig P226 under my left. The Fairbairn and Sykes was in my boot and all I needed was the bow, with a dozen hunting arrows, which I left in the bag with the remaining C4.

I sat a moment reviewing what there was of my plan, decided I had left nothing undone and dialed one on my phone.

Explosions don't roar unless there is a lot of flammable material involved. An explosion is most often a violent expansion of gasses that sounds and feels like a hard smack in the air. These four were practically simultaneous, like a vast door slamming above the forest. It was followed almost instantly by a huge shower of sparks above the treetops and then the screeching of tortured metal as the pylon keeled over and crashed among the trees. On the far side of the wall all the lights went out. The spots that flooded the lawns died and the house was plunged into darkness. Male voices started to roar and shout, dogs barked wildly. I smiled, and for the first time in a long while I started to have fun. I pressed nine on my cell and the air was smashed in half by an almighty explosion at the southeastern corner of the compound, and at the same time four small explosions among the barbed wire on the wall below me.

For a few seconds there was utter silence. Then dogs started wailing and howling. They were joined by men shouting in alarm. Some were crying out in pain. I waited and after a minute there was the roar and whine of diesel engines and I saw headlamps glowing green in the black ocean that was the lawn: two pairs moving in the direction of the gate, a third set cutting diagonally across the night toward the inside corner of the compound, where the explosion had taken place.

Another thirty or forty seconds passed and I was surprised to see the third set of lights converge suddenly with those that had headed for the gate. For a moment I was disoriented and wondered if they had stayed inside the compound, but then realized, as the shouts reached me through the night, that the mines and the C4 had blown a hole in the wall, and I was seeing the headlamps of the trucks on the far side. My smile deepened and I pressed the number eight.

Another violent explosion slapped the air. The headlamps jumped and rocked and several of them went out. There was a lot of howling and screaming. For a couple of minutes that was all that happened. Then there were more shouts. They sounded somehow more focused, more cautious. Two more sets of headlamps appeared, along with the sound of engines roaring.

I dialed seven and yet another almighty report tore the night in half. I lifted the night-vision goggles from my eyes and looked through the telescopic night-sight on the Heckler and Koch. There was a Wrangler with four guys in it approaching the inside corner of the compound wall in the southwest corner. A large chunk of that wall had collapsed and there was a gaping hole. The Jeep slowed and came to a halt and the men jumped out and took refuge behind it, fearful because of the booby-trap that had cost their pals their lives. They were joined by more men. I counted eight altogether.

Through the gaping hole in the wall I saw two Land Rovers pull up on the outside. Men got out and took up positions behind the vehicles, aiming their weapons out into the trees. I waited. It was hard to judge how close the vehicles were to the tree, but they were close. There were some shouts and the eight men on the inside started to approach the breach in the wall. A few more shouts and four men detached and started to run toward the first breach. I figured it was to guard it.

I looked back at the second breach. Men were picking through the rubble while other men scoured the forest with their scopes. Time for six.

I dialed six. Another violent explosion. I gave myself five seconds to observe what happened. One of the Land Rovers reared up on its front wheels and then crashed to the side. The other rocked sideways and its windows and windshield erupted into glittering spray. The men standing around, maybe eight or ten of them, broke into a strange kind of dance, twisting and writhing, raising their arms over their heads and faces, like they were being attacked by a swarm of wasps.

I pulled the goggles over my eyes again, scrambled to the middle of the branch and lowered myself to the wall where the wire was hanging in shreds. I paused for only a second to scan the lawn and listen. I saw nothing and the only sounds were the lingering cries and moans of the men injured in the explosions.

I dropped the bag with the bow and the C4 in it and lowered myself after it. I dropped, gathered up the bag and ran, crouching, the ten long paces through that strange green and black world to the box hedges that formed the nearest edge of the gardens. There I dropped on my belly and scrambled to the nearest opening in the hedge.

What the situation called for was to proceed slowly and with caution. However many I had killed or maimed in the explosions, I had no intel, and I was almost certainly still seriously outnumbered. But I was also acutely aware that I had to strike hard and fast while I still had the element of surprise in my favor.

So I got on my haunches and ran to the nearest rhododendron. From there I could see that I was in a series of walkways and paths, like a maze, flanked by box hedges among which were set flowerbeds and flowering bushes. From what I could make out there were also arbors draped with flowering vines. I was just thinking that if I was fast, the garden might just give me cover until I could make the house, when two guys stepped out of a set of sliding glass doors, waving a flashlight around, and headed for a shed with a satellite dish on the roof, over on my right, which I had already identified from the photographs as a likely place for the emergency generator.

Working fast, I assembled the takedown bow and fitted one of the carbon hunting arrows. The two guys were standing at the door of the shed. One was shining a glowing green light while the other was fiddling with a key. I could hear frantic shouts from the front of the house. Hazy green flashlight beams danced across the lawn and played along the walls. I went on one knee, drew, aimed instinctively and loosed. I didn't bother to see if I had hit the mark. I knew I had, and in any case, if I hadn't, there was nothing I could do about it.

By the time the barb thudded home through the target's chest, slicing through his heart, I already had the other arrow nocked and drawn.

And loosed. It whispered and vanished.

They were both frowning down at the bloody broadhead that was protruding from the first guy's chest when the second arrow thudded home through the second guy's back. Frowning at each other, they both knelt and lay down, like the last scene of a bad amateur production of *Swan Lake.*

I sprinted, vaulted a couple of hedges and came to the large shed. The key was in the lock. I stepped over the bodies, opened the door and dragged the two dead guys inside. The generator was there in the middle of the floor. I didn't pause. I slapped a pound of C4 on it, thrust in a detonator, set it as nine and stepped outside again. I locked the door, dropped the key in my pocket and made for the house.

There were a lot of shouts now, some coming closer, and the sound of half-crazy dogs pulling on their leashes, barking and howling. I fitted another arrow to the bow and, staying in the shadows of the house, loped toward the sliding glass doors through which the two guys had emerged.

A green flashlight danced at the corner of the house. I stopped and drew. The light glared right at me. I heard a voice call a name that sounded like "*Ivan?*" and I loosed the arrow, aiming an inch above the flashlight. A beat and suddenly the flashlight was pointing up at the sky, and beneath it I saw the diabolical form of a huge, black Rottweiler with glowing green eyes hurtling toward me. There was no time to nock another arrow. I grabbed the Maxim and dropped to one knee as it leapt, snarling at me, and as its huge, slavering wet maw closed on my hand I pulled the trigger, blowing the back of its head into spray and gore.

I jumped to my feet and ran, with the bag over my shoulder, and slipped inside the house through the sliding glass doors which stood open a couple of feet. I pulled it closed and dropped behind a large armchair, where I had a view of the shed outside. I gave it thirty seconds or so and was about to blow it, thinking I could not waste any more time, when three men ran past toward the generator shed, shouting instructions. There were also men with dogs running along the lawns, playing flashlights in all directions.

I heard a couple of shouts as the guys reached the door of the shed. There was the report of a gun and they hauled the door open and went inside. I dialed nine. Bright light flashed in the open doorway. The roof of the shed seemed to dance. There would be no light that night. Now I had bare minutes in which to find Yushbaev and the colonel, and get the hell out of there.

TWENTY

I HOLSTERED THE MAXIM 9 AND PUT THE HECKLER AND Koch with the grenade launcher to my shoulder. I moved fast across the room, taking care, but fairly sure that everybody was either upstairs locked in secure rooms, or out searching the grounds.

I opened the door and eased out. I was in a vast hall. A huge marble staircase that glowed green because of the night-vision goggles spiraled up from the center of the floor, over my head to a galleried landing above. Directly across from me the main doors to the house stood open and two guys dressed in black, holding flashlights stood at the door, staring out.

I dismissed a philosophical thought about how we always look out when the greatest danger is within, took three silent strides and shot one of them in the back of the head with the Maxim 9, and, while the other was still in shock I sprang forward, got his throat in the crook of my right elbow, gripped my left bicep with my right hand and grabbed the back of his head with my left hand, then squeezed. While he started to suffocate I dragged him into the cover of the spiral staircase, laid him on the floor and knelt on his chest with the Fairbairn and Sykes poised on his throat. He was wheezing hard and panicking, while I wondered whether Russian schools taught their kids English. When he'd caught his breath I asked him.

"You speak English?"

He croaked, "Little."

"Where is Yushbaev?" He swallowed hard. I sighed. "I have no time. I want to get what I came for, and leave. Fast. No problems. Understand?" He nodded. "So you help me, you go home tonight. You give me problems, I kill you and ask somebody else. Now, you have five seconds. Where is Yushbaev?"

He licked his lips. "Upstairs."

"Where?"

"Master bedroom, with armed guard. Top of stairs you make..." He hesitated. "Top of stairs you make left..."

I drove the blade through his throat and sliced hard to the side. I knew from that point on he would be lying. Yushbaev's bedroom would not be to the left. The left would be the southwestern corner and would get the evening sun. The master bedroom would occupy the southeastern corner to get the morning sun with views of the sea.

I stood and moved quickly and silently up the stairs with the rifle at my shoulder. On the sixth step I saw the faint glimmer of green, reflected light from the open front door. I paused half a second and instinct made me duck. A fraction of a second later they opened up and a hail of hot lead rattled down, striking the marble balustrade.

They couldn't see me. They were spraying the area in steady bursts of sick shots. My heart was pounding and my belly was on fire, but I stayed ice-cold and took careful aim. There were two of them and in the black and green world I could judge where their heads were. I took a full second over it, keeping just out of their line of fire. I double-tapped twice, heard the grunts and cries of pain and ran the rest of the way up to the top of the stairs.

The landing was a gallery that ran in a square all around the stairwell, overlooking the huge hall below. In addition, from where I was standing at the top of the stairs, a corridor branched off to right and left, into the west and east wings respectively. There was nobody there. I figured by now they were either searching the grounds or forming a protective guard around Yushbaev, Marianne and the colonel.

I was disabused of that idea as I saw, framed in the green light that spilled in through the front door, dancing black shadows approaching. They were obviously responding to the gunfire they had heard. It looked like it could be four of them, but it might have been six.

I let them burst through the door, then lobbed two grenades at them and sprayed them with fire, then ran hell-bent for leather toward the east wing. I came to a door. I had no time to think. I put four rounds through the lock, kicked it open and hurled myself to the side. Back at the stairs I heard boots tramping and lobbed two more grenades over the balustrade. They exploded and I heard screams. I dropped to my belly and peered round the door, training the rifle on the inside.

It was a large bedroom with windows looking south and east, bathing the room in that strange green light. There was a cold, marble fireplace at the far end; there were armchairs, a sofa and an elaborate coffee table. There were long drapes open on both windows and a high ceiling. And there were no people.

Except, that was, for the woman lying on the huge bed, sobbing.

I stepped back to the door and looked out. There were no tramping boots, no shouts, nothing. I closed the door and marched to the bed, wondering if it was the colonel. It wasn't. It was Marianne. She stared up at me from between her clenched fists.

"Please, Harry, don't kill me. Please, he made me do it. You don't know what he's like. Please..."

I snarled, "Where is he?"

She rose from the bed, hugging her arms. She was naked under a translucent negligee. She came around the bed taking hesitant steps.

"Are you going to hurt me?"

"Where is he, Marianne?"

"Please don't hurt me. He has hurt me so much since Koufonisi."

"I'll damned well hurt you if you don't quit stalling and tell me where he is!"

"He's downstairs," she said, and her face collapsed and she started sobbing, reaching for me with both hands. "Harry, he has hurt me so bad."

I snapped, "I haven't got time for this!"

"Please!" She grabbed hold of my arms and pressed herself against me. I grabbed her face with my left hand.

"Where is the colonel? Is she with Yushbaev?"

"No." She shook her head, staring into my face, surprised. "He believes you've killed her. He believes I conspired with you. He is going to kill us both, Harry, you have to help me. He hurt me so badly."

"Where downstairs? Where is he downstairs?"

She had stopped crying and was just staring up into my face.

"He has locked himself in the bunker, with the girls."

"What girls? What bunker?"

"And his praetorian guard. He knows that you will go there for him, and he will kill us both."

"*What girls? Where is this bunker?*"

"Didn't you know? He has fifty women here at any one time, Harry. He brings them from Russia, Poland, Turkey, from all over the place... I thought you knew."

Her hands were on my face and on my neck, stroking me, holding me. I gripped her wrist. "What are you doing, for Christ's sake? *Where is the bunker?*"

"Harry, he hurt me so much, he left me here, for you to kill me. You won't hurt me, will you?"

I snapped, slapped her face. "Cut it out! Where is this bunker?"

She turned away, holding her cheek. "He brings the women

and teaches them to be whores. At first they don't want to, but he gives them drugs..."

She stared up into my face, as though examining every feature. She looked strange, like a creature from another planet, luminous green among ink-black shadows, reaching up to touch my cheeks with her fingers.

"He laces their food with cannabis, they live in luxury, Harry, he gives them aphrodisiacs, caviar, all the alcohol they want, luxury all the time, and every day cannabis to smoke or eat or drink. He breaks them down with pleasure. Nobody can fight pleasure, Harry. It's not natural."

She smiled and I growled, "What the hell are you talking about, Marianne?"

"He sells them." It was almost a whisper. "He sells them, the ones who aren't special, to very exclusive clubs all around the world. They pay very high prices for them. They are for judges, ministers, archbishops."

There was total silence. Her smile was growing deeper. She was pressing her naked body against me. My belly was on fire.

"What the hell are you doing?"

She whispered, "I am trying to help you. You have to kill him. Only you can kill him, Harry. Then we can have all the girls for ourselves. The very special ones he keeps, or he sends them to the very exclusive clubs, for kings and princes, and presidents. And a few he keeps for himself. They are *very* skilled, Harry. You know what they are especially skilled at, *Harry?*"

I waited.

"They are *especially* skilled at blackmail, at extracting information, at feeding information, and at...," she pressed her lips to my ear so I could feel her moist breath, "...*assassination.*"

That was when I felt the prick in my arm and an intense, numb pain. I stepped back and looked down as something that looked like an EpiPen clattered to the floor.

"*What did you do? What was that?*"

She gave a soft giggle. "Even if I tell you, you won't know for sure, will you?"

"Goddamn it, *what was that?*"

I stepped toward her and the room seemed to move too, and when I stopped the walls bulged away from me. She was very erect and translucent. The green of the night-vision goggles suddenly terrified me and I ripped them from my head.

"It might be lysergic acid," she said from very far away, with no expression in her face or voice. She was just a black silhouette with a glowing, translucent aura, standing against a glowing window that overlooked the Black Sea. Black and white chasing each other into infinity, good and evil, life and death.

I wrestled to drag my attention back to what was important and focus it where it had to be focused.

"Where," I said. "Where should I be focusing my attention? Where is Yushbaev?"

"I told you." She took a step forward that brought her several miles through space and time to stand so close I could feel her breath and her warmth. "He is down, deep down, Harry, all the way down, in the bunker with fifty women. Fifty female assassins. Fifty very dangerous women who love him and adore him. But maybe—" She ran her fingers over my chest, up my neck and face and through my hair. "Maybe they can be yours. I used to love him, Harry. But then I met you, and you own me now."

I dropped the Heckler and Koch, and the bag with the C4, and gripped her fiercely to me. I bit savagely into her neck and growled in her ear, "I want to own you, I want to consume you."

"Yes, Harry, and the first step to do that is to confront Gabriel, destroy him and make all his women yours. You are the master of death, Harry. The master of death and destruction. He is weak, he is terrified of you, hiding in the basement like a frightened slug, with his women to protect him. Come with me," she pressed her lips to my ear again and breathed, "*come with me.*"

She turned me gently toward the door. The door swelled and somehow we passed through into the black passageway. She led me among the darkness to a wall that was paneled in wood, and that wooden wall opened to reveal two black beings with no face. They inhabited an oval of light and Marianne and I stepped inside the light and began to sink.

Marianne held me all the way, whispering in my ear that she was my slave, and I was the god of destruction, the god of death. The wall in front of me opened again and we stepped out into a vast cavern. There was a turquoise pool and tall columns, and gardens that smelt of neroli and jasmine. There were women, maybe a dozen of them, all beautiful. Most of them were naked, others were partially naked. They were all staring at me.

On the far side of the turquoise pool there was a large, elaborate chair, and sitting in it was Gabriel Yushbaev. He was scowling at me. He stood and his voice resonated like thunder across the dome of the underground sky.

"Make no mistake, Harry Bauer! I *hate* you! You have hurt me, Harry Bauer! You have hurt me a lot! And I want to kill you and eat your heart!" He pointed at me and his face went crimson. "*I hate you and I will eat your heart and drink your blood!*"

I saw the blood leach from his face and his eyes bulged, and suddenly I was huge. So huge that I wondered how that cavern could contain my vast size. And when I spoke my voice was immense and crowded out everything else in the cavern, making the naked women wince and cower away, and making Yushbaev shrink to the size of an ant.

"I will kill you, Yushbaev," I said it slowly and deliberately and with huge, heavy words, "and I will eat your heart and your liver and I will drink your blood, and I will have all of your women and your riches, because I am the god of death and destruction."

He turned and glared at Marianne. He pointed at her. "You have him for tonight. But tomorrow, he is *mine!*"

He watched us cross the chamber, past the pool and through an arched door. One by one, as we passed them, the naked women turned and followed us. We followed a dogleg passage with marble floors and walls of living rock that breathed and pulsed as we went, and eventually we came to a large, arched wooden doorway. Marianne unlocked the door and we went inside.

There was a table piled high with caviar, oysters, hams and cheeses and fruit of all descriptions. There was wine and ale and spirits, a bucket of ice and champagne. There was a huge, wooden four-poster bed and to one side a pool that was large enough for thirteen naked women and me. The door closed and the girls began to close around me. Marianne started stroking my face and unbuttoning my shirt. Other hands stroked my hair and began to unlace my boots.

"Poor Harry," Marianne whispered in my ear. "Life has been so hard for you, you deserve to rest. You deserve some pleasure. Allow us to give you pleasure, Harry. Please allow us to do this for you." Her lips found mine, and then my ear again. "Tomorrow you can fight, but tonight is for pleasure."

My whole world was soft, silky skin, soft hair scented with jasmine, exquisite curves under my hands. I was guided to the pool where I was enveloped by women. I didn't know which was which. Identity didn't matter. They all stroked me, they all kissed me and they all gave themselves to me among crazy wild images and a seemingly endless ocean of pure pleasure. At some point they moved me to the bed, and at some point, hours later, I sank into black oblivion.

TWENTY-ONE

MY MOUTH WAS SO DRY AND SWOLLEN I THOUGHT I was going to suffocate. There was a weight on me that was oppressive, and as I tried to push it off I found I was smothered by it on all sides. I panicked and struggled and realized that the weight was human bodies that had me pinned under a sheet. I pushed, heaved and scrambled all at the same time and found suddenly that I was sitting up in a bed.

There was a faint, pale blue light emanating from across the room. In its glow I could see not twelve but three women on my bed, one on my right, two spooning on my left. None of them was Marianne.

I had a sickening ache in my head. I slid to the foot of the bed and stood. The room rocked and spun, but then settled. A door over to the left was open and I could see it was a bathroom. I staggered to it, washed out my mouth at the tap and drank about a pint of water from my cupped hands. There was a shower there and I stepped in and stood under the hot water for five minutes while I lathered myself and shampooed my hair, then switched it to cold as I rinsed off. That made me feel better.

I stepped out of the shower cubicle, found a towel and dried myself off, then returned to the bedroom. The three girls were still sleeping. I took in the walls; they were uneven and the color of stone, like the place was a cave that had been hollowed out under the house. There was a table with drinks and food. It was not a vast banquet, but it was enough to feed a hungry man. Vague memories started to creep back into my mind, like timid rodents.

And that comparison made me pause. I had been given some kind of hallucinogen, and I wasn't absolutely sure the effects had worn off yet. It might have been my surroundings, but everything seemed, not so much surreal, as unreal.

I pulled on my clothes and went to the door. It was unlocked. I opened it and stepped out into the tiled corridor I had followed the night before. I retraced my steps and came to the area where I had emerged from the elevator. It looked different this morning, smaller, less imposing. The large pool was still there, and the high, domed ceiling. There was also a heavy, elaborately carved table in the center of a mosaic floor with six heavy chairs set around it. The artificial light mimicked sunlight, and there was jasmine growing up the walls, and garden areas with roses and other flowering bushes and vines. A passage disappeared on the far side of the cavern, and I could hear female voices coming from that direction, laughing.

Beside the elevator doors there were two men in black uniform holding assault rifles. They observed me without much interest. Over beside the pool was Yushbaev sitting in a large, comfortable armchair. There was a white, wrought-iron table in front of him, strewn with newspapers and magazines. I saw the *Economist, Time* and various others. He glanced at me and didn't look happy.

He picked up the *Washington Post* and spoke as he scanned the front page.

"You owe your life to Marianne. I was ready to kill you last night, but she convinced me to spare you."

"Yeah? Something tells me she didn't do that for my benefit. What did you give me?"

"A concentrated distillation of salvia divinorum, a mild, naturally occurring hallucinogen related to mint." He glanced at me. "Did you enjoy your evening?"

"I'm not sure. I don't remember much."

"That is a shame. Marianne said you were spectacular."

I scowled at the word. "Are you going to tell me what the hell this is all about, and why you *didn't* kill me last night when you had the chance?"

He sighed, dropped the paper and gestured to a chair across the table from him.

"Sit, are you hungry? You probably want breakfast after all your exertions yesterday." He fished a small brass bell from under the papers and rang it. "That is a good question, Harry. And I have no doubt nine hundred and ninety-nine thousand men in a million would have killed you,"

"Or tried at least."

"Or tried, as you say. But I have a very different way of doing things. I am dyslexic, you know? We tend to think differently."

"Really?"

He ignored the irony in my voice and plowed on. "The problem is, as you yourself have observed, people throughout the ages have relied on pain, brute force and violence to get what they want. But, you know, pleasure can have a far more detrimental effect on a person than pain. Constant, sustained, unrelenting pleasure twenty-four hours a day, day after day, becomes debilitating and corrupting. It can destroy a person."

I laughed out loud. "You're going to kill me with pleasure? Boy, you're the best enemy I ever had, Yushbaev!"

"Not exclusively. We will feed you drugs which you will enjoy immensely. We will be nice to you, you will be waited on by beautiful women who will do your every bidding. There will be nobody for you to fight with, and nothing to fight against. And one day you will realize you belong to me. Just like everybody else here. You will be unable to live without me. You will need me."

"Yushbaev—"

"Yes, Harry—"

"They'll be making snowmen in hell before I need you for anything but target practice."

He shrugged. "Bravado, but it changes nothing. If you want to eat, if you want to drink, you will have to consume a steady intake of cannabis in various forms, as well as salvia and some other, stronger, more addictive substances."

I squinted and shook my head. "But why? Why this elaborate setup, the expense—isn't it easier just to shoot somebody?"

"Certainly, and if you are a Neanderthal, why do anything else? But the whole point of investment, Harry, is to get returns. And if you invest in people, the returns can be tremendous." He gestured toward the room where I had slept. "Those girls cost me practically nothing. I kidnapped them from their homes, from their jobs, universities... For the first day or two they wept and fought and screamed. Within less than a week they were sullen but submissive, within two weeks they were responding, beginning to smile and be happy. By the end of a month they were devoted to me."

He gestured around him with both hands. "This place was a mine, then adapted by the Soviet Union as a nuclear bunker. It is very large. If you go down that way, where you hear the girls playing, there are caverns which we have converted to every kind of pleasure. There are dormitories for the guards and for the girls," his face darkened, "though usually we are upstairs. Induction and storage take place down here; *life* takes place upstairs!"

"Induction and storage?"

He grunted. "When the girls first arrive they are brought down here to be inducted. When they are adjusted and happy they move upstairs for training."

"In assassination, espionage..." I shook my head and laughed. "You are modeling yourself on Hassan i-Sabbah! The Persian founder of the Nizari Assassins. The words *assassin* and *hashish* both derive from his name. His killers were called the Hashishim."

"Very good."

"And you're doing the same, but using women. What will they be called, the Gabrielites?"

He ignored the joke. "Not all of them become assassins and spies. Some just get shipped to various high-class clubs around the world to be used as whores. Others have more potential and they become escorts, companions..."

"Spies."

"And assassins. This is one of my many products, Harry, and it has served me very well. When you get inside somebody's intimate life, it gives you a lot of control over them. I can influence government policy on four continents."

"Well I am glad I screwed that up for you a little bit last night, Yushbaev."

His face darkened again and for a moment he was the stereotypical Russian whose mood changes on a single word. One minute he is laughing, the next he's weeping, and the next he's wiping out the entire German army. He scowled and the lights seemed to dim.

"Screwed it up a little? You did more than that, Harry. You have hurt me and my operation very badly. You have killed almost all my men. I have a handful left down here. You destroyed my electronic security system, you have cost me millions of dollars in damage and lost business over the last twenty-four hours. And right now I have a very serious problem with the local police who want to come and investigate what happened last night. My lawyers in Moscow are fending them off, but you tell me, how do I clean up the mess you made last night?"

"I don't really give a damn, Yushbaev. I'll tell you something else, before long you're going to have an even bigger mess down here."

He leaned forward, like he hadn't heard me, narrowing his eyes. "It was *carnage*! How can you live with yourself? What you perpetrated on us last night was a *massacre!*"

"You're asking me how I can live with myself?"

He nodded. "Yes, I am."

"You kidnap free women and use narcotics to convert them into slaves, spies and assassins..."

He was roaring with laughter before I had finished.

"The melodrama! Free women! You make it sound so sinister and evil. But I do not cause them pain, or maim them, or amputate their limbs! I introduce them to a new life, to a new way of seeing life. They live in luxury and when the time comes for them to move to a club, or an assignment, they do not want to leave!"

"Because you have turned them into cabbages, Yushbaev! Because you have robbed them of their humanity! Of their free will!"

"But they are *happy* cabbages! What do they want free will for? They haven't the intelligence to use it! *I* have free will for them! It has always been that way, Harry! Open your eyes! A small minority of shepherds lead, and the sheep follow."

"You're full of shit. You live in a fantasy to justify the monstrous things you do. What about the children who have died cruel deaths because of the armaments you've sold? How do you justify that?"

"I did not create the wars."

"But you fueled them, and you exploited them, and you provided weapons you knew would be used against peaceful villagers, women and children."

"You think if I had not sold phosVX to the Taliban, they would not have massacred that village? They were going to massacre them anyway. You can lay that at the door of religion, Harry, not Gabriel Yushbaev."

"Bullshit! You rode the bandwagon so you could test your chemical weapons!"

"Not my chemical weapons. I don't make them."

"You can wash your hands all you want, Yushbaev, but you can't change reality. Every time you look at your hands, you will see the blood of children. And one day, soon, the blood you see will be your own!"

He gave a humorless laugh and shook his head. "That I

should have to receive lectures on morality, murder and massacres from you!"

There was a movement behind me and one of Yushbaev's half-naked women approached carrying a tray of coffee, croissants, toast, eggs, bacon and sausages. She set it in front of me and withdrew. The smell of the coffee and the bacon was intoxicating and I realized I was very hungry. I looked at Yushbaev. He was smiling.

"The world is changing, Harry. You belong to a dead age, the age of Pisces. This is the age of Aquarius, science and order. You deified the individual and his freedoms, but you know as well as I do that there is no such thing as freedom. Society works on the basis that people are not free. For society to work, people must obey. And even if man did not live in society, a man living alone in the wilds is no more free than a man in prison. We are bound by the laws of physics, chained by the laws of nature and ultimately subjugated by the laws of society. Where is your freedom? What I have understood, and you have failed to understand, is that there are only two options: obey the rules, or make the rules. And I chose to make the rules. Eat."

This last he said jerking his chin at my tray.

"It's drugged?"

He nodded. "But you will enjoy it. It will stimulate your dopamine production, act as an aphrodisiac and make the next seven or eight hours extremely pleasurable."

"So if you are doing this to me instead of killing me, that means you have a plan for me."

"Marianne believes you can be useful. I think she is wrong. I don't think you can ever be controlled. We'll see."

I thought about it for a moment. "What about upstairs?"

"What about it?"

"The mess. There are a dozen bodies up there, maybe more. How are you going to explain that to the cops? Those bodies are going to start rotting and attracting wild animals. You can't hide down here indefinitely. What are you going to do?"

"Why should you care?"

"I'm curious. Humor me."

He sighed. "I am arranging a team to come and clean up."

"That must be hard."

"You haven't made my life any easier by what you have done. As I said, I wanted you put to death."

"Who is Marianne? How come she carries so much weight with you?"

"I found her in Paris a couple of years ago. She is highly intelligent, brilliant, she is what psychologists call a sociopath but I call an enlightened person—"

"She is incapable of empathy or compassion."

"And she is, as you know, sensational in the sack. Since I discovered her she has become invaluable to me."

"Tell me something." I said it looking down at my tray. "What's to stop me shoving this tray up your ass, breaking your neck and walking out of here?"

He glanced at the two guys by the elevator. "Them, ten more of them down that passage where the girls are bathing, the fact that the elevator uses biometrics and you would never get out alive, plus the fact that if you don't eat that food, you will be force-fed intravenously."

I nodded once, upward. "Oh."

"Face it, Harry, you are beat. You have finally met your match. You have given me a hard time and caused me a lot of pain, you can be proud of that, but this was only ever going to end one way. I represent...," he sighed, shrugged and spread his hands, "I represent a higher level of evolution. You are a troglodyte, I am a man of the future." He gestured at my tray again. "Eat, enjoy it."

"Where is Marianne?"

"Up above."

"Why?"

"Why so many questions, Harry?"

"Well, I guess I am feeling insecure and I want to understand the situation I am in. Give me a hand here and I might even eat your damned eggs and bacon."

"She is contacting with friends and allies to come and help clear the mess upstairs."

"Why can't she do that from here?"

"Enough."

That was the answer I had expected, and it confirmed what I had deduced. I sighed and watched his face carefully. "So she went to the yacht? Where is the yacht moored?"

"In Gelendzhik Bay. Now, enough, Harry! Eat!"

"OK." I sighed, picked up the plastic knife and fork and looked down at the eggs and bacon, the sausages, toast and croissants, and I smelled the coffee. I was starving and I wanted really badly to eat it all and have the girls drag me back to the bedroom. Maybe I could kill him tomorrow. I smiled at Yushbaev. "I mean," I said with a laugh, "what the hell am I complaining about, right?"

He spread his hands and shrugged, and smiled.

TWENTY-TWO

I SET DOWN THE PLASTIC KNIFE AND FORK AND STOOD. I placed my left hand beside the tray and vaulted onto the table, landing, half crouching, on top of Yushbaev's papers and magazines. For a moment he stared at me in astonishment, but it was only for a second. Because as I stood erect I smashed the heel of my boot into his face, crushing his nose and sending his chair flying and him sprawling on his back. It was unexpected and it took the guards a couple of seconds to react, but by the time they were shouting and running toward me I was down beside Yushbaev, dragging him to his feet.

One of the guards was shouting something at me in Russian, the other was bellowing down the passage. I ignored them both, put a choke hold on Yushbaev and hauled him over to the tray of food. There I snapped the plastic knife by forcing the blade against the tabletop with my left hand. When it broke, I pressed the jagged point close beside Yushbaev's left eye.

"Tell your boys to stand down, Gabriel. You know me well enough to know that I will make a mess of your left eye, and when I am done I will make a mess of your right one. And I am more than happy to die breaking your damned neck. So tell them to stand down, now!"

He babbled something at them in Russian as his few remaining troops arrived running out of the passage. Behind them, in dribs and drabs, looking confused and worried, came the women.

"Now, you are going to do exactly as I say—"

"You cannot expect to get away with this." He croaked the words, like a frog. "Your position is impossible."

I ignored him. "First, I want all the women topside." I was watching the guards and saw one of them glance at the women. "You! You speak English?"

"Little."

"OK, understand this, I will take out Gabriel Yushbaev's eyes, first the left, then the right, and then I will kill him. Understand?"

He was looking nervous and nodding. "Understand."

"So you must put all the women in the elevator, and send them up to the house. Do it now!"

He babbled something to Yushbaev, who quickly answered, "Da, da!"

Then the guards were shouting at the women, herding them into the elevator like cattle. The women were shouting and whimpering too, more like frightened sheep than cows. Soon the elevator doors closed and half the women began to ascend.

I snapped at the English-speaking guard.

"You! What's your name?"

"Gregor!"

"Gregor, next time I give you an order, if you check with this son of a bitch I will take out his left eye. Understand?"

"Understand."

"I am the power now. You do what I say."

"Yes."

There was a big Slavic guy standing beside him with a walrus moustache. I jerked my head at him and said, "So take your pal's GSh and bring it to me."

He hesitated a moment and I pressed the jagged point of the plastic knife deep into the corner of Yushbaev's left eye. His scream was horrific and his arms and legs began to thrash. Gregor jumped and ran to his big, Slavic friend, snatched the semiautomatic from his holster and brought it to me, screaming, "Stop, mister! Stop, you must stop! I not check! I not check!"

I eased up. I had not damaged Yushbaev's eye, but I had cut deep into the very sensitive skin at the corner of his eye. Blood was running freely down the side of his face and he was weeping. Gregor handed me the 9mm Gryazev and Shipunov and I took it in my right hand, wedging the cannon hard under Yushbaev's jaw.

The elevator returned and I jerked my chin at the remaining girls. "Send them up."

There was more herding and a couple of minutes later the last of the girls were on their way to the surface. To Gregor I said, "Stairs?"

He shook his head. "No stairs. Only elevator?"

"OK, what about another elevator, a cargo elevator."

"No, no, only this elevator!"

He was looking real anxious and I thought maybe he was telling the truth. I nodded and turned my attention to Yushbaev.

"OK, Gabriel, now I need you to walk and I need you to talk, I do not need you to see or smell or use your arms or your hands. You're a smart guy so you know where I am going with this. You are going to eat my breakfast and drink my coffee, and you are going to do it like you were a starving wolf, and then we are going to take a ride. Give me a small problem and I will blow your hands off at the wrist, after taking your damned eyes out with a plastic knife."

He didn't argue. He was still sobbing, and with every sob I could see he was losing the respect of his men. That suited me fine. I let them watch him wolf down my breakfast and drink my coffee, then I spoke to Gregor again.

"Tell your guys to get down on the floor with their hands behind their heads."

He issued the order. They spent a couple of seconds looking at each other until Gregor screamed at them and they all dropped and adopted the position. I said, "Call the elevator." He did. "Now get on the floor, over there, with your back to me."

We climbed aboard and I told Yushbaev, "Take it up, Gabriel. I have no desire to break by an excess of pleasure. I am very happy to use pain. Do it!"

He pressed the button, the onboard computer read his biometrics and we began to rise.

"You have an underground power supply."

"Obviously."

"But sending and receiving signals depended on an antenna above ground which was damaged last night."

"When the generator was destroyed. It was housed on the roof of that building. I feel very strange."

"Yeah? Relax and enjoy it, that was the advice you gave me, remember? So Marianne had to go to the yacht to arrange things. That was the only place where you had secure communications."

"You said it, Rambo."

He giggled, I sighed and the doors opened.

We were in the master bedroom. It was as I remembered it. The light filtering through the windows said it was midmorning, maybe ten thirty or eleven. Yushbaev looked at the bed with an idiot smile on his face. "Where is Marianne when you want her? I think maybe she is in that bed. Shall we go and look for her among the folds and warps of space?"

"No."

I grabbed a cushion and dropped it in the elevator doorway to stop it closing. Then I bent and retrieved my bag. It still had the C4 and the rest of my gear in it. I took two cakes and stuck a detonator in one of them. I set it to self-detonate in thirty seconds, tossed them into the elevator car, removed the cushion and sent it back down. I counted thirty seconds and the walls shook, the wooden paneling cracked and the elevator doors rattled.

Yushbaev stared at me with no particular expression. "Trapped," he said, "in the heart of the world. In hell, maybe."

"Yeah, deep. Get moving. Walk and talk, Yushbaev, walk and talk."

He nodded thoughtfully as I propelled him toward the door. "They sound the same, and the meaning is parallel. Talking is the walking of the mind, Harry. This is an important realization. Talking is the walking of the mind. Walk and talk."

I resisted the temptation to slap him across the back of the head. Instead I asked him, "Where do you keep the information you have on the colonel?"

We had arrived at the galleried landing and he started to take the steps down. He repeated, "The information you have on the colonel. That phrase means nothing to me. Meaning, Harry, is something that we give to objects and phrases. They have no inherent meaning of their own."

"You learn that from a fortune cookie, Yushbaev? You think you might grasp the meaning better if I blow your kneecap off?"

"I don't like violence."

"You were blackmailing Colonel Jane Harris."

"Jane." He stopped dead halfway down the stairs, smiling, and sighed again. "I like Jane."

"Keep moving."

I shoved him and he started ambling down the stairs again. In the light of day I could see the carnage of the night before. There were eight dead and partially dismembered bodies lying in large pools of congealed blood and gore.

"I don't like violence," he repeated. "I am like Buddha. Gotama Buddha, Harry, wanted to remove suffering from human experience. I too wanted to achieve my ends by causing pleasure instead of pain."

I pushed him toward the door. "Fascinating. Now focus, Gabriel. You persuaded Jane to do what you wanted, right?"

He nodded and fell into step beside me. "Oh, it was not hard. She was the bait on my rod to draw you in. Marianne said, 'Kill him and torture her,' but I do not like causing pain, Harry."

"You just pay other people to do it for you."

"That's it," he said absently. "I thought, back then, if I had you both. If I could induce you both into my system, what an investment that would be!"

"You should have listened to Marianne."

"I should."

We came out of the front door onto a broad flight of shallow steps that fanned out down to the gravel drive. I said, "But you didn't. Instead you blackmailed Jane into working with you."

He snapped his fingers. "It was brilliant." His eyes were shifting here and there. "Please keep talking to me," he said. "I think the trees want to eat me."

I pushed him onto the lawn and we headed for the breach in the southeast corner of the wall. "You made deliberate public displays of her kissing you on the cheek, leaving your yacht alone and returning of her own free will, negotiating on your behalf..."

"It was guaranteed to bring you running."

"But how did you do that, Gabriel? You blackmailed her."

He was half-walking, half-running now, gaping at the trees beyond the big, redbrick walls.

"Do you think I can buy the trees, Harry? Do you think I can buy their souls?"

"Probably. Talk to your brokers. Tell me about Jane."

We arrived at the hole in the wall. It had caved in from the blast, crushing a couple of guys and a dog. We picked our way through the rubble to where there were two Toyota trucks and four guys, all six torn to shreds by the blast and the red-hot ball bearings.

"Jane, what can I tell you. She is beautiful."

"Tell me about her boyfriend."

He stopped and laughed, leaning forward with his hands on his thighs. Then he turned, wagging his finger at me. His pupils were huge, black discs.

"Oh, oh, oh," he said. "Who is her boyfriend/ I think you would like to be her boyfriend, huh, Harry? I think you have a soft spot for Jane. But be careful, maybe that soft spot will suck her in, all the way inside to that blackness you have in your soul, huh, Harry?"

I sighed. "Jesus! It's like talking to an insane asylum tripping on acid." I shoved him in the direction of the track where I had hidden the Jeep. "Bull, Gabriel. Remember Bull? Jane's boyfriend?"

He hunched his shoulders and hugged his arms. "I am afraid of these trees, Harry. They want to consume me. Can you see their mouths, up in the dark canopy, their mouths are looking down at me, and they want to suck me in."

"Keep walking and think about something else." We moved through the ferns, among the tall, straight trunks, weaving back along the path I had followed the night before. "Tell me the story of how Jane dropped out of college."

"Jane dropped out of college?" He giggled. "That's rich. You should tell me that story to keep my mind off these trees. These trees are really dangerous, Harry. I can pay you. I can pay you a lot to protect me. From the gaping mouths, the gaping mouths." He repeated it a couple more times, exaggerating the sounds of the vowels. "The *gaping mouths...*"

It continued like that as we moved down the slope. I wasn't sure the Jeep would still be there, but Yushbaev's lawyers had managed to keep the cops at bay and the truck was where I had left it.

"Get in the passenger side, Gabriel."

I shoved him and he clambered in. I got in behind the wheel and fired up the big engine. I smiled at him.

"I know what you want," I said.

He smiled back with arched eyebrows. "You do?"

I put it in reverse and spoke as I turned the truck around. "You want Marianne. In the Emperor Suite, with champagne and oysters. Am I right?"

He nodded, gazing out the windshield. "Oh, yes. That's good, Harry."

"She'll make you forget the trees and their deep, black

mouths. She'll put her arms around you and make you feel all right."

"Oh, yes, Harry. That is what I need right now. It has been very hard this week. It is kind of you to think of that."

"Yeah, kind of guy I am." I pulled back onto the track, followed it to the end and turned right toward Gelendzhik. "But it gets even better, Gabriel. I am going to take you to the *Bucephalus* now, where we are going to see Marianne, and you are going to make love to her for hours while I prepare lunch."

His head lolled back against the seat, he closed his eyes and sighed. "Oh, that is going to be just heaven."

"It's your special day, Gabriel. So while I drive us to the yacht, why don't you tell me about those two years that Jane was with Bull. That was real smart of you to track that down. Tell me how you did it."

He shook his head and shrugged. "I don't know. Must have been somebody else."

I drove in silence for a while, trying to control the anger and frustration in my gut. Eventually I forced a laugh into my voice.

"You didn't know that Jane had dropped out of college?"

"Nope. You think Marianne will fuck me? She was real mad at me."

"You didn't know about the marijuana and the coke?"

"Nope. I think if you tell her she might. She admires you, you know?"

"How about Bull?"

"Bull, there is something seriously wrong with reality, Harry. Did you know that? Reality does not work. I think I am going to fall into a hole in reality in a moment. Can I hold your hand? It's like the Philadelphia Experiment all over again."

I drove on in silence, with Yushbaev gripping my shoulder to stop himself falling through a hole in reality, while the red embers of anger were steadily fanned into a red-hot flame.

We came off the M4 onto *Ulitsa Lunacharskogo*, and followed that through semi-industrial wastelands to the intersection with

Ulitsa Ostrovskogo, which threaded its way among pretty apartment blocks, stores and cafés, and the eternal abundant trees, to *Ulitsa Lenina,* the port and the seafront, where two long piers thrust out into the water, with a few yachts moored to them, and anchored a quarter of a mile out, I saw the *Bucephalus,* massive and gleaming.

"OK," I said to Yushbaev, "let's go talk to Marianne, see if we can't arrange a little bit of paradise for you."

TWENTY-THREE

WE WALKED THE TWO HUNDRED YARDS TO WHERE THE launch was moored, with my arm linked through Yushbaev's, like we were old pals and he'd had had a few vodkas too many. We climbed in and I took the launch out to the boarding deck at the rear of the yacht. There, with some difficulty, we clambered aboard and moved to the sliding glass doors that gave onto the saloon.

Now I could see there was a screen beside the doors. Yushbaev placed his palm on it and, once scanned, he allowed it to scan his eye too and the doors hissed open. We went through. The doors hissed closed behind us and he turned and gripped my lapels, frowning hard into my face.

"Where am I, Harry?"

"On the *Bucephalus*, and we are looking for Marianne."

"Is this..." His face remained immobile but his eyes rolled around in their sockets, taking in his surroundings, "Is this *all* a reflection of my inner being?"

"I don't think so, there are too many trees and too much sunshine. Where is Marianne, Gabriel? Would she be on the bridge?"

"Then she is in control?"

"Probably. How about crew. Is there any crew on the yacht at the moment?"

"These questions..." He shook his head. "So deep. How have I been so blind? What, in the end, is control, Harry?"

I rolled my eyes and wondered if it had been worth it, feeding him my breakfast. "Come on, let's find that elevator."

"The *elevator...*," he said, nodding ponderously. "Exactly!"

We made our way through the luxurious lounge and found the elevator that led to the Emperor and Empress Suites. Yushbaev stood swaying and making unnaturally slow blinks.

"Gabriel, we are looking for Marianne. You want to see her, right?"

"Very much."

"So I need you to think, will she be in the suite, or will she be on the bridge?"

He just stood and stared at me, then turned and stepped into the elevator. I followed him and we rode up to the suites. The doors hissed open and we stepped out into the grotesque, crimson antechamber, with the rococo chairs and the passage that led down to the Emperor Suite on the right, and the Empress Suite on the left.

He walked unsteadily, across the room and down the passage. He stopped in front of the tall walnut doors and pushed them open. I followed him into the absurd drawing room and watched him cross to the bedroom door. He opened it and stood staring for a while then went inside.

I went and looked. He had crawled under the duvet and covered himself, and was moaning and repeating Marianne's name. He was about as useful as a paper parasol in a monsoon.

I turned and was not all that surprised to find Marianne leaning on the doorjamb. She was in a dark blue suit with a white blouse and a string of pearls around her neck. She said, "What have you done to him?"

"I fed him my breakfast."

She laughed. "Looks like I backed the wrong horse."

"Violence wins every time over pleasure."

"That's a bleak philosophy, Harry."

"It's not a philosophy. It's a fact."

She made a "maybe" face. "So what now?"

"So now I need to know what he had over the colonel."

She gave her head a tiny shake. "Nothing."

"You're lying."

"Maybe. You'll never know."

"You know where she is?"

"Yes."

I stepped toward her and she pulled a .22 from her jacket pocket.

"These babies get a bad press. Big guys are not supposed to be scared of twenty-twos. But if you know how to use them, they can do a lot more damage than a forty-five. And believe me," she smiled, "I know how to use one."

"What do you want?"

She gave a small frown, like she hadn't really thought about it till then. She gave her head a little shake. "You have made such a mess of things. The lawyers can't hold off the cops much longer, and nobody is prepared to send us a cleanup team. What do I want? I want out of this nightmare you have created."

"And you think you'll achieve that by killing me here on the boat?"

She shook her head. "No, I'd just rather you didn't kill me."

"There's no crew on the boat?" She hesitated a moment too long and I smiled. "You know how she works?"

"I could take her out of port, I couldn't sail her to New York, or even Istanbul." She frowned. "Why?"

"How sophisticated are the communication systems on this boat?"

She shrugged. "As sophisticated as they can get."

"Can you bank from onboard?"

"Of course, but like everything onboard it requires biometrics."

"Come." I crooked my hand at her and she followed me to the bedroom door, where I pointed at him lying in the bed. "He's crazy about you. Did you know that? He's been like this since he drank my coffee and ate my breakfast, fantasizing about you. Now I'll tell you what we are going to do. We are going to take this baby out a few miles into the Black Sea. On the way you're going to get his computer, and the same way you manipulated me last night, you are going to manipulate him into making a substantial transfer of funds. He is out of his mind right now, so it should not be too difficult. Then we are going to ditch this baby, take the launch and head for the coast of Turkey. From there we make our way to..." I spread my hands. "Belize? Brazil?"

"And what guarantee have I that you will not ditch me and leave with all the money?"

I slipped my arms around her waist and kissed her neck. "Have you looked at yourself recently? Besides, I'm assuming you have an offshore account. One transfer for you, one for me, and then we sink the boat."

"With him onboard?"

"Will you miss him?"

She smiled. "Not a lot."

She disengaged herself and she led me, by way of the elevator, across the open deck and up the stairs to the bridge. There she powered up the ship's computers and punched in a set of coordinates. After a moment the engines engaged and we started to move.

"Autopilot is engaged. This will now take us one hundred miles off Trabazon, on the coast of Turkey. It should take three hours. Trabazon has an international airport. We can fly out of there and be anywhere you like in a few hours."

"Sounds good to me. After that," I shrugged, "we can hang together for a while, or you can go your way and I go mine, whatever you like. You were never my target."

"Gabriel was?"

"That's for me to know, best if you don't. Let's go deal with Yushbaev."

We retraced our steps to the Emperor Suite and I stood in the doorway looking at Yushbaev while she went to the study and emerged a few moments later with a laptop, which she opened and placed on the bed. Then she started caressing Yushbaev's face and hair, and kissing him on the corner of his mouth. He opened his eyes and reached up, trying to grab her, but she pulled away, laughing.

"Darling, I want so much to be with you, but we have a little bit of work to do first."

"Work?"

"Work, my love, here, now press your finger on the pad... *voila!* So easy, my love. Now Harry is going to help us a little. Harry thinks you are wonderful, don't you, Harry?"

I took the laptop and tried not to let my eyes bulge at the numbers I was seeing. I made a few transfers, the biggest to Cobra, then to my account in Belize and another to my account in Panama. I used his fingerprint and eye-scan to execute the operations, then handed the laptop to Marianne.

"All yours." I stood. "Send me down to the lower decks. I need to prepare to scupper the boat. Meanwhile you can clean out the rest of his account."

She accompanied me to the elevator and as the door slid open I placed my foot in it to stop it closing and drove a straight right into the tip of her chin, just hard enough to put out her lights. I took the twenty-two from her jacket and laid her across the door, so it would stay open. Then I returned to Yushbaev and put two slugs in his head. Like she'd said, a twenty-two can sometimes do a lot more damage than a 9mm. A 9mm can go through and through, and on rare occasions you can survive the shot. But a twenty-two gets trapped in the skull, without the force to make an exit wound, and ricochets around, tearing up the brain.

I returned to the elevator, dragged Marianne to her feet and used her fingers to take us down to the main deck. There I used kitchen twine to tie her hands behind her back and her ankles and laid her on a sofa in the lounge.

I took her cell from her bag, showed it her face and dialed the brigadier. It rang a couple of times, then there was silence. He didn't recognize the number.

"It's me, Harry. I'm borrowing a phone from the girl who tried to kill me on Koufonisi."

"Progress?"

"Yushbaev is dead. Cobra is substantially richer. Yushbaev's operation is broken and as we speak I should think the Russian cops are swarming all over his so-called palace. I am on his yacht. It's on autopilot and headed for Trabzon, in Turkey. We are about twenty minutes out of Gelendzhik, and in the next twenty minutes I am going to blow the ship to hell and escape, with my prisoner, in a launch. Can you extract me?"

"I had anticipated your request. In fact, to be perfectly honest, Araminta had anticipated it. We have a plane on standby that should be with you in an hour or so. We'll track this number on GPS. What about the colonel?"

"She wasn't here. She didn't return to him." He didn't answer. So I asked, "Did you track down Bull?"

"Yes, he wasn't a Hell's Angel, Harry. He was just a biker, didn't belong to any club. A bit of a waster, but certainly had no record beyond a couple of speeding tickets and a couple of brawls."

"You spoke to him?"

"Not personally. He remembered Jane, said they'd had a brief relationship twenty years ago. She was just sixteen. One day she had stopped seeing him and that was all he could tell us."

After that I had a sense of déjà vu. I carried my bag down to the engine room and the storerooms, and found the section where the propane tanks were stored. I had ten pounds of C4 left. I wedged one pound against the tanks, and the remaining nine against the hull. I set the detonators for twenty minutes, then returned to Marianne. She was awake and as mad as an alley cat with a hornet up its ass.

"I'm going to untie you, but there is something you need to understand. I have set explosives on this boat that will blow it sky high in a little over fifteen minutes. I am going to untie you, and that will give us about ten minutes to get in the launch and as far from the *Bucephalus* as we can before it blows."

"You bastard!"

"No time for that. I can take you with me or I can leave you here."

"You wouldn't!"

"You're wasting time."

"OK! Untie me! I will behave!"

I untied her and we ran to the boarding deck, scrambled onto the launch, turned and sped away, putting a half mile between us and the vast, beautiful yacht. After twelve minutes it seemed to jump and expand. Then there was a huge shower of sparkling glass in the air before the entire yacht was engulfed in a fireball, after which it gradually subsided to the portside and was consumed by the Black Sea.

Marianne sat in silence as she watched the whole process. I didn't say anything to her. I had nothing to say to her. I had no understanding of her feelings, and she didn't care about anybody else's.

Half an hour later a DHC-6 Twin Otter appeared out of the south, circled us a couple of times, then came down onto the sea and taxied toward us. I took the boat up to his floats and the pilot leaned out.

"*You Harry?*"

"*Yeah! Buddy send you?*"

"Buddy" was Brigadier Alex "Buddy" Byrd. He gave me the thumbs up.

"Climb aboard!"

When we scrambled inside, I wasn't surprised to find Araminta there. Marianne glared at me. "Who is this?"

Araminta smiled at her. "Marianne Barbet?"

"Who are you?"

I slammed the door and we sat. The engines roared and we started to accelerate across the water with great walls of foam and spray rising up beside us.

Araminta pulled out her badge and showed it to Marianne. "Araminta Browne, Central Intelligence Agency. I am here to arrest you. I'll read you your rights when we get to Ankara."

"Under arrest what for? I have done nothing!"

"Oh, we have a long list. See, we picked up Ben Macleod in Yushbaev's office in Istanbul, and when we explained the situation to him, he had a lot to tell us. I am pretty sure you and I are going to have a lot to talk about too, Marianne."

Marianne closed her eyes and flopped back in her seat. I looked at Araminta for a while.

"It's good to see you," I said.

She patted my knee. "You too."

EPILOGUE

THREE DAYS LATER I WAS IN GILROY, CALIFORNIA, sitting in my rental car on the corner of Second Street and Princeville Street. It was a pretty, affluent neighborhood with lots of lawns and lots of leafy trees.

On one of those lawns a woman was tending to her roses. She was blonde, slim, in her mid-fifties. She was dressed in Levis, with an expensive white cardigan, the cuffs pushed up from her wrists. I climbed out of the car and crossed the blacktop, then the sidewalk and crossed the lawn to where she was hunkered down pruning dead branches.

"Mrs. Harris?"

She jumped, startled, and turned to look at me. I smiled and she laughed, one hand over her heart.

"Do forgive me!" She stood. "You startled me."

"Then I should apologize. Are you Mrs. Harris?"

"Yes, but," I saw the glint of her daughter's strength in her eyes, "who are you?"

"My name is Harry, Harry Bauer. I am a friend of your daughter's."

"I'm sorry, I am afraid..."

I interrupted her. "I know she is here, Mrs. Harris. I would not have intruded otherwise. I don't want to cause any distress. I have very good news for her, and it is really very important that she sees me and speaks to me."

She hesitated. The front door of the house stood open and it crossed my mind that I could simply walk in, but I dismissed the idea as a young girl stepped out and stood frowning at me with crossed arms.

"What is it, Mom?"

"Somebody asking for your sister, Helen."

Helen held my eye. "She's not here. We haven't heard from her for a long while."

I gave her a big, friendly smile. "Then who was that I saw bringing in the groceries half an hour ago?"

"You should leave."

I looked back at Mrs. Harris. "I know you have been through a lot of stress and anxiety these past couple of weeks. I know all about it. But you need to go and tell Jane that it is all over. You tell her this: Harry is outside on the lawn, Yushbaev is dead, the *Bucephalus* is at the bottom of the Black Sea, the palace is destroyed and Marianne is in jail. Even Colonel James Armitage is crying out for her to go back to work."

A shadow appeared at Helen's shoulder. Helen gave a small gasp and turned. Mrs. Harris said, "Oh, no..."

I approached. The colonel, Jane, was looking down at me with tears in her eyes.

"Is it true, or are you lying?"

"Not to you, Jane. Never to you."

"You'd better come inside."

We went in and Mrs. Harris closed the door. Helen asked, "Who is this man?"

Jane sat and gestured me to the sofa. She said, "He is a very good friend, and one of the few people I can really trust."

There were tears in her eyes and her nose was red. As I sat I pulled a handkerchief from my pocket and handed it to her. Mrs. Harris sat beside me but Helen remained standing, beside Jane.

"You should have told us, Jane."

"I know. But the Air Force back then was strict about that kind of stuff. And with time, I guess I figured it was nobody's business but mine."

"In Istanbul. You should have told me in Istanbul."

She shook her head. "It was too risky. And you are such a brute." She laughed a tearful laugh and I smiled. "I knew you'd start blowing things up and shooting people and the risk of things going wrong was too high. I am so sorry I hurt you—"

"When?"

"Oh, come on!"

"I was going to apologize for falling asleep on you."

She laughed and sobbed a little more, then said, "It was too late to go back to Yushbaev. I had to come back here, to my mother and," she hesitated a moment, "to my daughter. I had to protect them."

I nodded. "It was hard to buy your story." I smiled. "I'm not saying you're not badass in your own way, but a biker chick?" I shook my head. "And when Buddy said he had traced Bull and he was basically a nice if irresponsible biker dude, who said that you just disappeared one day, it kind of clicked into place. I had seen Yushbaev's palace. I saw what he had there, and I realized what he had threatened you with."

She nodded. "And it was all to get to you. They were desperate, Cavendish and Yushbaev. They were desperate to know who you were and who you worked for."

I glanced at Helen and Mrs. Harris. "How much have you told your mother and your daughter?"

"Practically nothing, and they don't want to know." She looked up at her daughter and took her hand. "I was sixteen, just seventeen when Helen was born. I refused to give her up for adoption, but Mom insisted that I should pursue a career. Dad was very ill. He was dying, and his dying wish was that, that I go to college and make something of myself. Mom was young and she said we would raise Helen between us."

Mrs. Harris broke in, "And she has done her father proud."

Jane smiled at her. "It's been our secret over the years. Until now."

"Buddy wants to know if you'll be coming back. So does Colonel Armitage."

She glanced up at her daughter, then across at her mother. They both nodded. She sighed.

"Perhaps, Harry. But we will have to make adjustments. I can't put my family at risk anymore."

I nodded and looked at her with meaning. "I know what you mean."

I stood and took a couple of steps to the door. "I'll be in San Francisco for a few days. Can I call Buddy and tell him you'll think about it?"

"Yes."

"And if you feel like a quiet dinner in a pizza joint, or a biker bar, just let me know."

She laughed. "You got it, dude."

I shrugged. "And maybe I could drive you back to New York, if you decide to go."

"Let's take it one step at a time."

I nodded. "OK, one step at a time."

Don't miss INVISIBLE EVIL. The riveting sequel in the Harry Bauer Thriller series.

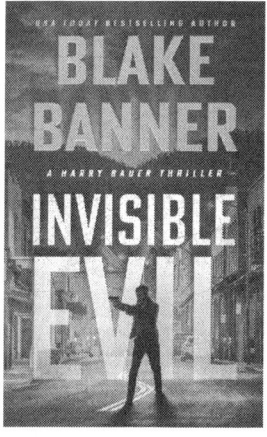

Scan the QR code below to purchase INVISIBLE EVIL.

Or go to: righthouse.com/invisible-evil

NOTE: flip to the very end to read an exclusive sneak peak...

DON'T MISS ANYTHING!

If you want to stay up to date on all new releases in this series, with this author, or with any of our new deals, you can do so by joining our newsletters below.

In addition, you will immediately gain access to our entire *Right House VIP Library,* which includes many riveting Mystery and Thriller novels for your enjoyment!

righthouse.com/email

(Easy to unsubscribe. No spam. Ever.)

ALSO BY BLAKE BANNER

Up to date books can be found at:
www.righthouse.com/blake-banner

ROGUE THRILLERS
Gates of Hell (Book 1)
Hell's Fury (Book 2)

ALEX MASON THRILLERS
Odin (Book 1)
Ice Cold Spy (Book 2)
Mason's Law (Book 3)
Assets and Liabilities (Book 4)
Russian Roulette (Book 5)
Executive Order (Book 6)
Dead Man Talking (Book 7)
All The King's Men (Book 8)
Flashpoint (Book 9)
Brotherhood of the Goat (Book 10)
Dead Hot (Book 11)
Blood on Megiddo (Book 12)
Son of Hell (Book 13)

HARRY BAUER THRILLER SERIES
Dead of Night (Book 1)
Dying Breath (Book 2)
The Einstaat Brief (Book 3)
Quantum Kill (Book 4)
Immortal Hate (Book 5)
The Silent Blade (Book 6)
LA: Wild Justice (Book 7)

Breath of Hell (Book 8)
Invisible Evil (Book 9)
The Shadow of Ukupacha (Book 10)
Sweet Razor Cut (Book 11)
Blood of the Innocent (Book 12)
Blood on Balthazar (Book 13)
Simple Kill (Book 14)
Riding The Devil (Book 15)
The Unavenged (Book 16)
The Devil's Vengeance (Book 17)
Bloody Retribution (Book 18)
Rogue Kill (Book 19)
Blood for Blood (Book 20)

DEAD COLD MYSTERY SERIES
An Ace and a Pair (Book 1)
Two Bare Arms (Book 2)
Garden of the Damned (Book 3)
Let Us Prey (Book 4)
The Sins of the Father (Book 5)
Strange and Sinister Path (Book 6)
The Heart to Kill (Book 7)
Unnatural Murder (Book 8)
Fire from Heaven (Book 9)
To Kill Upon A Kiss (Book 10)
Murder Most Scottish (Book 11)
The Butcher of Whitechapel (Book 12)
Little Dead Riding Hood (Book 13)
Trick or Treat (Book 14)
Blood Into Wine (Book 15)
Jack In The Box (Book 16)
The Fall Moon (Book 17)
Blood In Babylon (Book 18)
Death In Dexter (Book 19)
Mustang Sally (Book 20)

ABOUT US

Right House is an independent publisher created by authors for readers. We specialize in Action, Thriller, Mystery, and Crime novels.

If you enjoyed this novel, then there is a good chance you will like what else we have to offer! Please stay up to date by using any of the links below.

Join our mailing lists to stay up to date -->
righthouse.com/email
Visit our website --> righthouse.com
Contact us --> contact@righthouse.com

 facebook.com/righthousebooks
x.com/righthousebooks
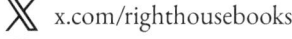 instagram.com/righthousebooks

EXCLUSIVE SNEAK PEAK OF...

INVISIBLE EVIL

CHAPTER 1

THE MOON, EVER A LIAR, PRETENDED TO SMILE. TO ME it looked like the smile of a radiant corpse. She was suspended, apparently weightless, over dense trees and bushes at the end of the garden; a fall moon, the trickiest of them all.

It was an early September night. We sat at a round table on the lawn at the back of the Cobra HQ, near Pleasantville, where nothing is what it seems. The table was set with white linen, the candles stood in eighteenth-century silver candlesticks that once belonged to Napoleon Bonaparte, the knives and forks and spoons had allegedly been used by Thomas Jefferson while he was plotting to secede from the British Crown, and the eight flaming bamboo torches that squared the circle around us, keeping the bugs at bay, were from Amazon, at forty-two bucks ninety-nine per set.

The food and the wine were not from Amazon. Brigadier Alexander "Buddy" Byrd had a chef who'd been with him for twenty years or more and was to sauces and roasting what Mozart was to flutes and pianos. Nobody knew his name, nobody had ever seen him, but he was a legend to those who had dined with the brigadier.

The brigadier managed to sit at the head of the table, even

though the table was round. It was not so much a case of where he sat, but the way he sat there. I guess he carried so much gravitas he distorted space so that round became oval. He was in a black dinner suit that probably cost as much as my TVR Griffith. The bow tie alone was so exquisitely understated it was all you could look at.

Unless you happened to be looking at the colonel. The colonel was in a black, sleeveless, strapless number I kept hoping would obey the laws of gravity and drop to the lawn. But it just clung tight to her body and smirked at me. She had a thin string of diamonds around her throat that, especially by candlelight, was distracting because it made me want to gnaw on her throat the way trolls were supposed to gnaw on bones.

A man in a white dinner jacket emerged from the house followed by two very pretty girls in French maid uniforms. The maids delivered plates of avocado and smoked Norwegian salmon to us and the man in the dinner jacket, whose name was Aitor, poured the wine, a *Marques de Murrieta, Castillo de Ygay,* 1986, which I knew came in at around six hundred and thirty bucks a bottle, plus tax.

The brigadier was saying, "You need a full-bodied white with a strong, oily fish like salmon. The whites from Rioja are greatly underrated."

"*Because* they're full-bodied," added the colonel, and I stifled a yawn by reaching for my whisky. "And, call me a philistine," she went on, "but that allows you to have it that little bit colder."

"I agree."

"I don't," I said. "I think you're a philistine."

She stared at me a moment, in shock, but when I smiled she laughed. I turned to the brigadier, who was spearing a piece of salmon and trying to skewer a piece of avocado with it.

"If we were at a restaurant in New York," I said, "I might convince myself that you'd invited me here because no sparkling dinner would be complete without me. But the fact that we are doing this at Cobra HQ makes me suspect you have some other reason, like a job."

He looked at the colonel, eyebrows arched and smiling, like she'd said something surprising. She smiled at her food and scooped a piece of salmon and avocado without piercing either of them, which just goes to show that women are smarter than men.

"I wish," he said.

"What's that supposed to mean?"

"Jane and I were discussing a job just last week. We were saying it would be right up your street. Unfortunately it is completely outside Cobra's remit. There would be absolutely no justification for giving you that job."

I carefully folded a piece of salmon, pierced it and put it in my mouth, then picked up a piece of avocado with my fingers and popped that in too. When I'd chewed, swallowed and sipped my wine, I raised an eyebrow at him.

"So your intention was to get my interest. You have it. Now you are going to have to explain."

He dabbed his mouth. "Some might say that what we do is technically illegal. On the other hand, I would argue, if I had to, that we are instructed by the executives of the Five: the United States, United Kingdom, Canada, Australia and New Zealand, on matters of national security which are beyond the jurisdiction of the courts, and, technically, it is *not* illegal. So, we occupy an ambiguous, gray area on the fringes of legality, because it is in the interests of national security of the Five. And all of that is for a simple reason—we deal in assassination, as opposed to murder."

"Meaning it's politically motivated."

It was the colonel who answered. "Political in the sense that our targets affect, or are capable of affecting, the balance of world power. Politics," she gestured at the brigadier, "as Alex is always saying, is the practice of accruing and *retaining* power. We are tolerated and retained by the Five precisely because we help to maintain the balance of power. We are in effect a covert, political weapon."

She reached for her glass and the brigadier took over, as though they were a couple of well-rehearsed TV presenters.

"But if we once started taking out targets because we had a vendetta, because they were standing in the way of the political ambitions of one of our clients, or indeed because we personally disapproved of them in some way, then we would be on the very slippery slope toward perdition."

"Who is this person, and what have they done?"

The colonel had her glass halfway to her mouth. She paused and set it down again.

"You have to understand, Harry, that we *cannot* ask you to do this job. And if you were to decide to do it, we could not pay you or bail you out if you got in trouble. You could not contact the brigadier or me for the duration of the job. As far as we are concerned, you would be on holiday somewhere."

"You make it sound so attractive. What's the downside?"

The brigadier took a deep breath and sat back in his chair.

"I am not a religious man, Harry. I try to take a philosophical, empirical view of the world. But this man..." He stopped, frowning at one of the torches that flickered in the September breeze, casting moving firelight across his face. "This man is evil. There is no other word for it. One can try to understand him from a psychologist's point of view, one can argue that good and evil are human constructs that do not exist in nature..." He shook his head. "I don't care. Whatever the circumstances that created and conditioned this man, he is now the incarnation of evil. He is evil made human, flesh and blood."

"What's his name?"

The colonel said, "I doubt you've ever heard of him. He is not famous. He is an American citizen, and killing him would be murder, plain and simple."

"What's his name?"

"His name is Oscar Larsen, known as Oz. In his youth he was a member of the Hell's Angels, but," she started to laugh, and by candlelight that was a nice thing to watch, "they asked him to leave because he was out of control!"

The brigadier laughed quietly and continued. "For the last few years, nobody is really sure how long, he has had his own gang. The basic requirement for joining seems to be that you are either a psychopath or a sociopath, and that you find ordinary organized crime too restrictive."

"Gang," I said, "what kind of numbers are we talking about?"

The brigadier looked at the colonel, who was mopping her plate with a slice of bread. She finished, sipped her wine and sighed. "It is very hard to be precise. He has ten to twelve men who seem to go with him everywhere. By which I mean, he might go to the bar down the road with all of them, or two of them, or four or six of them, but the others will be at home or within a couple of minutes if he calls them. But in addition to those twelve, he has a number of," she looked at the brigadier, "what would you call them?"

"Followers, disciples? It's very much like a cult. There are maybe twenty of them, fifty, a hundred? We don't know."

"Do they have a name?"

The colonel replied. "Apparently they call themselves simply Free Men. They have acquired a few nicknames in the local underworld, Ozwalds, Ozones..."

"How come I've never heard of these guys?"

"Because they keep a very low profile, and they are on the other side of the continent."

"California?"

"Not quite, southern New Mexico."

"Halfway across."

"It was a manner of speaking, Harry. The reason you have not come across them is because they keep to themselves, the press tends to steer clear of them, much like everybody else, and they are located halfway across the continent."

Aitor appeared again with his two pretty maids. They took away our empty plates, and the empty bottle of wine, and returned shortly afterwards with a large steak and kidney pie, a bowl of roast potatoes, Vichy carrots and buttered broccoli. To accompany this feast there were two bottles of red *Marques de Murrieta, Castillo de Ygay* 2001, which came in at a very modest two hundred and fifty bucks a bottle, excluding tax. It was like drinking ripe plums and whipped, full fat cream, with the added benefit of alcohol. It seemed a shame to spoil it talking about Oz, so we ate in silence till our plates were almost empty, and our stomachs were in a stupor of distended pleasure.

Then I sat back and sipped and sighed and said, "So, what has Oz done that has singled him out as the only human on Earth Cobra would stoop to murder for?"

The brigadier arched an eyebrow at his last remaining potato. "Nicely put. I'll tell you."

He put the potato in his mouth, set his knife and fork at six o'clock, the way Brits do, wiped his mouth with his napkin and concluded operations by sipping his wine.

"Oscar Larsen was born in Nogales, in Arizona, in November of 1981, which makes him forty years old. His mother was a prostitute and, without the benefit of DNA testing and a great deal of patience, his father's identity must remain a mystery. He, Oscar, was in and out of foster homes throughout his childhood and, at sixteen, he left home and became a prospect for the Hell's Angels."

He swirled his wine for a moment, sniffed it and then sipped it. After quietly smacking his lips he went on.

"As you probably know, when you are a prospect for the Hell's Angels you are required to do absolutely whatever you are told to do, even if that means taking the fall for a member and going to prison." He paused and smiled. "Oz did not take the fall for anyone. He was told by one of the senior members of his chapter that he, the senior member, was going to kill a member of the *Chupacabras*, a Mexican motorcycle gang not dissimilar to the Angels, and that Oz was going to have to take the fall and go to prison. This would involve serving a sentence of at least sixteen years."

The colonel took over while Aitor and the pretty maids cleared the table and delivered a cheeseboard, a bottle of twenty-year-old Courvoisier and another of the Macallan.

"Of course, if that senior member was caught and tried he could face the death penalty. But a boy of sixteen, his first offense, a good defense lawyer paid for by the Angels and good behavior, Oscar's sentence could be as little as sixteen years, of which he would probably serve thirteen.

"However, what Oz did was to tell the senior member to go to hell. If he was going down for a murder, he said, he would go down for a murder he had committed, not for one somebody else had committed. So he went to a bar where he knew the *Chupacabras* hung out, found the intended victim, stuck him with a ten-inch blade and disemboweled him right there in the middle of the bar.

"In court he pleaded guilty, contrary to his attorney's advice, but said that he had heard on the grapevine that this man planned to kill *him*, and he decided on a preemptive strike."

The brigadier poured me a glass of whisky and as I cut myself a slice of Stilton he continued the story.

"Oz served thirteen of the sixteen years. His first two years he got into several fights with the most feared and dangerous gang leaders in the prison. I assume he did that deliberately. He knew he had the backing of the Angels, but apparently he didn't care either way. What he wanted was to make sure everybody inside feared him, even the screws. And by the time he was eighteen he was universally feared. Nothing went down without his say-so, and he took a percentage of everything that came into the prison, booze, tobacco, drugs.

"By his third year he had settled down to an apparent life of good behavior. But this was in reality because anything he needed done, he got one of his boys to do it for him. So after eleven years of living like a king and running the biggest organized crime ring in the history of the prison, he was released early for good behavior."

The colonel balanced a piece of brie on a cracker and slipped it in her mouth, then picked up her glass.

"Two weeks after he was released, the Angel he was supposed to take the fall for was found dead, disemboweled in his house. He had been castrated and had his eyes gouged out. The Angels never managed to prove it was Oz who had done it, but they revoked his membership and made him leave.

"He soon surrounded himself, however, with the worst and most psychotic members of the Tucson underworld and, within a year, he had taken over the drug importation racket north of the border. He agreed terms with the Sinaloa cartel and secured exclusive distribution rights for anything coming into Arizona from Mexico."

The brigadier was nodding. "But that was not enough for Oz. For him, you see, it was not really about the money or the expensive cars or any of that. For him it was all about sticking it to the authorities. More even that that, I would say it was a challenge to himself to see just how evil he could be, just how far he could push the limits of his own inhumanity before anybody tried to stop him.

"He never challenged Sinaloa, because they were a source of enormous wealth and power for him. As the Angels had in their day, Sinaloa gave him a very valuable backing. But what he did do was to go far beyond simple drugs trafficking. Pretty soon he had moved into the prostitution and pornography industry, and within five years, using the money he was making from distributing for Sinaloa, he had moved into white slaves, not just from Mexico, but from Poland, Russia, the Philippines and Brazil. He owned a string of discreet, luxurious gentlemen's clubs in San Diego, Yuma, Phoenix and Tucson and that where he exploited these girls.

"He was good, and he had disposed of at least half a dozen

rivals. He was thorough and meticulous, and nobody was ever able to pin anything on him."

I was steadily working my way through the Stilton and the whisky, enjoying the little act they had prepared for me, but asking myself what was so special about this guy. In the end I interrupted.

"This guy, I agree, he's a son of a bitch and the world would be a better place without him. But there are thousands of guys like him. We can't just take it upon ourselves to start eliminating them all, one by one, much as I would like to."

The colonel shook her head. "That's what we said to you in the beginning. But what we are telling you here is just a little background so you understand how he got started. By the time he was thirty-seven, in 2018 or thereabouts, he had established himself as the most dangerous gangster in Arizona and Southern California, and nobody, outside the FBI and the local PDs, had ever heard of him."

The brigadier nodded, then looked at me. "But what he did next was what eventually put him on our radar."

CHAPTER 2

THE TEMPERATURE HAD DROPPED AND THERE WAS A slight, agreeable chill in the air. The colonel had wrapped a light stole around her shoulders and was holding her glass of cognac in both hands, watching the brigadier, apparently content to let him take over the story for now. He helped himself to a little more cheese.

"As I said, Oz was making enormous amounts of money, but the thing for him was never the cash. What motivated him, what excited him, was breaking the rules, pushing the boundaries and going as far beyond what was acceptable to any normal human being as he possibly could. So what he did was to set up a website, offering child pornography. He employed a couple of geeks to run the site and, I am no expert in these matters, but apparently, by using several VPNs, they were able to make it almost impossible to locate the server from which the site was hosted. In other words, for anyone trying to track them, they might have been in China, Russia, Mexico or in the middle of the Pacific Ocean in international waters. At this point all Oz did was to buy videos from stock that was available on the web.

"But in 2019, he made a major move. He relocated his HQ up into the mountains above Eden, and, as well as that, he set up a studio in the desert. The studio was separate from the HQ. It was essentially a prefabricated hangar kitted out as a basic film studio, and they would go there every couple of months or so, and make films. He had studied his market and knew what his punters were prepared to pay top dollar for. From there it was a short step to creating his own channel."

I had stopped eating and was studying my whisky. I muttered, "Now I'm beginning to understand." I frowned, "Wasn't there some Arab guy arrested and prosecuted for something similar recently?"

He shook his head. "I'm not sure. But I don't think you fully understand yet, Harry. Most child pornography relies on rings of parents who have brought their children up in that environment. That is sick and odious enough, but what Oz did next went well beyond that."

I could feel the burn growing in my belly.

"Where is this guy now?"

The colonel glanced at me and murmured, "Wait, Harry, you need to hear all of this."

"He created teams," said the brigadier, "whose task it was to travel the country—here and in Mexico—identifying vulnerable children, and in some cases families, and kidnapping them or luring them here for the purpose of exploiting them. I need hardly say that what they looked for was children who had never been exposed to this kind of nightmare. What he sought to capture with the camera was the fear. Fear and submission is what this monster is hungry for."

I set down my glass and snarled. "I thought the Feds were supposed to be on top of this kind of thing. Isn't this what they're there for? How the hell can they allow something like that to happen?"

He nodded. "I'm afraid, Harry, that sometimes the law is a self-defeating institution, because it has to protect people's rights and freedoms, and obey its own rules. The operation went on for over a year. The Bureau knew it was going on and they were monitoring it, but they were unable to get the kind of evidence they would need for probable cause. They had a team trying to identify where the HQ and the studio were located in the hope of being able to raid them. But they had very little success, until a field agent in Arizona informed them that he believed Oz was running some kind of operation in the hills north of Eden. Efforts were intensified, but they were still unable to identify a studio, or gather anything remotely like probable cause to raid the HQ."

"So what happened?"

"A team of federal agents eventually managed to follow four of his gang to the studio in New Mexico. They now had a location, but still nothing they could take to a judge and ask for a warrant. So, in frustration, they took matters into their own hands and broke into the studio after the gang members had returned to HQ in Arizona. They took photographs and video footage of everything they could find and grabbed computers, laptops, films—everything you could hope for. Their plan was to deliver it anonymously to their own team. That way the person acquiring the evidence would have committed a felony in breaking in and stealing it, but the investigative team would be off the hook and free to adduce it as evidence to the court."

"Good, what happened?"

"They committed that most cardinal of sins. They underestimated their enemy. He had concealed motion-activated CCTV cameras all over the studio. He filmed and recorded every move they made and every word they said." He paused, then intoned, "'If you know your enemy and you know yourself, you need not fear the result of a hundred battles. If you know yourself but not the enemy, for every victory gained you will also suffer a defeat. If you know neither your enemy nor yourself, you will succumb in every battle.'" He shrugged. "Obviously they had not read their Sun Tzu, and every bit of evidence they acquired was ruled inadmissible by the judge, and the case was kicked out of court, defeated before it had even started."

"Who was the judge?"

"Judge Casper Williams, but he only did what any judge in America would have been obliged to do, apply the law to the facts. It is, if you will forgive me saying so, one of the more asinine features of an otherwise sound legal system. By all means, punish the agents—punish them severely if you will—but the evidence should be judged admissible or not on the basis of its probative value, not on how it was acquired. Still, there it is. On the evening of the hearing in chambers, Oz was out on the streets of Tucson celebrating at the Three Points Casino."

He fell silent and after a moment the colonel said, "Of course, on the upside his operation had to stop, but on the downside he is now free to start another one. And knowing him, it will be even worse than the previous one."

I stared at her. "How could it possibly be worse?"

The brigadier grunted. "You've been in Helmand, use your imagination."

I went cold inside. I felt my skin crawl, and I knew that as long as that man was alive he would not stop pushing the limits of his own evil.

"What do the Feds say?"

He took a deep breath. "The Federal Bureau of Investigation says that the law must be upheld and enforced at all costs and under all circumstances. An alleged, un-attributable source claims that the team who were investigating Oz's operation are certain that his success has emboldened him and he is preparing a new operation in New Mexico. He has moved there, to Manuel Vazquez County, which is about as remote and isolated as you can get in the United States without moving to Alaska, and he has bought a property about thirteen or fourteen miles northeast of Dell City, about seven miles north of the Texas state line, as the crow flies, and not very far from his old studio. Rumor has it that he still has stuff hidden there."

I said, "If he's gone that remote it's because he doesn't want to be seen."

"Obviously."

"And if the Feds or the Sheriff's Department go anywhere near them, his lawyers will slap them with every kind of injunction known to man, and probably sue for damages into the bargain."

The colonel nodded. "You can bet your bottom dollar on it."

"And within the month this bastard will be preying on children again, not only with impunity, but protected by the law."

The brigadier refilled our glasses. "In a nutshell," he said, "yes."

"So, if I accepted this job which you are not offering me, how would this work?"

The colonel leaned forward and placed her glass on the table.

"For a start you would have to understand that you were committing murder, and there would be no get out of jail free card for you here."

"I get that."

"Second, whatever files you may remove from the brigadier's office, or mine, during your visit, cannot be traced to us and do not have our fingerprints on them."

"I understand all of that," I said, "what I need to know, in real, practical terms, is to what extent can you help me? Logistically, how much useful information can you give me—names, addresses, numbers, locations—and how do I get to this bastard?"

"In real, practical terms, I have a file with all the relevant information on where he is and what he is doing, to the best of the Bureau's understanding—which is not a great deal, and that is on my desk because I have forgotten to put it away. As to how do you get to the bastard..." He made a question with his face which involved raising his eyebrows and looking at the colonel. "Jane?"

"Wait," she said, "let's take one step at a time. In terms of weapons we cannot provide you with any hardware."

The words were incongruous coming from such a feminine face, decorated with diamonds and bathed in candlelight. I tried not to smile. If she noticed she ignored me.

"Whatever weapons you need you will have to secure either from your private arsenal or from a private supplier. In Arizona and New Mexico that is not going to be a problem. Now—" She looked at her glass and turned it around a few times, like she was looking for the best angle. "As to how you get to him, physically, he has a property about three and a half miles northwest of Hope, which is a census designated place about twelve miles northeast of Dell City. It's a farming community. There are about three hundred and fifty inhabitants all told. You can stay at the saloon. It's called the Horns of the Dilemma. There's not a lot else to tell about the town."

The brigadier said, "Oz lives at his property. It's called the Farm. Apparently they get whatever they need from the town. Sometimes they pay, sometimes they don't."

"What about the sheriff?"

"Sheriff Matías Olvera, he's based in Vazquez, the county seat, about fifty miles northwest of Hope by winding road. They get a lot of stray sheep up there, so he has his hands pretty full. From what I hear, the last time he went to Hope was about two weeks after Oz moved in to the Farm, about six months ago. He hasn't been back since."

"Right." I nodded. "He's not going to be a problem, then."

"I wouldn't have thought so."

The colonel drained her glass and slid it across the table toward the brigadier. As he refilled it she said, "Now, your main problems are two: first, how many men are you up against? We have zero reliable intel on that. It is unlikely to be less than twelve, and unlikely to be more than a hundred."

I laughed. "You're kidding."

"Not really." She shook her head. "Crazy cults like these can end up attracting a lot of people. What's the membership of the Hell's Angels? Two or three thousand? Koresh had almost a hundred people on his ranch when the Feds stormed it, and Bhagwan Shri Rajneesh had two thousand people living at his so-called Rancho Rajneesh, in Oregon. We just have no idea what he has going on out there, but whatever it is, it has the allure of plenty of money, sex, drugs and rock and roll."

"OK, understood, and my second problem?"

"Your second is going to be getting enough reliable intelligence to develop an executable plan. They are reclusive, largely self-reliant, well organized and they have the people of Hope terrorized. So getting reliable information will be difficult and dangerous." She raised a finger and nodded as another thought came to her. "*And*, he is IT literate and has skilled nerds working for him. He may be operating in Hicksville, but his techs are up to the minute."

I grunted. Neither problem was insurmountable. "What we're talking about is a period of recon and then developing a workable plan. That's standard operating procedure."

The brigadier nodded. "Yes, but in the kind of environment we are looking at here, in a standard operation you would have the support of three other blades. In this case you are alone. And I do mean alone. Much as we would like to, we *cannot* help you."

"You don't need to keep telling me that, sir, I understood it the first time. You drummed it into me in the Regiment. Never get into a fight you don't know you can win. I'll recon. If it's doable, I'll do it. If it's not, I'll nuke the place."

He smiled, put his hands on the arms of the chair and stood.

"I'd expect no less from you. I must excuse myself. And, Harry, my study is unlocked and I have a very sensitive file on my desk, with a duplicate beside it. Be a good chap and don't go in and filch it, will you?"

"I wouldn't dream of it, sir."

"Good night."

We watched him go inside, then sat in a silence that could have been comfortable and companionable, or uncomfortable and awkward, depending on how much you had drunk. I hadn't drunk enough. I gave her the kind of smile you give someone when you're not sure whether to smile or not. It didn't matter much because she was staring at her glass and didn't see it.

"Are we done talking about not-work?"

"Yup." She gave a single slow nod at her glass.

"Can I ask how you've been? I half expected you to quit. You haven't been in touch."

"No," she said, with unnecessary ambiguity. I waited for her to clear up the ambiguity but she just kept staring at her glass. Eventually I asked her, "No, I can't ask how you've been, or no, you haven't been in touch?"

"Alex, the brigadier, whatever, he told me what you did." She looked at me and frowned. "What you went through. I am very conflicted, Harry. I feel guilty."

"What about?"

She gave a quiet laugh and offered me a sardonic smile.

"Come on, Mr. Tough Guy. I know you play the indestructible man of iron, and I know to some extent it is real, but I also know you're human, and I know you suffered a lot. Not just physically. I know you went through a lot of anxiety too…"

Before she could finish I nodded and interrupted. "Yeah, that has a name, Jane." She paused and eyed me. I said, "It's called life. If you live in a three-dimensional, physical world, there is going to be pain. It's as unavoidable as time and space. We don't get to choose on that score. What we do get to choose is how we deal with that pain." I shook my head. "You won't hear me talk like this very often, so you had better pay attention, Colonel. If somebody I care about is in trouble, then I choose to deal with that pain by fighting to help that somebody. And I'll do whatever I have to do."

"Harry…"

"Wait. I'm not done. Your family were threatened and you did what you had to do to protect them. You should not feel guilty about that. You did the right thing. The only place you screwed up was in not telling me from the start."

She frowned and returned her attention to her cognac. "Thank you." She said it like she wasn't really sure. "Harry, you said," she hesitated, "you said 'a person you cared about.'"

"Yes."

"Do you mean care about as a friend?"

I sighed. "Honestly, I don't know."

"That can't be."

"I know. But we can only control how we behave, Jane, not how we feel."

She took a deep breath, seemed about to say something, then smiled an empty smile and said, "I had better go up."

She stood and I stood with her. She placed a hand softly on my chest.

"Good night, Harry. And thank you, for everything."

If she hadn't kissed me softly on the cheek, I don't know what I would have done. But she did, and that killed anything else that might have happened. Then she brushed past me and disappeared inside. For a moment I almost went after her, but the impulse never became action. Instead I sighed very deeply, sat back down under the sneering moon, and poured myself another dram of solace.

Scan the QR code below to purchase INVISIBLE EVIL.
Or go to: righthouse.com/invisible-evil

Made in United States
Orlando, FL
02 January 2026

76166241R10141